The Resurrectionist

By

Alex Cristo

Protognosis Press

Published in the United States by Protognosis Press

POB 52554, Tulsa, OK U.S.A.

Library of Congress Cataloging-in-Publication Data

ISBN 978-1-934613-47-4

Cristo, Alex, author.

The Resurrectionist

Alex Cristo

First U.S. Edition

[First Printing]

Printed in the United States of America.

ALSO BY ALEX CRISTO

Alabaster Sins

Crypto-Sapien

Crypto-Sapien: Sky Temple

Dracula Abridged

Pilate

To the person who always burns me with her sunshine.

Opportunity of a Lifetime

"Enough with all your damned questions, you annoying woman," boomed a voice from down the hall. The yelling was punctuated by a slammed door followed by loud footsteps. The claims adjuster and the rest of the insurance team were finally fed up with the stenographer.

Inspector Cass had been listening to the yelling and footsteps from a small roll-top desk. *I can pick out anyone, just by the sound of their footsteps*, Inspector Cass thought. *Those staccato clicks against the wooden floor must belong to the sales rep; sharp and close together.* He believed his hearing and perception was so sensitive, he could pick out a person's mood by the timbre of their footsteps. *You can tell a lot from a few footsteps. It shows character and industriousness,* Cass thought. *I bet I could pick out a murderer or a millionaire, just by the sound of their footsteps.*

Cass was part of a small group of insurance investigators from Philadelphia performing a follow-up investigation for a claim in their St. Louis office. Fidelity Mutual Insurance had a detective department of its own and Cass had been working out of the cramped St. Louis branch for the last few days.

He was surrounded by large, bound books of ledgers, invoices, aging reports and EOBs. It was a great deal of cross-referencing work that made everyone cross-eyed and on edge. Since joining the firm in the summer of 1890, Cass had quickly become one of the most hated men to work with.

The hard and uneven shoe clicks approached. *Definitely the sales representative*, Cass thought.

"Well hello, Mr. Jacobs," Cass said, without turning to look.

"Stop it, Mr. Cass. You can't tell us apart from our footsteps."

Cass was wrong; he was always wrong. It wasn't the sales rep, but one of the claim adjusters who had traveled from Philadelphia with him to St. Louis.

Everyone was fed up with Inspector Cass, as well.

Cass set aside his carefully stacked paperwork. *Must have been an echo that distorted the sound.*

The claim adjuster wrinkled his nose. The kerosene lamp Cass was using must have had a small leak and it was burning the inside of his nostrils.

"How's your head? I have something for that," Cass said. "I told you. It's the most powerful headache tonic on the market. You must tell all your friends about it." Cass had been trying to sell his special headache tonic to everyone he saw.

"I thought you weren't allowed to pedal your tonics at the office anymore."

"Yes, but we're not at *our* office, are we?" Cass asked.

"Do you remember the Pitezel case?" the adjuster asked, trying to change the subject. Cass had to be the most tiresome person anyone had ever met. That was until a few moments ago when the adjuster had met the odd woman down the hall.

"It was a few weeks ago. I remember I wasn't satisfied with the events, but the company paid out the claim very quickly. I wasn't satisfied one little bit," Cass said.

"A messenger called here with a letter from Major Lawrence Harrigan, Chief of the St. Louis Police. He received a communication from a prisoner about the Pitezel case."

"A prisoner?"

"Are you familiar with a man named Marion Hedgepeth?" the adjuster asked.

Cass's eyes burst with excitement.

"The Handsome Bandit? The Wild West outlaw? *That* Marion Hedgepeth?" Cass became as excited as a little boy at a circus.

"The same."

"Yes, I love his dime novels! He usually robs greedy train owners who steal from farmers and ranchers."

"Exactly. You read all their silly Jesse James and Billy the Kid dime books, right?"

"They're not silly!"

"Anyway, Mr. Hedgepeth makes some very outrageous claims about the Pitezel case. We were going to throw it away but then I thought this would be a great way to get you out of the office. I want you to take his interview."

"What about my work here?" Cass asked.

"Don't you worry about that," he said, set on getting Cass out of his hair for a few hours.

"That's very exciting! What does he claim? I'll leave right now. Baker can come along as my stenographer."

"He's out on assignment. I'll send Whitsett to meet you outside; we all need a break from Whitsett and all those damned questions. Remember, take as long as you like. No rush. In fact, you and Whitsett shouldn't even come back to this office. You two can even take a separate train back to Philadelphia when you're done." The sales rep handed Cass his black coat from the back of the chair.

Who is Whitsett? Cass thought to himself. He didn't know everyone who had traveled to St. Louis with him. Few people would sit next to him on the train, or in the office in Philadelphia, or even outside the office in Philadelphia. Whitsett must have been the tall man with the blonde mustache. *He will most likely have deep, firm footsteps.*

Cass was too excited to think about Whitsett long, he was meeting Marion Hedgepeth, the Handsome Bandit.

Cass sent a message to Major Harrigan of the St. Louis Police and arranged for a coach to take them to the prison. He waited for the stenographer to meet him on the curb. The cool breeze blew the hot odor of horse manure from the piles burying almost every part of the street. Cass had to wave his hand to keep the flies from his face.

He began to think about meeting one of his favorite dime heroes, 'The Handsome Bandit.' He had collected all of his books. *What do I say?* he thought. *I better run through the Pitezel case notes before I meet him.*

His notes outlined the accidental death of a man named B.F. Perry—real name Benjamin Freelon Pitezel—on September 4th, 1894, just a month ago. A smoking pipe exploded in his face, killing him instantly. The body was identified by the man's daughter Alice and somebody named Mr. Holmes. The claim was paid out against the recommendation of Cass to the amount of $9,715.85. Everything about the death seemed to be just a little jagged at every point, like the rough sketch of a poor artist.

Who is Mr. Holmes? was scrawled across his notes.

I take amazing notes, it's like I'm there, Cass thought, pleased with himself for his exemplary record keeping. If something wasn't written down, it was like it never happened. He always kept very good records. *It's impossible to remember everything. The trick is to get the important details that make you feel like you were there. And of course, penmanship. A good man can't be a good man unless his writing is readable. Penmanship and posture are the most important things.*

There was a poke on Mr. Cass's shoulder. He turned around and saw a short woman with large eyes staring at him. She had a green bag filled with paper and pencils and an excited smile. She wore a faded white shirtwaist and a large black skirt with a dirty hem from being dragged along the ground.

"Hi," she said.

"Good day."

She stood in silence, blinking at him.

"Can I help you?" Cass asked.

"I'm ready."

"Ready for what? Do I know you?"

"Yes. I rode on the train with you. From St. Louis. I'm Whitsett."

"You're a woman."

"Very good, inspector," she said with a careful smile. "I'm Miss Whitsett. I'm going to be your stenographer."

"I see." Cass coughed and straightened his jacket. He didn't have very much experience working, or speaking, or not speaking with women. "I thought you were the adjuster's secretary."

"Nope, stenographer. You sound nervous. Are you nervous? Why are you nervous?" She had a high, soft voice that most struggled to hear. Her brown hair was stuffed into a bun like a bale of cotton.

"I didn't realize we had woman employees who weren't secretaries. How did you get the job?"

"Black magic."

"Really?"

"No, I just applied for it. How'd you get your job?"

"Are you allowed outside? I mean, out around the town?"

"Sure, I'll be with you, it's okay. I'm a woman, not a demon. Ready to interview the Handy Bandit?" she asked.

"Handsome Bandit! He's a famous outlaw. Like Billy the Kid, or Jesse James."

"Oh, those are those dime books for kids. They are fun though, I like them."

"They're not just for kids. They're heroes. They're outlaws, they fight injustice and evil along the territories and wild west. The Handsome Bandit is one of the fastest guns in the wild west. He once gunned a man from his holster who already had his gun drawn."

"Drawn?"

"He's the leader of the Hedgepeth four. He's known for his bowler hat and having polished shoes."

"Is this our coach, inspector?"

"I've probably read more books about Billy the Kid and Jesse James, but the Handsome Bandit is one of my favorites."

"Okay, calm down."

"I'm going to go out west someday and have a ranch just like in the books."

"And raise cows?"

"No, get into adventures. Explore. Find treasure. Ride my horse."

"You wouldn't last five minutes in the west," she said.

"What! Why would you say that?"

"Your hands are too smooth, and your skin is white and milky, like a woman's. If the sun didn't kill you, some roughneck would. I wonder if a cow can kill you. I bet a cow could kill *you*. I really like it here in St. Louis, there's so much grass. There's not much grass in Philadelphia. I wonder if that's because there's always so much building going on. Ready to go?"

A horse-drawn fly coach pulled up and the driver helped Whitsett climb inside.

"Grass?" Everything was moving too fast for Cass. Whitsett spoke faster than he could listen. He quickly followed her.

As the coach rocked from side to side on the road, Cass fussed with his tie.

"Need some help, inspector?"

"You know that as my stenographer, you are to write down everything we say. The questions and the answers."

"Yes."

"And stenographers aren't allowed to talk. Just take notes. You have to blend into the background. Do you know how to blend into the background?"

"I've read about it," she said.

"You must have good penmanship. I'm trying to decide if I should wear my bowler hat. It's the same kind he wears. What do you think?"

Whitsett looked Cass over. His grey suit and double-breasted vest hung loosely over his body like a coat on a hook. His jacket was open, revealing his waistcoat and heavily-starched shirt. His buttons had buttons. *Buttons, buttons, glorious buttons*, Whitsett thought. "Are you paid by the button?" she asked.

"No? Do I not look presentable? Does the hat make me look feeble?"

"It's not the hat."

The Handsome Bandit

They ascended the dirty stone steps into the prison while policemen glared down at Whitsett. She just smiled and walked past them, leaving them confused. She was unbothered in her own little world. The interior walls were large bricks that were crumbling away. Everything was dirty and it smelled of manure.

Realizing where she was, Whitsett pulled a ring off her pinky with a painful tug and placed it on her wedding finger, turning the amber stone to her palm so it looked like a wedding band. The small ring was tight and began to cut off the circulation.

"Are you married, Miss Whitsett?" Cass asked, noticing her discomfort.

"Hell, no!"

"But, why have you put that ring around your wedding finger?"

"The ring will make 'em think we're married and keep everyone on their best behavior."

"Why would it keep them on their best behavior?"

"Because if you're a married woman, you have value. But if you're an unmarried woman, you're garbage."

"That's not true," Cass said.

"Married women get hospitality; unmarried women get the door. This will help keep everyone's mouth and mind clean. It's okay, I use this con all the time."

"Um, Miss Whitsett. Should I have a wedding ring too?" he asked.

"One hour with an unchaperoned bachelor and I got a proposal. They're right, single men are dangerous," she said.

"I don't mean to be inappropriate," Cass said, oblivious to her teasing. He was still fussing with his tie. "Do I not look respectable?"

Whitsett untied Cass's necktie, putting it in her pocket. Then she unbuttoned his stiff stand collar. "There," she said. "Now you don't look like such a starched bureaucrat. They won't be so hostile now."

"They get hostile?" Cass suddenly became more nervous.

"Can you look tougher?"

"I don't look tough?"

"I'm sure the tie will do. Is this the first time you've spoken to a roughneck?" she asked.

She was so excited to be able to walk through a prison. Her smile calmed Cass, setting him at ease.

"Yes. Is this your first time?"

"From inside a prison, yes," she said.

After showing a letter of introduction to the warden from the Fidelity Mutual Office, they were led to the cell of the Handsome Bandit. They walked past cell after cell, seeing prisoners with vacant expressions on their faces. The entire facility was lit by small holes in the tall ceilings that let in harsh shafts of white sunlight.

Cass expected the prisoners to be snarling beasts, but instead, they were pale and feeble, malnourished with sunken cheeks and heavy eyes. They were living corpses with dead eyes and sharp faces. One prisoner was hanging by his wrists as he coughed and wheezed. Another prisoner's hands were bound behind his back, attached to his feet with shackles. He had been forced to urinate in his pants.

The prison's stone walls had bloody scratch marks and vulgar graffiti. They could hear far off yells and screams. The misery of this place was painted on wet and thick.

The Handsome Bandit was lying on the hard, damp floor of his cell. Cass and Whitsett entered and sat down on two wooden chairs. When the bandit heard the creak of the wood on the concrete floor he stirred and sat up. Whitsett took out her writing material as she tried to ignore Hedgepeth's coughing and hacking.

Cass was let down. The Handsome Bandit looked nothing like the dashing drawings in the dimes and comics. He was emaciated, bones poking through his skin, coughing and drooling. His thick black hair was now gray. He finished his coughing fit by spitting yellow mucus onto the floor. He looked more like a hospital patient than a frontier hero. His tattered, striped prison clothes were stained yellow and red.

"Mr. Hedgepeth, I'm Inspector Cass. I work for Fidelity Mutual Life Association. I was lead investigator on the Pitezel case that you referred to in your letter. This is Miss Whitsett. She's a stenographer. She's going to be recording our conversation. Is that alright?"

"Sure thang, boss." He had a raspy voice, hoarse from coughing.

Whitsett noticed he was covered in bruises and wire marks, just like the other prisoners. Their wrists bled from sores made by the shackles. She pulled her shirt sleeve tight over her wrists and hoped no one noticed her own marks.

"What's that screaming?" Whitsett asked the bandit.

"Must be the guards workin' someone over."

"Why?" she asked.

"What's today?"

"Wednesday."

"I guess because it's Wednesday."

"Now, for the sake of her hands, we should speak slowly so she can record everything," Cass said.

"Whatever you say, boss."

"What do you mean my hands?" Whitsett asked, furiously stretching her sleeves over her wrists.

"So your hands don't cramp up."

"Oh, right, okay. Thanks." No one had ever asked an interviewee to speak slowly for her sake before; they mostly just pretended like she wasn't there.

"Off the record, I just want to say, I'm a big fan of yours," Cass said.

"Fan? Oh yes, the little books." He finished his sentence with a coughing fit and the expectoration of mucus.

Cass was at a loss for words.

"What're ya in for?" Whitsett asked.

"Train robbery, ma'am. Waiting to get my sentence. Maybe this will help the judge give leniency, ya know."

"Train robbery! Was there a shootout? Did one of your gang turn you in?"

"No, Pinkertons caught me."

"How did you out draw that other outlaw?" Cass asked.

"What outlaw?"

"The one with his pistol already pointed at you."

"I don't 'member that," Hedgepeth said with his rough drawl. "I'm surprised they sent ya'll the way out here from Phil-delphia."

Cass motioned for Miss Whitsett to begin recording again. The tight ring had made her tingling finger go numb and she flexed it to relieve the pressure.

"We were already in St. Louis, Mr. Hedgepeth—on another assignment."

"You married, miss?"

Whitsett looked up and pretended to be surprised. "Umm. Yes."

"Well, how 'bout that. He treat ya right?"

"This is my husband, sir!" She grabbed onto Cass's arm. "I would appreciate you being civil. Especially if you're trying to get leniency from the judge." Her soft voice took on a hard bite.

Cass's eyes opened wide and his cheeks blushed. "Umm," Cass said.

"My apologies, boss."

The distant sounds of iron doors slamming and painful screams echoed through the halls. Whitsett noticed Cass was still trying to process the outburst and she wanted to give him a little help.

"Inspector?" she asked.

"Umm," Cass said.

"You've been swindled," Hedgepeth said.

"What makes you say that?" Cass asked.

"I'm in on the swindle."

"Mr. Hedgepeth, you rob from greedy landowners and unscrupulous railroad men. You don't 'swindle' insurance agencies."

"Son, I rob anyone that gots money. And what your insurance company gots is money. Money and a body that isn't Mr. Pitezel."

"Whose body do we have?"

"Hell if I know."

"How are you involved in this, Mr. Hedgepeth?" Cass asked.

"About two months ago, a man named H.M. Howard was in heres with me. We got to talkin' and he told me he had a scheme to make $10,000. He needed some lawyer who could be trusted. I said, don't we all. He said if I knew someone like that he would see that I got 500 for it. I told him I knew a lawyer that would work with him. A Mr. J.D. Howe."

Cass suddenly perked up. He remembered that name from the file. He always took excellent notes.

"How was the scheme to be executed?" Cass asked, leaning closer.

"Executed?"

"Carried out?"

Flush with the inspector's full attention, Hedgepeth sat back against the wall.

"How long you been married?" Hedgepeth asked Miss Whitsett.

"I would appreciate it if you behaved like a gentleman or I'll end this interview right now."

"And the two of you work with each other? Must be a real treat."

Whitsett stood up. "Do I need to get the guard?" she said.

Hedgepeth's face went white and he pushed himself against the wall like an old work dog. "No, please," he said, his voice a whisper. "Don't get the guard. I'm sorry. I'm sorry."

Whitsett's hand was still tingling from the tight ring and her mouth went dry. She realized that a word to the guard meant he would get his own Wednesday working over. She sat down and tried not to look at him.

"The swindle, Mr. Hedgepeth," Cass said.

"Howard said that Mr. Pitezel and him were gonna work the insurance company for the $10,000. He said he was an expert at this sort of thing and had done it before. He said he was a druggist and could easily swindle the insurance company by having Pitezel fix himself up according to his directions and appear he was mortally wounded by an explosion, and then put a corpse in place of Pitezel's body and then have it identified as that of Pitezel. I thought he was a liar. After a few days, he made bond and I thought that was that.

"Then a few days later, that dog of a lawyer, Howe, come to me and said Howard said I recommended him. Howard had told Howe the entire scheme and the lawyer was impressed by it. He said Howard was smooth. He told me he never heard of a finer or smoother piece a work. Slickest man he'd ever seen, and that's from a goddamn lawyer. Pardon my language, ma'am.

"Then Howard went east to pull it off. Sent in the premium to make sure the policy was up to date. Then a notice appeared in the *Globe Democrat* and *Chronicle* of the death of B.F. Pitezel. Howe said the policy was paid out to the wife. The wife paid Howe $1,000. He wanted $2,000. Pitezel and Howard are alive and well living in Germany. And I don't have my goddamn $500."

Whitsett poked Cass with her elbow. He was frozen with his mouth open and eyes bulging.

"I see, and Howard, what did he look like? Can you describe him?" Cass asked.

"Like every other pecker in a tie. Pardon my language, ma'am. He did have bright blue eyes though."

They rode back to the office in the same uncomfortable fly coach. Cass was silent and moody. He rolled his hat in his hands, tapping it against his thigh.

"What was it like meetin' your hero?"

"I don't want to talk about it," he said.

Miss Whitsett wanted to buy him a balloon to cheer him up. She took his tie from inside his jacket pocket and began to tie it around his neck.

"Well, Mr. Cass, you've done a lot of growing up this afternoon."

"What did you think of his story?" Cass asked her.

"Sounds like a cart of horse shit," she said in her soft voice.

"Ladies aren't supposed to talk like that," Cass said, shifting uncomfortably.

"And men aren't supposed to cry like little girls, but I won't tell anyone if you don't."

"I didn't cry."

"Exactly, your secret is safe with me."

Cass could see she was smiling at him, but he didn't know if she was mocking him. They exited the coach outside the insurance office.

"I'm sorry you had to hear all this, Miss Whitsett," Cass said.

"Hear what?"

"As an insurance inspector, I am accustomed to thinking about all manner of death. It must be troublesome to you."

"It doesn't bother me either," she said.

"Why not?"

"I don't know, would you prefer I gasp every time someone says something?

"No, that wouldn't do," Cass said. "Well, I guess we better get back."

"I don't think they're gonna miss us. Why don't we walk around?" she said.

"We should probably do some follow up."

"Oh, that sounds better," Whitsett replied. "What does that mean?"

"We should go and see if anything the Handsome Bandit says is true."

"Fun!" Whitsett was so excited she bolted away, walking without knowing where she was going. Then she suddenly stopped and turned around. "Why wouldn't this Howard person just pay him the $500?"

After a carriage ride to the police station, Cass and Whitsett were shown to the superintendent's office. He was a thick man with yellow teeth who didn't become superintendent to take meetings with insurance agents and women. He chewed on his cigar to keep from spitting on them.

The entire office was covered in boxing match playbills. Most of them had been faded by the harsh sun. In the corner was a small mounted plaque with two colorful butterflies pinned to the cork board.

"Did you have a Mr. Howard incarcerated?" Cass asked the superintendent. Cass thought he would be a frightening man to a young woman like Miss Whitsett but she did not seem the least bit intimidated. She looked at the grim police and jail mementos around the room with a pleasant smile.

"Do ya think I could buy a cigar from you?" Whitsett asked.

"Excuse me?" the superintendent asked.

"A cigar. Could I buy one from you? No one will sell me one."

"That's because ladies shouldn't smoke. Now sit there and be quiet." He looked through his files.

"I like your butterfly," Whitsett said with a wry smile.

No one had ever mentioned or even seen the butterfly before. The superintendent felt ridiculous scowling at a smiling young woman and began to relax. "Yes. There was a man here by that name."

"Really?" Cass was surprised the Handsome Bandit's story was true. "What was his crime?" Cass asked.

The superintendent searched the notes.

"Fraud. He bought a drug store using borrowed money, a mortgage. Then he sold the drug store, which is a mortgaged property. He had no right to sell it. And he did a real number on the people he sold the drug store to. He hired fake customers to make the place look busy when he was showing the property."

"Good con," Whitsett said. "I'll bet he raised the prices for that too, made it look like he was making it hand over fist."

"Exactly, a real character that one. I see you have an eye for it, miss."

"And may I say," Cass added. "I am very impressed with your record keeping. Very good note taking."

"Thanks?" the superintendent said, unsure of what to make of Cass's enthusiasm for paperwork.

"Do you have a sketch of this Mr. Howard?" Cass asked.

"Yes. I'll have a copy drawn up for you. The police made it while he was imprisoned to collect evidence on a number of frauds he had supposedly committed."

"Do you have an address for him?"

"He was staying at a boarding house of some kind. Not a local."

"So, I can't talk you out of a cigar?" Whitsett asked.

The superintendent smiled at her directness and persistence; she reminded him of himself as a young lad. He wouldn't have taken no for an answer either. And she did have an eye.

"Well, as long as you don't tell anyone where you-"

"Thank you very much for your time. And, if you don't mind me asking, do you suffer from any ailments?" Cass asked, leaning forward. He had been preparing his pitch and jumped in like a bucking horse.

"Ailments? Why?"

"Because I have a special tonic with me that will help with most physical discomfort. It's the most powerful tonic on the market."

"I don't think so, Mr. Cass."

"I promise, one swig of this tonic and you will be able to go about your day in peace."

"I assure you, I'm quite fit."

"Perhaps your wife suffers from headaches."

"My wife? Guard, will you please show Mr. Cass to the artist for his sketch."

"I'll make sure he gets there, sir," Whitsett said, pulling Cass up by the arm. She knew she wasn't getting her cigar now. "Are you a madman?" she whispered to Cass. "Those men will belt you."

"Do your duty and a little more and the future will take care of itself; Andrew Carnegie," Cass said as she pulled him down the hall.

"Calm down, inspector."

Follow Up

Cass found the address for Mr. Pitezel's widow in his files and they rode the coach across town to the boarding house. Whitsett looked at the sketch of the man in question.

"So, this is the man who wouldn't pay the Handsome Bandit $500? I guess his story wasn't a cart of horseshit after all. He's good lookin'," she added.

"No. No, he isn't. He was in jail, Miss Whitsett."

"He's still good lookin'."

"No."

The old wooden building was congested with women in dirty clothes and smelled of spoiled meat. The wood was rotting away and creaked like an old ship.

After five minutes of knocking and shouts by neighbors to 'piss off,' Whitsett was resolved to the fact that no one was home.

"I think you can stop knocking now," Whitsett told Cass.

"I have to be thorough."

"I guess you're a thoroughbred," Whitsett said, laughing to herself.

"What does that mean?"

A mother holding a small baby opened the door next to Mr. Pitezel's apartment. Her face was yellow, and she looked as though she were about to waste away to nothing.

"What are ya lunatics doing?" she asked, bouncing her crying baby.

"Do you know when Mrs. Pitezel will be home?"

"No idea. She hasn't been back in a week."

"A week?" Cass said. He turned to Whitsett and motioned for her to start recording. "Do you remember the exact date?"

"Who are you?"

"I'm sorry. I'm with Fidelity Mutual. You may have heard that Mrs. Pitezel's husband died recently and we're here doing some routine follow-up on her insurance claim. Did she tell you where she was going?"

"No, she just took her little boy and daughter and left."

"I see." Cass presented the sketch of Howard. "Have you ever seen this man before?"

"Oh yes, was here all the time. He would come over with another man named Howe."

"This man? He was here all the time? Regarding what?"

"I don't know."

"How do you know the other man's name?" Whitsett asked.

"He would scream it all the time."

Cass helped Miss Whitsett into the coach.

"I'm beginning to think there was a lot more to the Handsome Bandit's story than we gave credit. Imagine if we found evidence of an insurance fraud. Could mean a promotion. Maybe a bonus."

"I would very much like a bonus," Whitsett said. "Where are we going?"

"To talk to that lawyer and see what he has to say for himself. His account isn't adding up either. How are you faring, Miss Whitsett? Is this work too strenuous?"

"It'd be a lot better if I had my goddamn cigar."

"What cigar?"

"Never mind, inspector."

"Do we need to stop?"

"Why, do you need a nap?"

"Me? Do I need a nap?"

"Am I talking too fast for you?" Whitsett smiled. Cass burst into laughter.

"Talking too fast," Cass said. "You speak so directly. Like Calamity Jane or Annie Oakley."

"I'm sorry. Is that too rough?" she asked.

"No. Not at all. I think I get it now. You're teasing me, yes?"

"Yes, inspector."

"Very amusing."

"I'm glad you think so," she said. "But you have to buy me a cigar. Seriously."

Cass held his side from laughing so hard.

They drove to the office of Mr. Howe, the lawyer 'who would work with you.' He was very gracious and invited the investigators to sit.

It was a modest office with papers piled on the desk. The lack of organization made Cass ill.

The only window in the cramped office overlooked an alley filled with rotting vegetable products. Howe rented the small office space from the accounting firm that occupied most of the building.

"How can I help you?" Mr. Howe asked. He had thin, blonde hair and suffered from toe pain due to shoes that were too small. He flipped through Cass's letter of introduction from the insurance company.

"Do you remember a client named Mr. Pitezel?"

"I'm afraid I don't. I have so many clients."

"A man died in Philadelphia named Mr. Pitezel. A pipe exploded in his face and killed him. It was ruled an accidental death. The life insurance claim was paid out against my recommendation. This person named Holmes came with Pitezel's daughter to identify the body; along with you. In my opinion, everything about the death was too convenient and very suspect. But the company paid it out anyway to the dead man's widow, Mrs. Pitezel; your client."

"Oh yes, I remember now."

"Do you happen to know the location of Mrs. Pitezel?" Cass asked.

"I have her boarding house address written down somewhere," Howe said.

"She isn't there anymore. She's just vanished as of last week."

"Vanished? Well, I haven't had any contact with her since the business with her husband."

"You've concluded your business with her?"

"Yes, thankfully."

"A difficult case? Did she pay you?"

"Yes. Not as much as she should. But that's the same story for all my clients." Howe laughed nervously.

"May I see your contract?" Cass asked.

"What contract?"

"Your paperwork. She was a client, I assume she signed a standard letter of engagement, fee schedule, etc. You can't run a practice without paperwork. If you don't write it down, it didn't happen."

"No, we didn't have any paperwork."

"No paperwork!" Cass was offended. Whitsett had never seen someone get so animated over paperwork. "That's a very big oversight. Especially for a lawyer."

"Some people just don't believe in them."

"You can tell a lot about a man by how he keeps his paperwork," Case said. "And his penmanship."

"Can I help you with something?" The lawyer asked, struggling to keep his irritation at bay.

"Why did Mr. Pitezel go by a different name?" Cass asked. "He was living under a fake name."

"He assumed the name of Perry to escape embarrassment from a bad business deal."

"Ever meet Marion Hedgepeth, the Handsome Bandit?" Cass asked the lawyer.

"No."

"Are you sure?"

"Never met him."

"Doesn't it seem a little suspicious for a family to up and move just a few days after getting a life insurance payout?"

"No, not necessarily," Howe said. "The death uprooted the family, maybe they went to stay with relatives."

"Yes, but if you recall, Mrs. Pitezel was too sick to travel to Philadelphia to identify the body. As a result, *you* had to bring her daughter. That's what I have in *my* paperwork."

"Oh yes, she was quite sick."

"Yet after receiving $9,000, she is suddenly healed and endowed with a wanderlust?"

"Mr. Cass, your company paid out the claim. Business is concluded," he said, brushing his hands together.

"Who is this man?" Whitsett asked, holding up the sketch.

"That's the man I met in your office before we went to the morgue. While I was there with the girl to identify the body."

"He seems to be showing up all over the place in the worst ways," Whitsett said. "He was in prison and was also seen visiting the 'sick' widow. Where else should we look for him? Apparently he goes by the names Howard or Holmes."

"I don't know anything about him."

"You've never seen him before?"

"No," Howe said.

"Except when you identified the body, right?"

"Well, yes..."

"You seem to be confused. Mrs. Pitezel's neighbor says she saw you with him at the boarding house," Whitsett said.

"She must be mistaken."

"Are you sure? I hear he is the 'smoothest piece of work,'" Whitsett said, copying the Handsome Bandit's drawl.

Howe's face became pale, recognizing he had used those exact words with Hedgepeth. "I'm afraid I have to get back to work." He stood up and showed them to the door.

As they walked out onto the curb, Whitsett was in a great mood. Usually she was stuck in a hot building all day and a cold boarding house all night. She really enjoyed riding around in a carriage and asking people uncomfortable questions.

"That was fun," Whitsett said. "For a lawyer, he wasn't very good at bullshit."

"These people think they're so smart. The lawyers and the doctors and the politicians. They just don't realize-" Cass stopped himself.

"How smart you are?" Whitsett laughed.

"I'm an inspector. It's my job to be smart. I'm known for being able to differentiate a person from their footsteps alone."

She made fake pistols with her fingers. "Inspector the Kid, smartest gun in the west," She laughed so obnoxiously, it made Cass smile.

The following day, the six visiting agents took a train back to Philadelphia. Riding on the train was like going to church except the narrow seats faced each other. Everyone was dressed in their Sunday best and anything but polite conversation was properly looked down upon.

Cass and Whitsett sat together the entire way. Their obnoxious laughing and conversation boomed over the sound of women fanning themselves, men coughing politely into their fists, and the chug of the engine. Cass told Whitsett of his belief in the importance of good penmanship while Whitsett mocked other people on the train, giving them voices and silly scenarios. The Fidelity Mutual employees, as well as the other passengers, were silently outraged.

"This was the first time I'd ever been away from home," Whitsett said. "I loved it. If I could do anything, I'd just spend all my time traveling. I was gonna move to Chicago for the World's Fair."

"Wouldn't you miss your home?"

"Christ, no. It'd have been so amazing. The White City. I coulda made tons of money and lived in a house with beautiful marble. Real books and a nice hat. Oh, I could get a real respectable hat in Chicago I'll bet."

"Marble?"

"They remade the entire city with marble and rivers and statues. Like the temple in Jerusalem. It'd have been like living inside a marbled dream with frosting."

Cass smiled at her enthusiasm. "Did you have family there? Why didn't you go?"

"No family, just couldn't afford the damn ticket. Maybe I could afford the ticket with our bonuses."

"Bonuses for what?"

"For uncovering the insurance scam," she said.

"No, we don't have enough to bring to the firm. Just a lot of conflicting stories from less than reputable people."

"We'll find somethin'. What about you, inspector. What would you do with your bonus?"

"I would have a nice big office." Cass reached into his coat pocket. "Which reminds me, if you have a headache, you should take this special tonic. It's called Sampson and Carlisle's Pain Tonic. Tell all your friends about it."

"It work?"

"Of course it works. Hypothetically."

"What's hypothetically mean?"

"As an idea, it should work. It has minerals from the orient."

"Oh, I see," she said. "You sure this isn't a con?"

"This is a viable product."

"You're probably not very good at doing things, are you?" she asked, opening the bottle and smelling the contents.

"What! Why would you say that? I'm an inspector. I've worked as the lead on three medium-term projects. I keep detailed notes and have excellent penmanship. I have my mineral water-"

"Got it, you wanna be a rich businessman so you can sit in an office and not do things."

"This product is going to help thousands of people," Cass said in earnest. "I'm going to be like J.P. Morgan."

"I hope it becomes very successful," she said.

"Me too. I've put a lot of my money into it."

"I'm surprised you haven't tried to sell this to everyone who works at Fidelity," she said.

"I have tried but I was told not to sell my tonic on the premises."

"Were you reprimanded? I'm sorry," she said, trying to hold back a smile as she imagined Cass being scolded like a little puppy.

"The entire situation was outrageous. I wasn't disrupting anything. What's more disrupting—my tonic, or an employee with a headache?"

"Outrageous, inspector. How much is this tonic?"

"You can keep the bottle," Cass said.

"Thank you very much. I wanted to get a cigar while I was in St. Louis, but you ruined it."

"Smoking isn't very ladylike, is it?"

"No, but it's the first time I've ever been away from Philadelphia, so I wanted to celebrate. I actually wanted to drink whiskey, but I thought they'd arrest me."

Cass smiled at the thought of this little girl trying to find whiskey. "You know what?" He rolled her a cigarette using McRae's fine Tobacco and Tip Top rolling paper. "To celebrate your travels." He lit the cigarette and handed it to her. Since deciding to roll his own, he was able to save almost $1.60 a month from buying the tobacco and paper in bulk. *I'm already on my way to becoming the next JP Morgan*, he had thought.

"Thanks," she said. "You have to have one too." The other Fidelity agents did not approve of a lady smoking. It was inappropriate. But they were trapped by their own social conditioning and didn't say anything. They were also happy they didn't have to sit next to Cass or talk to Whitsett.

After Cass rolled his own cigarette, he slapped the breast of his coat and his pants, dusting the small leaves onto the floor.

"What I need to do is to invent a new cigarette. A square cigarette. It will last longer and be easier to roll."

"You want everyone to walk around with a box in their mouth?" She laughed. "I'd go back to the well on that one."

"What part of the city do you live in?" he asked.

"I live with my family just outside the city. I'm surrounded by trees and quiet neighbors and grass. Miles and miles of grass. And books."

"That's nice. What does your family do?"

"They love me. My father retired and he bosses my mother and me around all evening when he isn't reading or chatting with the neighbors or wanting to discuss art and theater and fashion and things with us. They're always fussing over me, but they do love me. I don't think they will ever let me move out. Because they love me so much."

"I'm sure they will when you get married."

"That's twice in one day you've proposed to me, inspector."

"Oh no! I wasn't trying to be rude," Cass said, turning red.

"I know, inspector. I'm teasing you."

Cass laughed and brushed his knee.

The ticket taker walked through the train car calling out the stops. "Next stop, Chicago! Next stop, Chicago!"

"Chicago. Didn't you say that man in the sketch was from there? Was it Howard or Holmes that lives there?" Whitsett asked. She was so distracted she dropped her cigarette onto Cass's lap.

"They are one in the same person. Yes. I think he goes by Holmes there," Cass said, holding a cigarette in each hand.

"We should stop. Do you have the address? Maybe there'll be something there that will get us our bonuses."

"It's in the file. I try and keep the best notes-"

"See, we'll just stop off and have a quick chat."

"The company won't sanction interviews that aren't authorized."

"Ain't you curious? We can do some more follow up." She visibly shook in her seat with excitement. "They won't ever know about it."

"They will when we report the information we discover."

"But it'll be helpful information. They won't be able to be mad at you. We can see what this Mr. Holmes has to say for himself."

"I don't know. That's quite a breach of conduct." Cass's heart began to pound at the thought of breaking a rule.

"Conduct. Psh." She waved her hand. "You're a man of industry. What would J.P. Morgan do? What would Billy the Kid do?"

Unannounced Visit

Cass and Whitsett got off the train at Chicago station and hired a coach to take them north of the city. The other agents didn't see them disembark as they were too busy hiding their faces in the morning editions, praying Whitsett and Cass wouldn't sit near them.

Chicago was large and crowded. All manner of people raced up and down the boulevards causing the city to undulate with frenetic excitement. Cowboys and roughnecks walked along the streets next to men and women in the latest European fashions. There were shops and shops and shops. Wagons crossed through large groups of people and streetcars. Anything you wanted could be obtained in abundance, as long as you could get through the crowd.

"Look how tall the buildings are! The city goes on forever in every direction. Including up," Whitsett said.

The noise on the street was overwhelming. Trollies moved hundreds of passengers. Buildings were being erected along the horizon like metal shoots. Carts of bricks and lumber were being driven to work sites. The streets were so crowded with people, carriages and carts that from the tops of the buildings, humanity flowed like a river rapid. Whitsett almost lost Cass a couple of times, as the mass threatened to swallow him away from her.

There were piles and piles of horse manure that baked in the sun, topped with thousands of flies. Dozens of dirty, small children ran from corner to corner begging and pulling on gentlemen's coattails. They were swatted away with canes and gloves like pests. Whitsett remembered how it felt to be hit with those canes and gloves.

The hansom cab they took had rubber tires which made for a smoother ride. *This city is so advanced*, Whitsett thought. *Welcome to the 20th century*.

After an entertaining ride, they found themselves in Wilmette. The white stone and concrete of the city had given way to brownstone townhouses and lawns. The address in the file took them to a two-story, red-framed house outside the city. It was the kind of house that most people would be happy to settle down in. It was clean and comfortable, out of the way of the city's noisy construction. It was almost the house Whitsett had pictured in her mind when she planned to move to Chicago, but it didn't have any marble. *Where is all the damn marble?* she thought.

Cass rang the bell and a young woman servant answered the door. She wore a white apron over her black dress and a white shirtwaist, almost exactly what Whitsett was wearing.

"Can I help ye?" the servant girl asked.

"Hello. My name is Inspector Cass. This is Miss Whitsett. I'm with...*we* are with Fidelity Mutual Insurance. We're doing a routine follow up on one of our claims. Is Mr. Holmes in?"

"No. Not at the moment, sir."

"Would Mrs. Holmes be available to speak with me? Us?" Cass corrected himself again.

"Please, come in."

Cass and Whitsett sat in the well-appointed parlor while they waited. The room was elaborately draped in fabrics and silks. The only light came from two small windows. Peppermint tea and sweets were served to them.

"All very respectable so far, isn't it?" Cass whispered.

"The vision of Christian modesty," Whitsett said as she gritted her teeth. "These teacups are fancy." The teacups were brought back from Europe by Mrs. Holmes' grandaunt Jean before the war.

The servant informed the ladies of the house, Mrs. Belknap, Mrs. Holmes and Lucy, of the guests and helped them prepare themselves for entertaining. The servant cinched up the ladies' corsets in their afternoon clothing and tied ribbons in their hair. The ladies then snuck a peek at the callers. *They are obviously lower class, possibly even tradesmen,* thought Mrs. Belknap. *Not worth the effort of any real hospitality. But all this will be good practice for little Lucy as she learns to be a lady.*

"Serve them the unsweetened biscuits," the lady of the house ordered.

The ladies entered the living room drenched in respectability. Tea was poured and introductions were made. The older woman spoke first in a polite and cool formality.

"My name is Mrs. Belknap. This is my daughter Mrs. Holmes."

Mrs. Holmes was a beautiful blonde woman with the face of a doll. She wore a crisp blue dress with bright blue ribbons in her hair. The jaeger corset she wore gave her the respectable, slight s-curve silhouette.

In contrast, Whitsett's grey skirt and white shirt were straight and without poofs and loops. They were presentable, but only for a working-class woman, or a servant. She looked like an animal rooting through garbage in comparison.

"And this is my granddaughter, Lucy."

Lucy was a small seven-year-old, the image of her mother. She was blonde and white and perfect. Whitsett wanted to spit on them. She stared at the women of different ages. She could see the stages of respectable life embodied in them; child, adult and old woman. It was a life she had never had, and never would have; a comfortable, respectable life. She pressed so hard with her pencil that she broke the tip.

"Hello, little Lucy," Cass said. Then he turned to the women. "I am Inspector Cass, and this is Miss Whitsett. We have some questions about Mr. Holmes."

"Why don't you go play with your dolls, Lucy?" Mrs. Holmes said.

"Yes, mommy." She took a biscuit and the servant girl escorted her upstairs.

"Little bitch," Whitsett said under her breath.

Everyone froze in shock.

"What did you say?" The old woman stood up and folded her hands under her stomach, protecting herself from the toxicity of the word. Such words had never been spoken in her presence, and certainly never directed at her, or for that matter, any lady she knew.

"I didn't say anything," Whitsett said. She made her voice higher and softer.

"I just heard you!"

"I don't think so." Whitsett began to act like the woman was hearing things. "Little Lucy said 'okay mommy,' is that what you were talking about?"

"She said 'yes mommy,'" Mrs. Holmes added.

"Did she? Are you sure? What did you hear?" she asked Cass.

Cass's eyes were open all the way. The situation was flying by him at incredible speed and he was having difficulty keeping up.

"Now I don't remember. Do you remember, Mrs. Holmes?" Whitsett said.

"No, I can't be certain," Mrs. Holmes said, struggling to remember what had happened only a few moments ago.

"What about you, ma'am?" Whitsett asked.

The older woman felt everyone's eyes on her. She coughed politely. "What's all this about, inspector?" She sat down, stripped of her confidence.

That was a close one, Whitsett thought. Good con.

"We're just doing a routine follow up on the investigation, ma'am," Cass said. "Would you mind if Miss Whitsett takes notes?"

"Not at all," she said.

"When did Fidelity Mutual first contact you?" Cass asked Mrs. Holmes.

"It was in the middle of September. Around the 15th I think. Someone from the company came here and gave me a list of questions and some news clippings about the death of someone my husband knew. I sent the notes to my husband and I forwarded his responses to your office."

"Do you expect your husband home anytime soon?"

"I'm afraid not. He's away on business. He's a busy and very important man."

"My son-in-law has a great deal of assets to see over," Mrs. Belknap quickly offered.

"I see, what kind of assets?"

"Property and real estate. All over the country. He even owns a famous property in Englewood. They call it 'the castle.'"

"Do you know what cities these properties are in?"

"No," Mrs. Holmes said.

"It isn't proper for husbands to discuss business and politics with their wives," Mrs. Belknap said.

Miss Whitsett snorted derisively. "Then what do you talk about?" she asked.

"Is there any address where we could reach him?" Cass asked, hoping to move on from Whitsett's breaches in propriety.

"I don't know where he is at the moment, inspector. Why don't you just leave whatever questions you have and I will forward them to him. He moves around so often it is hard to know where he will be."

"It is very important we reach him. There's no way we can get in touch with him?" Cass asked.

"I'm afraid not," Mrs. Holmes said.

"It must be very difficult having your husband so hard to reach. How did you meet him?" Cass asked.

"We were living in Minneapolis at the time. He was there on business. He was so exciting and full of energy and spirit." Mrs. Holmes's face began to glow with excitement as she remembered. "We had a wonderful courtship."

"All chaperoned and public," Mrs. Belknap added.

"He is so full of life. So vibrant." She couldn't stop smiling. "Once we were married, I worked as a clerk at his drug store. But then..." Her glow extinguished. "I live here now with my parents and our daughter. He comes here when he can."

"You have no idea where he is?"

"I'm afraid not, I'm sorry. I'm just a simple mother." She leaned towards her servant. "Could you refresh everyone?"

"Yes, ma'am," the servant answered as she began to pour. Cass and Whitsett had forgotten she was still in the room.

Miss Whitsett slammed her hand over the teacup and wouldn't take another drop of peppermint tea from this poor, simple mother and her servant on principle.

"Well, thank you so much for your time, so sorry to have troubled you," Mr. Cass said.

They were seen to the door and made their way to the street.

"That was a waste of time. I can't believe we got off the train for this. Please don't tell anyone we did this," Cass said. He was furious. "I'll have to pay for the extra expenses. I can't afford that; I spent all my money on my headache tonic. I'm going to get fired!"

"Calm down. Don't be angry, inspector. We aren't done just yet. Do you have two dollars?"

"Yes."

"Give it to me."

Cass handed her two dollars from his pocket.

Whitsett grabbed Cass's arm and led him around the back of the house. Through the kitchen window, she saw the servant girl cleaning up the dishes. Whitsett waved to get her attention and motioned for her to join them outside.

The servant girl cracked open the door leading to the kitchen. "Yes?"

"Hey," Whitsett said. "You got a few minutes for a smoke?"

"Sure." Her Irish accent cracked as she inched forward.

"Mr. Cass." Whitsett nudged him with her elbow. Cass took out his pack and rolled a cigarette for her. Whitsett handed the girl the smoke together with the bills.

"Thanks." The servant girl pocketed the money and lit the cigarette. "I almost died when ye called the little one a bitch," she said, laughing. "I thought for sure they were going to throw ya out. I can't believe you got away with it."

"How are they?" Whitsett asked, pointing to the house.

"They's al'right. You know how tis."

"Yes. When was Mr. Holmes last here?"

"Few days before the last insurance man come out." She did her best to blow the smoke out of the side of her mouth to keep the smell off her clothing.

"Last September?" Cass asked. "Is he here often?"

"Nah, he's never 'round here. Sends 'is monies and maybe a Christmas present for the little'n."

"What's he like?" Whitsett asked.

"Real charmer, that one. Fast talker."

"Do you think he has all these properties?" Cass asked.

"I wouldn't know about that. But the misses believe everything he says. If you ask me, he isn't what he seems at all."

"Why do you say that?"

"There was a wire before he went to Philadelphia to look at the dead man. It was a request to wire funds to him in New York. The misses had to sell some of her silver pieces. Not happy she was."

"What was the money for?"

"I don't know. But it was a lot. $157.57."

"That's a lot of money," Whitsett said. "Do you know why she stopped working at his drug store? Why she moved out here?"

"Mr. Holmes loves the ladies if you catch my mean'n. Fights a lot with his misses about it. But she's devoted. Makes no sense, as you can see, the misses is the most beautiful woman in the world. Makes me sad for the little'n."

"Not very respectable, is it?"

"Not the word I would use. Thanks for the smoke." She put out the cigarette and went back to her work.

Whitsett and Cass caught the next train to Philadelphia. She teased him the entire trip. When they disembarked, Whitsett said goodbye to Cass at the station and started to walk towards the trolley that led out of town. When she was sure Cass was out of sight, she turned around and walked back the way she came, into the muddy street. She had to hurry before it became dark. If she walked the street, unaccompanied at night, she knew the cops would stop her, thinking she was a prostitute.

She could already see the public women beginning to line the alleys for dark. They wore buttoned shirts that revealed their chests, which they kept covered with wraps. They had long dresses and had painted their faces white with chalk or flour. Whitsett kept her head low and avoided eye contact with them.

After a few blocks, she arrived at the boarding house for single women. This neighborhood saw no new construction or skyscrapers. There was just an old, drafty wooden building where the sewage ran freely in the street and people covered their mouths when they walked to avoid catching an illness.

Whitsett made her way up the stairs. She entered her apartment, took off her boots, and placed them in a bucket which she hung out the window to keep the smell of wet garbage away. The room was barely two strides across, and the floorboards creaked with even the slightest thought of movement.

One of her neighbors had a squawking bird that would screech profanity in Hungarian. Her other neighbors were Italian and Greek immigrants that would yell and scream at each other constantly. Miss Whitsett would beat the walls to try and get them to shut up, but it never worked.

She grabbed her bed sheet and shook it. Bugs and pests were sent flying across the room. The building didn't have gas and she couldn't afford any candles. Perhaps once Cass discovered what the $157.50 was used for, she could buy a few candles with her bonus.

She didn't have any clean clothes after the trip so she decided to just wear a less dirty blouse and dress. But, as usual, she would have to wait until morning to be able to see. Once she got her bonus, she was moving to Chicago.

Fidelity Mutual Life Association

Inspector Cass arrived at work early that morning. He was anxious to get into the files and do what was most comfortable to him—research. He wanted to see if the Handsome Bandit's claim about the outstanding premiums being paid up to date before the 'accident' was true.

He thumbed through the past invoices and aging reports. All the notes were presented in alphabetical order; it was like reading a history book.

Cass froze. The bandit was telling the truth. The premiums hadn't been paid in half a year. Then, just before the death, the outstanding payments were paid in one lump sum of $157.50. The exact amount the servant said Holmes had his wife send.

This was no accident. It was an insurance scam!

He had to inform the president of the company immediately.

Inspector Cass knocked gently on the president's door. It was a warm day in Philadelphia and the windows were open. The sounds of construction could be heard from the streets. The neighborhoods of four-story red-brick buildings were being replaced by steel skyscrapers. The city just kept getting taller and taller, like a garden of untended weeds. Ten years ago, the president had a great view of a small patch of trees from his window. Now he could only see the middle floors of the building across the street.

"Come in."

Cass took a deep breath and entered. He stepped so lightly that the warm wind from the window almost knocked him down.

"Mr. Cass!" President Fouse said. "I don't like my agents conducting unauthorized interviews. You were supposed to take a statement for the file, not reopen an investigation. The claim has been paid. I approved it myself. I am going to dock you two days' pay. What do you have to say for yourself?" The president was an old man with a turkey neck. He was so fat his waistcoat buttons were stretched, hanging on for dear life.

Cass looked around the office trying to find something to say. He had been carefully researching the Pitezel case ever since he returned to Philadelphia, but he was too nervous to respond. The clangs of the construction work outside rattled him.

"Go on, what have you to say?"

"Everything Mr. Hedgepeth said could be substantiated," Cass said. He was so nervous his voice could barely be heard.

"I need not remind you that all these claims are made by a known criminal and degenerate," Fouse said. "Most likely, he is trying to scheme himself into a position for selfish purposes."

"The premium *was* paid from New York on the same day it was due; wired directly. Until that point, it had been behind in payments," Cass tried to explain. "If Hedgepeth was making up this wild story, how did he know where and when the premium would be paid?" Fouse wasn't interested in any of it.

"I don't understand why you insist on impugning this man, Holmes. I met him myself. He was completely respectable. A very astute and well-bred gentleman. We're going to have lunch the next time he's in town. He is incapable of such degenerate behavior."

"But this Holmes person also goes by the name of Howard. He seems to be involved in some criminal activity," Cass said.

"I have been in this business for almost 30 years, Mr. Cass. I have met a great deal of respectable men and degenerate men. I have come to know the difference." It was clear Fouse had been charmed by this strange gentleman, Mr. Holmes. He had even put in a rush to pay out the claim at Holmes' request.

Cass's heart was pounding.

"Go on, say something, man."

"The wart." Cass was finally relieved he was able to say something concrete.

Fouse was caught off guard. "The wart?"

"During the identification of the body, Holmes removed his coat, produced a scalpel from his pocket, cut away the clothes and sliced the wart from the corpse's neck. A very odd thing to do."

"Yes," Fouse said, slightly disgusted. He sat up in his chair. The leather hissed against his round body. "But the man is a doctor, he's simply used to that sort of thing."

"How did he know it was there?"

"How do you mean?"

"The wart was covered by a standard collar and hair. How did Holmes know there was a growth there? Had he seen this man naked?"

The thought of a man seeing another man naked was so scandalous that it caused Fouse to grab onto his desk in shock. "My God, man. Are you trying to be indecent?"

"No, sir. It just means he had a suspicious knowledge of the deceased that was intimate in nature. One that he conveniently produces when the deceased can't be positively identified due to the extensive burns on the face. Perhaps he wanted to present the mole in order to secure the payout of the insurance claim. He was very eager about everything. Why else would he do something so bizarre?"

"Did you try and find Mr. Holmes?" The thought of such indecency sent Fouse into a rage. Looking at other men! Without clothing! To think, I was going to have lunch with this pervert, he thought.

"Yes, sir. It appears to be an alias. I couldn't find any trace of him in St. Louis or Chicago. Holmes kept a domicile in Wilmette, Illinois. Rarely seen in the neighborhood. Rumor is, he is well known in Englewood, Illinois-"

"What rumors? I don't want to look at naked men!"

"I didn't say you wanted to look at naked men, sir."

"We will engage the Pinkertons," he said.

"Sir, there's no need to use them. I can easily run the investigation," Cass began to ramble. "I'm known for being able to differentiate a person from their footsteps-"

"No, I want the Pinkertons. Find Mr. Holmes."

By the time Cass had calmed down enough to explain all the outstanding questions he had uncovered about the case, Fidelity Insurance had already hired the Pinkertons.

The Pinkertons were a private detective agency and security force. They were known for getting results as well as serving as the private guards to presidents. Famous for chasing outlaws like Billy the Kid and infamous for brutality against labor unions, they were the private army of the rich and powerful, their slogan was "We Never Sleep."

The Pinkertons quickly mobilized their vast information network of officers and detectives in every major city. They employed more agents than the standing army of the United States. Their information network bled into every town with a large collection of details on criminals and a vast library of mugshots and sketches. They were brutal and organized.

After a few months of investigating, and a rather large bill, the Pinkertons were able to track down Holmes in Boston. Mr. Fouse decided to send Mr. Cass to Boston to interview Mr. Holmes and act as a liaison for the firm to help bring him back to Philadelphia for insurance fraud. Cass was pleased Fouse was in such a good mood, mostly due to the relative ease and simplicity in which they had found Holmes. *What an easy and straightforward case*, he thought.

Cass would need a stenographer. He was able to convince Mr. Fouse that using a woman was a good idea because they are paid so much less than a man; the firm would be saving money. Cass used his new business knowledge, just like J.P. Morgan.

The women were made to work on the top floors of the office building. *Why is it so hot on these top floors?* he thought as he climbed the stairs. He went into the supervisor's office and asked to see Miss Whitsett. As the supervisor fanned himself with a silk fan, he called in the gang leader, Mrs. Sappington.

Mrs. Sappington was an old, broad-shouldered woman with glasses that sat perched on the end of her nose.

"Yes, sir," she said politely in her thick Welsh accent.

"Inspector Cass would like to speak with Miss Whitsett."

Mrs. Sappington left the room and returned with Miss Whitsett. Cass felt as though he was entering a dungeon from one of his dime novels. Miss Whitsett was drenched with sweat and her face was flushed from the heat.

"Hey! It's Inspector the Kid," Miss Whitsett said, laughing to herself. Both Mrs. Sappington and her supervisor were outraged with Whitsett's familiar tone in the workplace. Mrs. Sappington gasped and pinched Miss Whitsett's ear. Whitsett had to stop herself from turning around and punching the woman.

Whitsett was put into a chair by Mrs. Sappington who stood behind her, clutching the seated woman's shoulders. The supervisor sat behind his desk with a careful eye on Cass.

"I'd like to speak to her alone?" Cass said, clearly uncomfortable with two people watching him like a hawk.

"Oh my!" Mrs. Sappington exclaimed.

"That would be inappropriate," the supervisor snapped.

"It's alright, we've spoken alone before, in St. Louis. We even went on an interview alone."

"Well you weren't supposed to," the supervisor said. He gave Miss Whitsett an angry look. "I don't know how they do things in St. Louis, Mr. Cass, but here, we don't let our women speak to men unsupervised."

"I see. Well, everyone, I need Miss Whitsett to accompany me to Boston for an interview."

The supervisor and Mrs. Sappington laughed in amusement.

"Mr. Cass, I can see you have no experience in working with women. It's not like working with another man. You can't just come in here and pick one out for yourself. It would be considered improper. It would even be scandalous. Can you imagine if anyone outside caught word of this company letting men and women work freely with each other? This isn't a bordello, sir."

"Heaven forbid if the customers found out," Mrs. Sappington added in her thick accent.

"Yes! Precisely! Thank you, Mrs. Sappington. And what of the customers, Mr. Cass? I'm sure they have stenographers in Boston for you to engage. You see, managing women in the workplace is like raising chickens. If you keep the-"

"I hate to interrupt you, but I'm rather pressed for time. We're unfortunately unable to go outside the company for this due to the high cost of the Pinkerton consultation."

"Then it just so happens we have perfectly good male stenographers for this situation."

"They are engaged on other assignments and can't be spared for a job in Boston," Cass said.

It looks like Mr. Cass is actually going to be able to talk them into it, bless his heart, thought Whitsett. They might serve whiskey to girls out east. Look out Boston, here I come.

Boston

Fidelity Mutual Life Association sent Inspector Cass and Miss Whitsett on the earliest train to Boston to interview the mysterious Mr. Holmes. They were both displeased at the insistence of taking Mrs. Sappington with them as a chaperone. She would position herself between them; there would be no funny business. She sat like a wooden statue throughout the long, uncomfortable trip.

Whitsett smiled the entire time, dancing in her seat as she stared out of the window and watched the countryside whip past her. She wanted Mr. Cass to roll her another cigarette but knew Mrs. Sappington would hassle her.

She ran out of reading material and Cass let her borrow his western dime novel. *This is garbage*, she thought. The plot was silly, and the characters were over-simplistic. But she enjoyed simply reading and riding on the train. *I'll bet Billy the Kid was really a shy person if you actually talked to him*, she thought. *He might have been fun to talk to. He probably wouldn't have liked the train.*

They arrived at the police station in the afternoon. The streets of Boston were winding and confusing. Whitsett wondered how anyone could know where they were going. The station was a three-story, red-brick building that had been there since before the states were united. The rooms were small and stuffed with old wooden desks. They were shown upstairs and pointed towards a small crowd.

"Who's that rooster?" Whitsett asked.

"A Pinkerton agent," Cass said. "Private investigator."

The Pinkerton wore an expensive, crisp suit. Many police officers stood around him laughing at his jokes and listening to his stories. Everyone was enamored with his nice clothes and hoped for a job offer. Miss Whitsett thought they looked like they wanted to ask him to dance.

"You must be Mr. Cass," the agent said, walking towards them. He was a broad man with a shining bald head.

"Nice to meet you. This is Miss Whitsett, my stenographer," Cass said. "And Mrs. Sappington, our chaperone."

"You let your company-women out on assignment?" the Pinkerton asked. "It really is the wild west out there in Philadelphia, isn't it?"

"And who let you out of *your* cage?" Whitsett asked.

"I beg your pardon!"

"What she means is that she isn't alone. I'm here. And that's why Mrs. Sappington is here," Cass said.

"Yes, we need to make sure you feel comfortable. I know how scary women can be," Whitsett said.

"I'm not scared of women!" the agent yelled. He stepped closer and Cass had to step back.

"Alright," Whitsett said. "No need to get angry, you old goose. This is a special occasion. The other man was on assignment and everything was last minute."

"I could have spared you the trouble. I have my own *male* stenographer and I could have easily provided you a copy of the transcript, for a small fee."

Whitsett forced a smile. "I'm already here, aren't I? The boss wouldn't want to pay twice for the same transcript."

"Here's our final report and invoice," the Pinkerton said, handing Cass an envelope.

"Thank you very much," Cass said. "How did you catch him? Did he put up a struggle?"

"Struggle? No, he was already in jail."

"In jail! We paid you to catch someone already in jail? What's he in jail for?"

"Stealing horses," the Pinkerton said. "He's decided to confess to the insurance fraud and surrender to you."

"What a jackass!" Miss Whitsett said. The Pinkerton looked at her hatefully for speaking.

"Go wait over there while the *men* talk," the Pinkerton told her.

"I will when I see some," she said.

The Pinkerton jolted. "What did that woman say to me?" He had never been spoken to in such a way from a woman. Cass couldn't get his mouth closed.

"She was just making a joke, sir." He tried to think of something to distract the Pinkerton. He moved in front of Whitsett hoping to hide her from the large, angry man.

"Why would Mr. Holmes surrender to me?" Cass asked.

"How long is the prison sentence for insurance fraud?"

"Less than two years."

"He's wanted in Texas for stealing horses. And they'll hang a man down there for that. Your two years will be a gift to him." Then he added, "I'm not afraid of women."

"You're a hateful little pecker, aren't you?" Whitsett asked. The Pinkerton was stunned. Cass quickly pulled Whitsett away from the agent. The Pinkerton returned to his police admirers in a huff and stared at Cass and Whitsett.

"Was that necessary?" Cass asked Whitsett.

"It felt that way at the time," she said.

"We can't afford to lose our temper, Miss Whitsett. No matter how rude they are to you or me, we must project the utmost professionalism."

"I'll do my best," she said.

"I'm going to read through this report."

"I'll keep a lookout," she said, quietly teasing him.

Cass opened the report and scanned the pages.

"What is this nonsense?" Cass yelled.

"I thought we couldn't lose our tempers?"

"But these are the worst notes I've ever seen! They don't tell us anything. It gives no details. It just mentions his wife and his real name! What a waste of time and money!"

Georgiana Yoke

The interview of Mr. Holmes couldn't start until the superintendent was back from his meeting with the district attorney. They had a couple of hours to spare. As Cass tried to breathe away the anger over the Pinkerton's report, two officers brought in a set of trunks and suitcases.

"These are for you, sir," the officer said.

"What are they?"

"The luggage of the prisoner and his wife. You'll have to take these with you." They were large and well worn, trimmed with a stenciled pattern of maple leaves. The luggage of a respectable couple.

"That's right, his wife is with him," Cass said.

"She probably won't be so condescending now, will she?" Whitsett said. "Little bitch."

"Miss Whitsett, please. Don't call her a bitch again."

"I didn't. And I can't promise anything."

The officer handed Cass the prisoners' personal items. They were keys, wallets and smoking pipes wrapped in newspaper and tied together with string.

"We would like to speak to Mr. Holmes's wife," Cass told the officer.

"I'll arrange it, sir," the officer said as he left.

Whitsett opened one of the trunks and began looking through the personal items.

"Don't look in there, Miss Whitsett."

"Why not?"

"It isn't proper. Only the police should look in there now. It's evidence."

"It's just clothing," she said, feeling the quality of the fabric. "Nice clothing." There was a large metal box stuffed under a jacket. She tried to open it, but it was locked.

"Stop it."

"Alright!" she said, closing the trunk.

The officer prepared a small storage closet for the insurance agents.

"Can't we use one of the interrogation rooms?"

"No," the officer said curtly, closing the door behind him.

The room was so small and cramped that Cass could reach out and touch both walls simultaneously. The space was stacked with wooden chairs and boxes of folded raincoats. The officer returned to the room with the prisoner's wife. Cass and Whitsett stood up to greet Mrs. Holmes. It wasn't the same woman they had met in Chicago.

"This is Mrs. Georgiana Howard," the cop said.

"Holmes's wife?" Cass asked.

"Yes, sir."

"It's a completely different bitch," Whitsett whispered.

Georgiana sat in one of the wooden chairs and waited with her hands folded properly on her lap. She wore a trumpet-shaped skirt with a wasp-waist cut that widened just above the knees. Her hair was tightly tied up in a bun and decorated with a fashionable sunbonnet—the latticed and tailored look of a refined modern lady. Cass and Whitsett realized they were still standing and tried to sit down simultaneously, fumbling over each other, struggling to negotiate the tight quarters. They sat gawking at each other.

Whitsett would have loved to have a sunbonnet. She could only manage to put her hair into braids behind her head like a mule.

"Mrs. Howard, I am Inspector Cass. I work for Fidelity Mutual Life Association. I was lead investigator on the Pitezel case. This is Miss Whitsett. She is going to be recording our conversation. Is that alright?"

"Yes, of course," Mrs. Howard said politely in an affected accent.

"Your name is Mrs. Georgiana Howard. What was your name before you were married?"

"Georgiana Yoke."

"And what is your husband's name?"

"Mr. Henry Mansfield Howard," she said proudly.

"Howard? How did you meet your husband?"

"I was only in town for a year or so, in Chicago that is. I wanted to see the big city before I got married. My parents gave me some money, but it wasn't enough to really experience the city, so I was forced to get a job."

"What a burden," Miss Whitsett said.

Cass looked at her with surprise.

"You're not supposed to say things like that," Cass whispered.

"Excuse me?" Mrs. Howard asked.

"Sorry, dear," Whitsett said. She started flexing her writing hand. "Just a small cramp. Please continue."

"I was working as a salesgirl at Schlesinger & Meyer department store in Chicago. He was one of my customers. We instantly fell in love and were married. I've been his faithful companion ever since."

"And what does Mr. Howard do as a profession?"

"He is a businessman and a gentleman. He manages his estate and other properties."

"Such as the castle?" Cass asked.

"No, sir, no castles that I know of," she said.

"No, not castles. *The* castle. The property in Chicago. It's quite famous," Miss Whitsett said.

"No. Sir, why is your servant addressing me?"

"I'm not his servant."

"She works for Fidelity Mutual. Did you know your husband goes by a different name?" Mr. Cass asked, trying to get the conversation back on track.

"Yes. His mother and father passed, leaving his uncle as his only relative. His uncle promised to leave his nephew all his property if he would take his name and continue his line."

"I see. And you've been traveling for some time. Did that not appear peculiar to you?"

"My husband is a prosperous businessman, sir. He must travel to oversee his various properties and holdings."

"Naturally. Such as Texas, Fort Worth. What holdings did he have there?" Cass asked, reading from a report.

"Some of the properties his uncle bequeathed to him. We also took our honeymoon there, if you must know."

"How romantic," Whitsett said with a small laugh. She flexed her hand again. "Cramp, sorry."

"I detect a condescending tone. Please keep in mind that my husband is a very important businessman and gentleman. I will not sit here and be ridiculed by a mere clerk and his servant girl."

"Hey, lady, there's the door, if you can make it past the cops," Miss Whitsett said. "Little bitch."

"Miss Whitsett, please." Cass tapped her shoulder to try and calm her down.

"I promised nothing."

"Mrs. Howard. I apologize. We are not meaning to be rude. We've heard a lot of conflicting accounts and are simply shocked at your version."

"The truth can be shocking, Mr. Cass."

"Amen, sister," Miss Whitsett said.

"I would like this interview to be over now."

She stood and the guard escorted her out of the room.

"Well, that was interesting," Whitsett said to Cass.

"You have to stop calling the people we interview little bitches," Cass said.

"Can I be the one to tell her?"

"You want to be the one to tell her that her husband is a fraud?"

"Oh yes. I think it would be very proper coming from a mere servant girl, don't you?"

"I thought she was rather respectable," Mrs. Sappington said. Cass and Whitsett had forgotten she was standing in the corner, watching over them.

"Mrs. Sappington!" Whitsett said. "It's very rude to speak without being addressed." Whitsett turned back to Cass. "She thinks she's so much better because she married a rich man. I bet she isn't so smug when she finds out that she's married to an insurance scammer."

"They aren't married at all," Mrs. Sappington interjected.

"Mrs. Sappington, please!" Whitsett said. "We're talking."

Cass was furious. He flipped through the Pinkerton's report a few more times. The lack of information only enraged him further. He stormed out of the office and presented the report into the chest of the Pinkerton agent.

"Excuse me. Why didn't your report say he had another wife?" Cass yelled. Whitsett had never seen him this agitated.

"It *is* in the report," the Pinkerton agent said.

"No, it isn't. I've met the real Mrs. Holmes. She lives in Chicago. There's no mention of a second wife in the report. When were you planning on disclosing this finding?"

"I guess the wife we have here is the third wife then because there's another wife. A Mrs. Mudgett. We think Mudgett is his real name."

"A third wife?" Cass was furious. "What is Fidelity Insurance paying you for?"

"To find this man. And we did. We don't run a wedding register, you pencil neck."

Mr. Cass turned crimson and began to stutter uncontrollably.

While Cass yelled at the agent, Miss Whitsett walked over to the policeman in uniform watching over the room. He was a young man barely in his twenties.

"Hello officer, do you have a cigarette I could sneak off you?"

"Sure thing, ma'am." The officer had a thick Irish accent. He lit a cigarette for her. "Want me to go help him out?" the officer asked, pointing to Cass.

"No, he's alright. I think. What do you think of our Pinkerton man here?"

"A bastard in a suit who punches people for rich bastards," he said. "Pardon my language."

"Do you have the key to open that metal box?" she asked.

"No. He didn't have a key on him."

"Oh. I heard a tinkling sound in Holmes's suitcase. Is there anything fragile in them?"

"No ma'am, just that bogus medicine water he peddles."

"He sells medicinal tonic water?"

"Yes ma'am. Just another street scam, it is. Like 'find the lady' or ectoplasm."

"What's ectoplasm?"

"Supposedly a type of mucus emitted from spirits and ghosts."

"You don't think Holmes is the gentleman he claims to be either, do you officer?"

"I'm more likely to believe in ectoplasm, ma'am."

Cass held up the Pinkerton's report.

"Your paperwork is the worst I have ever seen. There is no summary, no appendix, you didn't even keep a time log. The worst paperwork I have ever seen!"

The Pinkerton agent had never been yelled at for his paperwork before, he wasn't even sure if he had been insulted. Feeling he had made a very dramatic point, Cass turned on his heels and entered the office with Miss Whitsett.

"I'm sorry you had to see that, Miss Whitsett."

"See what?"

"My fight with the Pinkerton agent." He tried to compose himself and straighten out his tie.

"That wasn't a fight," she said with a laugh.

"Of course it was a fight. What would you call it?"

"Yipping."

"Yipping?"

"Like a small dog through a fence."

"I know that male dominance and aggression can be overwhelming, Miss Whitsett. But you're being a bit ridiculous. Now take a few minutes to compose yourself and we'll get ready for Holmes's interview."

Whitsett brushed off her sleeve. "I'm ready."

Confession

Tables and desks had been pushed aside to create something that resembled a theater. Officers had to suspend their work and stand up against the walls. The police, Pinkertons and insurance people sat in a group facing one chair. A guard escorted a man with a thick mustache into the main work room. With a large, friendly smile, he shook hands with the deputy superintendent and the Pinkerton. He patted the guards and police officers on their shoulders and backs. At first, Cass and Whitsett thought he was their cousin or a famous actor.

The gentleman was Holmes, the prisoner.

He was short and slight. Whitsett almost laughed at his small and vaguely effeminate aspects.

Cass and Whitsett sat on a wooden bench behind the Boston officers and the Pinkerton. Whitsett leaned into Cass and spoke softly to him. "This looks more like a gentleman's club meeting than a police interview. Everyone looks like they have a drink in their hand and a stick up their ass."

"Miss Whitsett," Cass said under his breath. He nodded for her to begin recording.

"Today is November 19th, 1893. We are in the Boston police station. With us is Mr. Hanscom, Deputy Superintendent of Police of Massachusetts, and John Cornish, Superintendent of the Pinkerton Detective Agency of Boston, Massachusetts. Today we are intervewing Mr. Holmes, Aka Mr. Howard. Aka Mr. Mudgett. I am Inspector Cass of Fidelity Mutual Life Association. This conversation is being recorded by Miss Whitsett." Cass sat back then leaned towards her again. "And Mrs. Sappington is sitting in the back corner."

The men finally settled down and took their seats, casually lighting their foul-smelling cigars. A front of cool seriousness had moved into the room and chilled the good humor.

"He's handsome, isn't he?" Whitsett whispered.

"What!" Cass yipped.

"Shhh." Everyone looked at him as though he had spoken in a theater.

"Now, Mr. Mudgett. I would like-" The deputy superintendent was interrupted.

"My name is Mr. Howard, if you please, sir," Holmes said politely. He was slumped over and lethargic. He rubbed his eyes and looked to almost be weeping.

When did he get sad? Whitsett thought. He was just making jokes.

"Mr. Howard. Excuse me. I'm told you go by other names as well?"

"I prefer Mr. Howard," Mr. Holmes said.

"Is Mr. Pitezel dead? Aka Mr. Perry," the superintendent asked.

"No, sir," Holmes said frankly.

"So, there was a conspiracy to defraud the Fidelity Insurance company of $10,000."

"Yes, sir."

"What part did you play in the conspiracy?"

"I was brought in to provide a substitute for the body of Mr. Pitezel."

"When was the last time you saw Pitezel?"

"I can't remember the day exactly. We can just leave that blank for now and I'll fill it in later."

"Where was the last time?"

"I saw him last in Detroit and it was in the neighborhood of three weeks ago, but I can give the exact date by consulting my wife," Holmes said.

"When was the last time before that that you saw him?"

"Only once since the Philadelphia occurrence and that was in Cincinnati, probably two weeks before that. I went from New York with the trunk that held the body. When I saw him, I gave him the check that would pick up the trunk at the depot."

"What date was that?" the superintendent asked.

"No, it was the Sunday nearest the 1st of September."

"You turned the check for the trunk over to him. When did you see him next?"

"About 10 days or two weeks later, in Cincinnati."

"Is that where you gave him the instructions as to how to proceed with the body?"

"He had those before," Holmes said.

"So, you didn't see him after turning over the check for the trunk until you met him in Cincinnati?"

"No, sir. Not for those two weeks. No, it must have been nearer to five weeks, ten days after the payment of the money."

Cass was hopelessly confused by the dates and locations. Holmes was speaking so fast and reversing himself so many times, it was difficult for Whitsett to get it all down. Her hand was stiffening.

"How did he get possession of the three children? Alice, Nellie and Howard. These are the three Pitezel children. Alice was the one who identified the body. The mother says they were with you."

"Well, one he got in Cincinnati and the other in Detroit. The boy he took there," Holmes said.

"And when did you turn the other children over to him? I'm sorry, Mr. Howard. I'm confused. Can you start from the beginning?"

"The beginning? New York the beginning or Cincinnati the beginning? Am I going too fast for you?" Holmes asked. His condescension caused the deputy to shrink back in his chair. Whitsett's ears perked up. This was the same con she used to confuse Holmes's wife after calling the little girl a bitch.

"Could you begin in Philadelphia?"

"After we came to Philadelphia to identify the body, little child Alice, who was there at the identification, went as far as Indianapolis with me and I left her there and went further on to St. Louis with the mother, and as soon as the money was paid over to the attorney and given to this woman, a portion of that I took and the other two children and I went to Cincinnati calling for this one in Indianapolis."

"What woman? You mean his wife?"

"Yes, sir. Now, when I landed in Cincinnati, I had three children; two I took at St. Louis—a boy and a girl—and one from Philadelphia. I just stepped off the train at Indianapolis and took her from where she had been at the Stebbins Hotel."

"Okay, so you took the three children and went to Cincinnati where you met the father?"

"The father and the mother, yes sir."

"Wait, was the mother with you?"

"No, not then, she was to follow. I was to go to Cincinnati and rent a house for the winter. Then the father was to see the mother for a few days before he went south. But he had been drinking. I took the other two to Chicago, because I had business there, thinking it would not call attention so quickly if he traveled with the boy alone as if there were three. Then I took them to Detroit and he was already there and I took the other two, dressed the smallest girl as a boy, but this girl Alice is dressed, I supposed now, as a girl and there are two boys and one girl."

"Wait, you took two boys?"

"No, there's only one boy. I dressed one girl up as another boy."

"Which other one?"

"The youngest girl."

"Why?"

"So he could travel."

"He? You mean the little girl?"

"Yes, sir."

"Okay. How long did you remain in Detroit with him?" he asked, hoping to move on past the confusion.

"Him? The boy? Which boy?" Holmes asked.

"No, Mr. Pitezel...wait, I thought there was only one boy."

"Exactly," Holmes said, with a confirming point of his finger.

They sat in silence. The deputy superintendent had forgotten the question. The Pinkerton leaned over and whispered into his ear to remind him of the question.

"Right. Okay. It is still not clear to me why the family should be broken up. Why did three children go one way and she with the two children the other way?"

"The first intention was to have them all go to Cincinnati and stay there for the winter until any noise might blow over. He was going to the south on lumbar business. I had the three children and he had been waiting there for some days and I stayed there with him that night."

"So you put off the mother by telling her that her husband was in different locations around the country?"

"That was his reason, I acted under him."

The superintendent rubbed his eyes in confused fatigue. "Under what name was he traveling at that time?"

"Well, T. H., or anyway it was made out of the name he used in the south, only he turned it around. He was there under the name of Benton T. Lyman, and I think it was L.T. or L.B. Benton. Benton was the name which was agreed upon."

"And that is the name he uses to correspond with you?"

"No, we were going to use a cipher code through either the Chicago or New York personal ads," Holmes said.

"A cipher code?"

"Yes, sir."

All the men looked at each other silently. Everyone was confused and dizzy by the mention of a cipher. They began whispering to each other.

Whitsett shook out her hand and leaned over to Cass.

"He's screwing with them," Whitsett said with a giggle.

"So, he's alive and well with the children?" the superintendent asked, clearing his throat. "Mr. Pitezel and his three children?"

"Yes, sir."

Everyone breathed a sigh of relief. They had finally received an answer to the heaviest thought on their minds. The thought that no one dared to consider out loud. There was another long pause and a few yawns.

"That should be enough, don't you think, superintendent?"

Everyone was eager for the interview to be over. They had been there for hours and yet didn't feel like they had any better grasp on any of the events.

"Oh yes. Most certainly. And I would like to thank you Mr. Holmes for your confession. I know it was difficult, but it saves us all a lot of trouble and paperwork. We can send you off to Philadelphia in the morning. I'm sure the judge will be lenient because of your cooperation."

Everyone stood up and was getting ready to leave. Inspector Cass was very upset he didn't get to ask any questions or participate.

"Why didn't you send Mr. Hedgepeth the $500? You must have known that he would inform on you once he felt he was swindled?" Whitsett blurted out.

Everyone swung their heads around to glare at her.

"I've never met anyone named Hedgepeth."

"The famous outlaw. You spoke with him in prison in St. Louis."

"I've never been to St. Louis, ma'am," Holmes said dismissively. "I think you have your names confused."

The men took the opportunity to laugh at her. Holmes spoke with such certainty that Whitsett began to doubt herself. She felt everyone's hateful eyes in her stomach. She was so embarrassed at the possibility of being wrong. Feeling she had been put in her place, she tried to keep her back straight while everyone began to pile out of the room.

Whitsett stretched out her arm and shook out her hand.

"You don't have your names confused," Cass said, pointing to his notes.

"I know. I was just…it's fine. He's full of it," Whitsett said. "Good con."

"Con? Nonsense, he's just an energetic gentleman. A very charming fellow. Bright. Never flustered. Lots of energy. The most industrious fellow I have ever seen. He's very sure of himself. Very polite.

Just the model of the perfect gentleman. A businessman modeled from the best of them."

"Ciphers? Putting people in trunks? Dressin' up girls as boys?"

"Indeed, what an intricate heist. He seems a very industrious man, indeed. After he is reformed in prison, I can see him becoming very successful in a legitimate setting. He has the spirit of J.P. Morgan."

"J.P. Morgan? Are you insane?"

While Cass filled out some paperwork, Whitsett sneaked back into the side room. She snapped open the latches on Holmes's luggage trunks as silently as she could manage. She found small trilby hats, kid's gloves, corsets and underthings. There were shirts with large poof shoulders and tailored suits. Someone would have required access to a lot of money to pay for these nice clothes.

She thought about taking one of the hats. She could never afford a nice hat and Mr. and Mrs. Holmes had bigger problems than a hat with feathers on it. *No*, she thought. *I really want to, but I'm not going to give that bitch the satisfaction. She won't be able to say, that low woman stole my hat with the feather on it.*

"Miss Whitsett!" Cass yelled. "I said we couldn't look in their luggage!"

"I know, sorry. It was just a peek."

Journey to Philadelphia

Mr. Holmes, aka Mr. Howard, and Mrs. Pitezel, who was brought from Burlington Vermont by a deputy, volunteered to be extradited to Philadelphia, saving days of requests from governors and transfer paperwork. Mrs. Pitezel had two of her five children who were not taken by Holmes. The extradition would be leisurely, and everyone would go back to their respective office with an inexpensive victory. They thanked Holmes at every opportunity.

Everyone was to travel by train. From Boston, they took the New York and Northern Railway to Jersey City and then transferred over to the Pennsylvania Railroad, which would take them into Philadelphia. The train ride would take all day and they would arrive in the middle of the night.

The migration almost filled an entire car. Along with Holmes, Mrs. Pitezel and a police officer from Philadelphia, there was Inspector Cass, Miss Whitsett, Pitezel's remaining two children and a Pinkerton. Poor Mrs. Sappington, who was not handling travel very well at all, took Mrs. Pitezel and Miss Whitsett along with the children into a separate car, refusing to ride with criminals.

Holmes sat by the window and the police officer took the seat next to him, pinning him in. Cass grabbed the seat directly across from them. He was very curious about Holmes and wanted to find the secret to his energy and enthusiasm. Cass thought it was something in his diet or posture. Maybe Holmes's behavior would give Cass some insight as to how to obtain the charisma he so desperately wanted. If only he could hear his footsteps or see some of his handwriting. *Perhaps I should grow a mustache*, he thought.

As the train jerked into motion, Miss Whitsett sat down next to Cass.

"What are you doing here?" Cass whispered.

"If you think I'm going to spend another moment with Mrs. Sappington, you're crazy, mister. You might as well throw me off the train. Will you roll me a cigarette, please?"

Mr. Holmes smiled at her, flashing his bright blue eyes. Whitsett was mesmerized by how deep and vibrant they were. He was very attractive and had such an air of confidence and competence about him. She smiled, though she didn't mean to. Cass passed her a cigarette, hoping to distract her from Holmes.

For the first couple of hours, Cass and Whitsett stared at Holmes. Once the train was further away from the city, Holmes began to fidget. He turned to the officer next to him.

"Say there. How much longer do you guess we have on this train?"

"Be quiet. I'm reading the paper," the officer said. It was clear he didn't care about the paper though; he was upset he had been made to travel away from his family.

"May I borrow the paper when you're done with it?" Holmes asked.

"No," the officer said.

"Why not?"

"Because I said so."

"Interesting reason," Holmes said. "I will buy it from you."

"No."

Holmes turned to look at Whitsett. They shared a glance and a smile. He ran his eyes over her.

"What about you? Can I buy your paper?"

"I'm sorry, I ain't got one," she said.

"Just as well, papers only print lies. Black and white lies. Good for you."

Holmes spoke as though they had been friends forever, as though he had every certainty he and she would be life-long friends. He had a bright smile and sparkling eyes, boiling over with energy.

"All I have is this book about pirates."

"Pirates don't write things down," Holmes said.

"These do."

Cass began to fidget. He thought he might distract Whitsett if he rolled another cigarette.

"You're the folks from Philadelphia, yes? From Fidelity Mutual," Holmes said.

"Yes. And I guess you're my prisoner," Whitsett responded with a smile.

Holmes laughed. The officer looked at Whitsett from the side of his eye. He didn't find that remark as entertaining as Holmes.

"And your name?" Holmes asked.

"I'm Miss Whitsett."

"Very nice to meet you. Miss? And you're the stenographer?"

"Yes."

"That's wonderful. I'm so glad they let women work now. Industrious little creatures, given the right direction."

"They let women work in the open in Chicago?" she asked.

"Yes, we're very progressive in Chicago. I run a lady employment agency. Are you interested in Chicago? Perhaps when this entire business is settled, you could come and work for me. I have a hotel where you could stay as well."

Whitsett was so excited. A job and a place to stay in Chicago. It was a dream come true. There was something about the entire thing that felt weird in her gut, but she decided to ignore it. Who could resist such an opportunity in Chicago?

"So, Mr. Pitezel is in South America?" Cass interrupted, finally able to say something.

"Somewhere down there."

"And the children are with him?" he asked.

"I gave him $1,600 and sewed $400 in Alice's dress. I left Alice in Indianapolis after taking her to Philadelphia, and then I got the other two children and brought them to her. I took them all to Detroit, where they met Pitezel, and then they sailed to South America. I was able to keep track of him with our cipher in the *New York Herald*."

"Yes, the cipher," she said. The idea of a cipher irritated her, it had the bitter tang of a con. She wiped the smile off her face and leaned forward. "I'm surprised he hasn't contacted you. Especially about his wife and other children," Whitsett added.

"Well, our man Pitezel isn't the most competent person. He leans to the drink and can have problems with simple tasks." Homes began to laugh. "I had instructed him on how to place the body and put the chloroform in its mouth and to press the sides, so as to work it down the throat," Holmes said, snickering to himself. "Oh, how he botched the whole thing. The man knows nothing about handling bodies. How do you mess up killing a dead person?" He laughed.

"And you brought a body from New York?" Whitsett asked. She noticed that Holmes's blue eyes grew brighter when he spoke. They were expressive and alluring. She couldn't help but smile for him. But his explanations were just so damned irritating.

"I brought the corpse from New York."

"How? Did you buy him a ticket on the 9:35 train?" Whitsett laughed, mocking Holmes with her sarcasm.

Holmes stopped smiling. He was not accustomed to being laughed at.

"No, I folded him up into a trunk and shipped him," he said with a sudden intensity.

"Was that supposed to make me faint?" Whitsett asked.

"No, just make you think," Holmes replied.

Holmes looked over and noticed the officer was nodding off. When the officer was finally asleep, Holmes grabbed the folded sections of the paper with his thumb and finger. He gently pulled and the paper slid out easily into his lap. He smiled at Cass and stuffed the paper between the seat and his thigh.

Cass froze. He just took the paper. He wasn't supposed to; the officer told him no. But Holmes just took it.

"Do you believe in hypnotism?" Holmes asked Cass.

"No."

"I can hypnotize people very easily. I would be more than happy to test my powers on you."

"No, thank you."

"Amazing thing, hypnotism. Hey, would you be willing to hold $500 for me?" he whispered to Cass.

Cass felt the question hit him like a nine-pound hammer. He wasn't sure how to respond.

Whitsett knew Holmes didn't have $500 on him. She wondered why he would offer. Maybe it was to see what the response would be or to see if Cass could be bought. He could also be messing with them, as he had done in the interrogation.

"No. I don't think that would be appropriate," Cass said, his voice creaking.

"Nonsense. You already have my trunks and suitcases."

"Who helped you double up the body in New York and put it in the trunk?" Whitsett asked, changing the subject to help relieve the pressure of the hard sell from the stuttering Cass.

"You ask a lot of questions, don't you? I did it alone. It's not a small task to fit a body with rigor mortis into a trunk. It's a trick I learned at the University of Michigan while studying medicine there."

"Oh, you studied medicine?" Whitsett asked.

"Yes, ma'am. Do you have something that ails you? Do you suffer acute pain? I have a special tonic that can help. I developed the chemistry myself."

"A tonic?" Cass felt as though the train had spun off the tracks. "You have a tonic too?"

Whitsett knew Cass wouldn't react well to the news that Holmes was his competition for medicinal tonics.

"Do you have an ailment?"

"Not directly, but I've got a medical question," Whitsett said.

"Very well."

"What is rigor mortis?" she asked.

"Good question. It is the stiffening of the joints and muscles of a body after death."

"Why does it stiffen?"

"Inquisitive, aren't you?"

"I like knowing things."

"The muscles contract and are unable to relax, this causes the joints to be fixed in place."

"I've seen a few dead bodies-"

"Miss Whitsett!" Cass interrupted.

"The bodies could be moved with no trouble," Whitsett continued. "Do some bodies not have rigor mortis?"

"No. All bodies go through it, everybody and every body. But rigor mortis only lasts for a couple of days. Three at the most. Then it loosens up again. You are intelligent for a working woman."

"Thank you," Whitsett said. "How was it you were able to make it seem that Mr. Pitezel's substitute body was going through rigor mortis? The body should have loosened up by then, from what you just told me," Whitsett said.

"It's a special trick I learned."

"Oh, really? How?" Whitsett asked, taking out a pencil to write his answer down. "How do you get a body to go through rigor mortis twice?"

Holmes gave no answer, clearly unaccustomed to that kind of question. The silence left a ringing in their ears.

Holmes grabbed the paper and began to read, ignoring them. Whitsett nudged Cass with her elbow. She had done something the Boston detectives and the Pinkertons had been unable to do—she had backed Holmes into a lie. Cass was extremely impressed with this little smiling woman with her frizzy hair. He lit her a cigarette and enjoyed the rest of the ride.

A few days after the transfer, the lawyer Howe was brought in on the charge of conspiracy and his bail was set at $2,500. Mrs. Pitezel was brought in as well. Her baby and daughter were placed in the care of

Benjamin Crew, Esq., Secretary of the Society to Protect Children from Cruelty.

Once the prisoners were taken to the county prison, District Attorney George S. Graham Esq., met with all the parties and an indictment was prepared, charging H.H. Holmes, Benjamin F. Pitezel in absentia, Carrie A. Pitezel, and Jeptha D. Howe with having fraudulently and willfully conspired to cheat and defraud the Fidelity Mutual Life Association out of the sum of $10,000 by means of substitution of a body for that of Benjamin F. Pitezel.

Mr. Cass received a firm handshake from the president of the company. No one received any bonuses.

Case closed.

Research

Miss Whitsett cleared her workspace and turned to the women around her. The top floor, where the women were made to work, was cramped and hot. Dozens of women were hunched over high slang-top desks, pushed haphazardly into the corners to accommodate even more desks. Every wall was covered with pigeon-hole files.

Every day they were sequestered upstairs to make copies and transcribe notes for Fidelity Mutual. The ceiling slanted from the pointed roof and everyone had to cock their head to one side as they worked. They might as well have been shoveling coal for how hot it was.

"If I'm not back in time, everyone remembers what to do, right?"

Everyone nodded and giggled. Whitsett pushed in her chair and walked towards the door. Like a hound, Mrs. Sappington put her nose in the air and stood to intercept.

"Where are you off to, Miss Whitsett?" Mrs. Sappington asked.

"I have an appointment."

"Is that so? And you think you can just take off an hour early?"

"No. I worked through my lunch the past two days to make up the time for today's lunch appointment. I'll be back before the bell."

"Miss Whitsett, women workers must eat at their workstations. We can't have one of our women trotting about on the streets during the day like some public girl. What would our customers say? Now I know you've been given preferential treatment lately, but don't think you're special. You're just like everyone else. And you know what that means?"

"Yes."

"Tell me what it means."

"I know what it means."

"Tell *me* what it means."

"That I am replaceable," she said. She had heard it so many damned times.

"You are replaceable. And if you're not back before the bell, I'll recommend you be replaced instantly."

Whitsett hated hearing that. She hated Mrs. Sappington and everything about the top floor.

"I am recommending that you be docked half a day's pay for leaving and having an insubordinate tone. Hurry back," Mrs. Sappington said as she slammed the door to her office.

Miss Whitsett walked down the stairs towards the side door and could smell Cass's cigarette as he waited for her. Her shirt was almost soaked through with sweat and she was a bit dizzy from the drastic change in temperature.

Cass watched two of his co-workers walk past him, not bothering to greet him.

"Hello, gentlemen," Cass called out to them. "Where are you off to?"

"To the saloon," they said. They nodded their heads and quickly moved along.

"I want to go to the saloon," Whitsett said.

Her voice startled him, and he spat his cigarette onto his coat. He began to slap his chest to brush it off.

"Calm down, it's just me," she said, helping to brush the ash from his tan cloth. "We need to hurry. I have to be back shortly."

"Are you sure you don't want me to talk to your boss?"

"No, absolutely not."

"It wouldn't be any trouble."

"No, it's hot enough up there without all those ladies thinking I get special treatment. Plus, I can handle my own business, thank you. I don't need anyone's help. Saloon?"

"They don't allow women in saloons, Miss Whitsett."

"They do in Chicago."

"Do they? Who cares? All those big cities are rotten."

"I assume they do. It'll be so great when I move there. I'll have a job, and live in a hotel, and go to saloons. That's why I need that bonus."

"Are you doing this for a bonus or because you're curious?"

"Both. I mean, do you believe his crazy story? Where did he get a dead body? The market? And what about that rigor mortis nonsense? Who is this guy Holmes? Now let's get this done, Inspector the Kid. Did you find a doctor we could speak to about rigor mortis?"

"I found something even better. Holmes said he went to the University of Michigan. But they've never heard of anyone named Holmes in their medical program. But then I looked at the Pinkerton's awful report and they said his name is really Mudgett. Herman Webster Mudgett graduated from the University of Michigan in 1884."

"He's really a doctor? I thought the doctor bit was a con."

"And one of his classmates works a few blocks from here."

"Hot damn!" Whitsett said.

"Don't go and work for Holmes."

"Why not?"

"Because." Cass had tried to roll another cigarette, but his hands were quivering. "Chicago is a terrible town."

"Is it now? Are you nervous, Inspector Cass?" Whitsett asked with a smile.

"I don't know if I can do this," Cass said. "I was directly told by the president of the company that the case is closed. He shook my hand. We aren't supposed to be doing this. I could get fired."

"Don't be silly, of course you can. Did Carnegie ever say that? Did J.P. Morgan?" She brushed the ash from his jacket. "You didn't want to interview that woman in Chicago. But you showed a little initiative and you got a trip to Boston. Imagine what you can get if you can show that this insurance scam went deeper than just grave robbing. Remember, you're 'Inspector the Kid.'" She took the cigarette from him.

Whitsett and Cass were shown into the office of Dr. Bishop Price. He had a full red beard and a linen detachable collar. The collar was so tall Dr. Price had trouble turning his head. Whitsett was fascinated with the collection of scalpels and saws Dr. Price had displayed on his desk. They were presented on a large felt mat.

"Are these your knives?"

"Those aren't knives, they are surgical equipment, my dear."

"So, they're yours?"

"Dr. Bishop Price? My name is Inspector Cass. This is Miss Whitsett."

"How can I help you?"

"We have a question about dead people," Whitsett said.

"My goodness," Dr. Price said with a gasp.

"We want to know if it's possible to re-stiffen a body after rigor mortis has been broken?" Cass asked.

"No," Dr. Price said confidently.

"There's no trick or procedure to re-stiffen a body?" Whitsett asked.

"No. Once a body has gone through rigor mortis, that is it. It starts to decay. You can't 're-stiffen' it as you say. Why do you ask?"

"A doctor, who attended the same medical school as you, claims he knows a trick to re-stiffen a body after rigor mortis," Cass said.

"He's a liar or a fool. Who told you this?"

"Herman Mudgett."

"Of course he would tell you that. What did he do?"

"Why do you say that?

"He was always a little adventurous."

"What was he like?" Whitsett asked.

"I didn't know him personally. He seemed smart. But he was a terrible student. They had to hold secondary votes to see if he should graduate. But he passed."

"Typical. Spoiled rich kid didn't take his opportunity seriously," Whitsett said.

"No, actually, he was quite poor. He couldn't afford the tuition and had to take side jobs to help pay for it. There was actually a rumor that he stole bodies from the anatomy suites and sold them to help pay for tuition. But that sounded like a farfetched story. Actually, now that you bring him up, he had a friend in our class. A close friend. Robert Leacock. Those two were inseparable. I remember when he died, Mudgett was very upset. Again, there were gothic rumors that he stole the body from the grave out of sorrow. I didn't believe that."

"It was hypothetical?" Whitsett asked, winking at Cass. She had learned that word from him when they first met. Cass smiled.

"Yes, exactly. Those two were always up to schemes. Causing trouble. He was just out of control when Leacock died. One time an insurance man came around the campus asking questions. Something about Leacock and a life insurance policy."

Whitsett and Cass perked up.

"Insurance policy? What did this friend die from?" Whitsett asked.

"No one knew. His face and body were all torn up. It must have been some terrible accident. It's interesting you would ask me about him though."

"Why?" Cass asked.

"Mr. Mudgett is dead. I heard he died a few years ago. A nasty death. He was in a fire and burned his face beyond recognition."

"It seems Holmes has a history of insurance frauds," Cass whispered to Whitsett.

"We're going to get a bonus," Whitsett whispered back.

"I have an unrelated question," Cass said to the doctor.

"Alright."

"I have a special mineral tonic that can help with aches and pains. I was wondering if you would like to buy some for your patients?" Cass pleaded.

The doctor laughed, believing Cass had made a joke. "Very good, inspector. I'll tell my colleagues that one."

"Yes?" Cass was confused. Whitsett laughed along with the doctor as she pulled Cass out of the office by his arm.

As they walked along the street, Cass smoked a cigarette to help him relax.

"You did very well, inspector," Whitsett said. "That was very brave of you. I told you Holmes was a con." She tried to grab the cigarette but he waved her hand away. "Are you okay?"

"Oh, I'm fine," he said. His hands were still shaking.

"Now we should go interview them," Whitsett said.

"Who?"

"Holmes, his wife and Mrs. Pitezel."

"They're in prison," Cass said.

"I know. We'll go see what they say."

"We can't get in the prison. We don't have any authority. And what if the boss finds out? It's against the rules."

"Ha, rules!" She laughed. "We'll be real quick."

"How are we going to get in the prison with no permission or credentials?" he asked.

"With your silver tongue."

"My what?" Cass was beginning to panic.

"Just be sure to speak with a firm tone."

"Why do we need to bother? We already have him in jail."

"Obviously, this wasn't his first insurance fraud. We need to know more about him, see how deep this goes. Walk yourself through what happened. Shipping dead bodies, rigor mortis, ciphers? Why didn't he give the handsome bandit his $500?"

"But he's already admitted to his crime."

"If he was lyin' before, he's probably lyin' now. What other things is he lyin' about?"

"Okay, I guess this is a good idea."

"And we should talk to Mrs. Pitezel," she said.

"Why her? What can she know? What do I tell the officers at the prison? What do I say?"

"It doesn't matter what you say. You just have to know your customer."

"Customer?"

"Yes. If they are polite, be very polite to them. If they are aggressive, be firm. Just act like you are supposed to be there."

Prison

"My name…my name is Inspector Cass. This is my stenographer. Mrs. Whitsett," Cass said with a slight stutter.

"Inspector?" the officer asked with an accusatory tone.

"With Fidelity Insurance." Cass was stiff and fighting his compulsion to run away and hide.

The officer wrote down the name 'Mr. Cass' in his logbook. Insurance pencil pushers aren't inspectors. "What can I do for ya?" The bright brass buttons on the cop's uniform were like giant gold eyes looking into him.

"Pitezel," Cass said, coughing. "Mrs. Pitezel…I would like to interview her."

"Interview? You work for the newspapers?"

"No, sir. I just said I am an inspector with Fidelity, didn't I?" Cass said. Whitsett wanted to put her head in her hands.

"People say a lot of things. Don't mean it's real." The officer looked directly into Cass's blinking eyes. "Can I see some identification?"

Cass showed him his Fidelity identification.

"Why do you want to see her? She is an unstable motherly lady and I don't want some nosy pencil pusher bothering her."

"Pencil pusher! I'm an inspector with Fidelity Insurance. I have worked as the lead investigator on three medium-term assignments with three people as support staff. I'm not a pencil pusher."

Whitsett could see the situation was spinning out of control and stepped in.

"Hi. Sorry about him. He's been working really late. Boss givin' 'im hell. If you check your records or ask Detective Miller, you'll see that we traveled and interviewed with the prisoners. The district attorney has asked that we come. We just need to get a couple of questions cleared up for the file. It would really help us out. We signed the book and everything."

The officer disappeared into the back of the station. Cass leaned in towards Whitsett.

"How was I?" Cass asked.

"Very intimidating," she said.

"What's the district attorney's name?" the cop called out from the back.

"Graham," Cass said softly.

"Graham!" Whitsett called out.

The officer mumbled to someone in the back. When he returned, he closed the logbook with a clap.

"Alright, you can talk to her and the lawyer. But if I hear you've upset that poor woman, I'll have you for it, understand?"

"Yes," Whitsett said.

They were pointed to the cell that contained Mr. Howe, the lawyer. He looked rattled and had bruises around his eyes and on his neck.

"You can have your interview with him while I arrange Mrs. Pitezel. She's fragile and takes some time to motivate," the cop said.

"Thank you," Whitsett said.

The officer stomped away and they sat down in front of the iron bars.

"Why didn't you pay the Handsome Bandit?" Whitsett asked.

"Surely you must have known he would inform on you?" Cass asked.

"I was just the lawyer."

"Ah, now you're just a lawyer," Whitsett said.

"Stenographers aren't supposed to speak," Howe said.

"And lawyer's ain't supposed to be in jail, but here we both are," she said. "Who arranged everything? You're the lawyer, you're the smart one. Did you plan the entire swindle?"

"No, that Holmes character did. He had the whole thing planned out from beginning to end. I'm not that kind of smart. Holmes is that kind of smart."

"And did he say they were using a replacement body for Mr. Pitezel?"

"Yes, said he had done the scam before in Chicago and knew all the ins and outs."

"I told you!" Whitsett said, slapping Cass's shoulder. "He's been doing this con since medical school."

"Where did he get the body?" Cass asked.

"Don't know. Didn't want to know. My only job was to help execute the proceedings with the insurance company."

"And Holmes's job was to secure the body?"

"That and more. He had the whole thing planned out from beginning to end. Real pushy son of a bitch."

"What about Mr. and Mrs. Pitezel?"

"No, they couldn't post a letter by themselves. And Mr. Pitezel was a drunk besides. Holmes was the man in charge."

"What happened to your face?" Whitsett asked.

"Nothing."

"What d'you mean nothing? Your face looks like you've been belted. It's completely black, like your face is in mourning."

"I must have fallen on the ground while sleeping," Howe said.

The lawyer was looking past her, towards the door. She turned around and saw a large cop standing behind them. Clearly the lawyer was reluctant to buy another beating by pointing fingers.

"I have Mrs. Pitezel ready for you," the cop said.

The cop brought them to a special apartment upstairs. They didn't want to put Mrs. Pitezel in a cell like a criminal. She was kept on the top floor, away from everyone else. They had turned a small file-storage area into an apartment with a cot, a rocking chair, and a freshwater basin that was dutifully refilled every two hours by the cops.

"It appears all the police officers here are protective of Mrs. Pitezel. I find it unlikely that she would have any information of criminal activity beyond what Holmes has told us," Cass whispered.

"You'd be surprised," Whitsett said. "She's just acting the part of the poor, victimized mother, but she probably planned the entire thing herself. You'll see. I rather like speaking to criminals." Miss Whitsett was smiling and singing to herself. "I wonder if they like talking to us. How much are bonuses by the way?"

"I don't know, a couple of dollars."

"What! That's it? That's a tip, not a bonus."

The young cop led Mrs. Pitezel into the room by the hand. They weren't expecting her to appear so ghastly. The grieving woman didn't look like a criminal mastermind. She had dark circles under her eyes and appeared to have been crying. With one firm grab, she would probably crumble away like rotted wood.

"Mrs. Pitezel, I am Inspector Cass. I work for Fidelity Mutual Life Association. I was lead investigator on the Pitezel case. This is Miss Whitsett, the stenographer. She's going to be recording our conversation. Is that alright?"

"Yes," she said with a sniffle. She was so frail in her black dress. She looked like curtains draped over a ladder.

"I'm not here to entrap you or trick you, I'm just trying to get the facts. Okay?"

"I don't know anything."

"Anything about what?"

"Any of this." Mrs. Pitezel was so nervous, her hands were white.

"Before the news in the press, did you know anything about this scheme?"

"Nothing. They didn't tell me anything about it."

"They told you nothing?"

"They didn't tell me anything about it," she repeated.

"Did you know your husband had life insurance?"

"I knew that, but not whether it was all paid or not. You know, all paid up."

"Did you know the amount?"

"$10,000."

"Who collected that money?"

"Lawyer Howe. And Mr. Holmes got some of it."

"What portion of the 10,000 did you get in the end?" Cass asked.

"About $500."

"Out of the whole business, you only got $500?" Whitsett said. She was so shocked she almost laughed. "Sounds like they just gave you a bonus."

"Where's your husband?" Cass asked.

"I don't know." She was noticeably frustrated and began to cry.

"I know, I'm sorry I have to put you through this. Did you have a cipher, a special way to communicate with your husband privately or a special system of numbers or characters?"

"No."

"No ciphers of any kind?"

"No."

"How many children do you have?"

"Five."

"During this traveling, how many of them were with you?"

"Two. The little girl and my baby."

"Where were the other three?"

"Covington."

"With whom?"

"I don't know. Mr. Holmes said it was a widow who was a nice woman."

"When did you part with the children?"

"Mr. Holmes took Alice first to identify the body."

"And the other two?"

"Mr. Holmes took them."

"Why?"

"He said I could go home and pay my parents a visit, and not be bothered with them, because my parents are getting along in years, and he would take the children and then I could go over there when I got through visiting."

"Did he ever tell you about dressing one of the girls in boy's clothing?"

"No."

"Never?"

"No."

"Where are the children now?" Whitsett asked, sure their mother would know where they were.

"I thought they would be here with him," she said.

"Do you mail your children?" Cass asked.

"I wrote them letters, Mr. Holmes mailed them for me."

"Who suggested that you employ Jeptha Howe as counsel?"

"Mr. Holmes."

"Tell me about Mr. Holmes."

"He was my husband's employer. For a few years now. My husband responded to a newspaper ad for construction of the castle."

"The castle?"

"That's what they called it. It's Mr. Holmes's large building in Chicago. It's the size of an entire block. The first floor is all shops; jewelers, barber and a pharmacy. The second and third floors are offices and rooms. Mr. Holmes owns them all."

"He owns all these businesses, he's the man in charge?"

"Yes."

"Why did you let someone take your children?" Whitsett yelled.

Mrs. Pitezel began to cry uncontrollably. She did her best to pull herself together, but it was too late. She was gone. Cass finished the interview and the cop was so angry with Whitsett for upsetting the poor woman he almost cracked her with his club. The cop couldn't hit a woman, so he shoved Cass in the stomach as he carefully escorted the weeping mother out of the room.

"Why did you do that?" Cass asked Whitsett, coughing and holding his stomach.

"I think this woman has no idea what's going on." Whitsett tried to shake the tightness from her hand. "She doesn't want to reveal anything and get her husband in trouble. Where are the children?"

The police officer from the front desk stomped down the hallway. He was visibly unhappy.

"I just sent word to the district attorney. He said your story was bullshit," the officer said.

Before the Bell

The bell chimed and Miss Whitsett's station was empty. Mrs. Sappington had stared at the workstation for two hours without blinking.

Five minutes after the bell, Whitsett burst through the door and scrambled to her seat. She was short of breath from running up five flights of stairs. Mrs. Sappington strolled up casually with her stiff smile beaming from her wooden face. Whitsett tried to swallow her deep breathing.

"My watch reads five past, Miss Whitsett. The bell sounded yet you were nowhere to be found. That is not your work area any longer. I shall be recommending that you be terminated immediately from Fidelity's employment. Maybe this will teach you a lesson." She turned and walked away.

"I was here before the bell, Mrs. Sappington."

"I beg your pardon."

"I was here long before the bell."

"Bad enough you are unreliable, but lying as well. You embarrass yourself."

"I was here the entire time. Ask anyone. I was here, wasn't I, ladies?" She asked the girls around her.

Each woman nodded her head and answered yes.

"Maybe your watch is fast," Miss Whitsett said.

"How dare you." Mrs. Sappington stomped away to her desk.

The women gave each other congratulatory smiles and happily went on with their work. "Good con, girls," Whitsett whispered to them.

Suddenly, Sappington threw a large bible down onto Whitsett's desk. The sound rumbled like a thunderstorm.

"Each and every one of you will put your hand on this Bible and swear that this woman was here before the bell. If you choose to continue with this abomination, then you'll have to answer to the good

Lord for bearing false witness and burn for eternity. Miss Carols! You first."

Miss Carols slowly stood up and inched forward. Whitsett watched the woman's face turn red. Before she could put her hand on the bible, Whitsett stood up and grabbed her hand.

"Alright, you cow," she said. "I was late."

Whitsett walked home to her boarding house for single women. As she passed saloons and bars, she could see working men settling themselves inside. She heard laughing and an out-of-tune piano. She bought the evening edition of the paper from a barker on the corner. Across the street she saw finishers pouring concrete and men in straw hats cooking tar. Down alleyways she could see young street children digging through heaps of trash and filth.

Whitsett passed the public women. Mud stained the bottom of their dresses, the higher the stain, the longer they'd been working on the street. The drunks and degenerates that lined the curb waited for the women to come home; they would grab and whistle and offer a price for the night. *I'm not dressed like a prostitute, leave me alone*, Whitsett thought. *My dress is clean.* Whitsett did her best to push and kick. She was more accustomed to fighting off the men later in the evening when they had more alcohol in them and less access to balance. She had been sent home early today, fired.

Whitsett entered her apartment, took off her boots and placed them in the bucket she hung out the window. She wasn't used to being home while it was so light outside. Her first thought was to make use of the light by reading. But her punishment for losing her job would be to sit on the end of her bed and think.

The headlines in the evening edition described the amazing Mr. Holmes and his great swindle of the corrupt insurance company. She opened the paper and began to look for a new job. There were no listings or openings for a stenographer. The only listings for young women were for personal secretaries, servants and nannies.

She had worked those jobs before and the thought of returning to them made her nauseous. Being a servant meant working for no money and living at the pleasure of some horrible woman like Mrs. Holmes and her little brat. *Those jobs don't pay anything, and you can look forward to a slap in the face for talking back. No thank you*, she thought.

Her neighbor knocked on her door asking why she was home so early. "You're not sick, are you? Are you sick?" Anytime someone was sick, people feared the illness would spread through the building.

"No, I was fired, Mrs. Jacobs."

"I'm sorry," Mrs. Jacobs said, crossing herself as she entered. She carried a small baby on her hip. Mrs. Jacobs had moved into the boarding house when her husband lost his hand in a factory accident. He disappeared into a liquor bottle and ended up dead in a workhouse.

"Do you need your apartment cleaned?" Whitsett asked. She felt so ashamed to ask, there was a pinch in her stomach.

"Sure."

Whitsett walked into her neighbor's apartment. It was spotless.

"Why don't you just get married?" Mrs. Jacobs asked, handing her a broom.

"No family will have an orphan raised in an institution with frizzy hair," she said, sweeping the clean floor.

"You're pretty enough, I guess. I'm sure they would overlook your hair. There are plenty of pretty girls on the block with muddy dresses. Straight hair didn't help them, did it?"

Down the street, she could hear her immigrant neighbors yell for their husbands. The piano music in the saloons would make it impossible for them to be heard. *The saloon must be a great place*, she thought.

"My cousin's son is still looking for a wife," Mrs. Jacobs said, bouncing the child in her arms. "He's no prince charming but he has steady work. It's good fortune you were fired, no man wants to marry a working woman, it isn't proper."

Whitsett realized her neighbor had only agreed to let her clean so she could try and con her into marrying her cousin's son.

"Your place is spotless. Why don't you let me take your baby for a few hours while you sleep? We can go for a walk." Whitsett had watched the baby a few times before and knew it was a great way to politely escape the conversation.

Whitsett took the baby for a walk. He wasn't as heavy last time. Usually she took him to a candy shop a few blocks over to watch stripped candy being made. But not today. Today she had been fired and needed money for rent. She wasn't going to be anyone's servant.

Whitsett rubbed dirt on the boy's face and wrapped him in a torn cloth. She had worked this con a few times before.

She walked around the streets and approached men in top hats.

"Excuse me, sir. Can you spare something for the little one? He's awfully hungry," she said with a pathetic voice.

The younger men gave what they could out of indignation, the older men wanted something extra for the effort.

She made out alright, but this con wasn't bringing in what it used to. *Maybe he is just an ugly baby*, she thought. *If not ugly, then not handsome enough to earn rent on.*

She became dizzy. No job, no prospects and no family. She would end up in a poor house. She wasn't going to end up in another institution and she wasn't going to be someone's servant. She drudged through the muddy streets back to her boarding house.

"Mrs. Jacobs. Tell your cousin's son I'll marry him."

Mrs. Jacobs was thrilled. "Wonderful! You stay here with Thomas and I'll go and tell them right now."

"I don't have money for next week's rent," Whitsett said. She was desperate and she sounded desperate. She was out of cons.

"You can stay with me until the wedding. A betrothed woman shouldn't live by herself anyway. I can show you how to care for a baby. You'll need to learn. It will also give me some time to figure out what to do with that hair."

Whitsett watched the baby until Mrs. Jacobs returned. Mrs. Jacobs spent the rest of the evening giving tutorials on marriage and clearing a place in the apartment.

Whitsett returned next door to her room and stared at the wall all night. It was her last night in her own place. She would soon be Mrs. Something or other. Dread and bitterness swelled over the side of her stomach. She had to set aside how miserable things were and do what she had to do.

Let Them Print That

"Do you know why I wanted to see you this morning, Mr. Cass?" the president of Fidelity Insurance asked, looking out the window, his hands clasped behind his back. He watched horses pull carriages of lumber to work sites and barkers selling morning editions.

"Does it have anything to do with my interviews at the prison?"

"It does, as a matter of fact. I was going to fire you. Do you know that the company could be charged with a crime for your conduct? The district attorney was furious with me. Then something happened over breakfast. Can you imagine what that was, Mr. Cass?"

"I have no idea, sir."

"Over breakfast with my wife this morning, I had to read about the wily Mr. Holmes and his heist of $10,000 from the evil insurance company. They stopped short of calling him Robin Hood. Robin Hood! The press has gotten ahold of the story, Mr. Cass, and Fidelity Mutual has been cast in the role of the villain."

"It was actually $9,715.85 and Holmes only took $6,700 of that."

"I must say, Mr. Cass, I am very impressed with your thoroughness."

"Thank you, sir."

"Shut up, Mr. Cass."

"Yes, sir."

"Why do you continue to work on this case, Mr. Cass? Even though I told you otherwise. You must have known that you would get fired. We have our fraud. We have our fraudster, he's in jail awaiting sentencing from the judge. Case closed."

"I'm not satisfied."

"I tell you when you are satisfied," Fouse said, leaning his fat body back into his leather chair. "What have you found?"

"I don't think Mr. Holmes, or Mr. Howard, or Mr. Mudgett is telling the truth."

"About what?"

"Everyone we interviewed said Holmes was the leader and the organizer, not Pitezel. Insurance claims on men with burned faces follow him everywhere he goes. Where did he get the dead body? Where is Mr. Pitezel? Who is this man?"

"This is turning into a nightmare, Mr. Cass." Fouse put his head in his fat hands.

"Am I still fired?"

"Not yet. What do you recommend?"

"That I not be fired."

"About Holmes."

"I would like to do some follow up research to try and corroborate some of these outrageous claims he makes. He might have only admitted to the crime of fraud to cover a more egregious crime. If we can uncover his fraudulent history, the papers may be less disposed to glorify him."

"Very well. I'll get in touch with the district attorney's office and let them know of our suspicions. Now that everything about this case is being publicized, we can't afford to appear as though we don't turn over every stone...we can't not turn over...we must turn over every stone."

"Yes, sir."

"The newspapers are making him out to be some kind of folk hero. The clever bandit stealing from the evil insurance company. What nonsense! They wouldn't be so excited if they knew he looked at other men's naked necks! I want every lie of his unearthed. He can't avoid justice by hiding in jail."

"Yes, sir."

"Spare no expense in finding the truth on this matter, Mr. Cass. And if a reporter wants a story, tell them that I said that. 'Spare no expense in finding the truth on this matter.' Let them print that in the paper."

"Yes, sir."

"Right, off you go," Fouse said.

"There is one thing that could really be helpful, sir."

Cass climbed the stairs to the top of the office building where the women were kept. He couldn't imagine having to climb these stairs multiple times a day. And the heat! *Why is it so hot up here?* he thought.

"What can I do for you now, Mr. Cass?" the supervisor asked.

"Miss Whitsett will be working under me on the Pitezel case."

"Will she now?"

"Yes, I have a letter from the president authorizing her to work for me."

The supervisor read the letter three times with his glasses. He was noticeably perturbed. The supervisor called in the gang leader, Mrs. Sappington.

"Will you bring me Miss Whitsett?" the supervisor asked Mrs. Sappington. She whispered to the supervisor that Whitsett had been terminated the previous day. The supervisor fanned himself with his silk fan. "Mr. Cass, why do you want this particular stenographer?" he asked. "What is it exactly you are up to?" Cass remembered what Whitsett had told him before they conned their way into the prison: *If they are polite, be very polite to them. If they are aggressive, be firm. Just act like you are supposed to be there.*

"You're a hateful little pecker, aren't you?" Cass asked, thinking of Whitsett's use of the phrase to the Pinkerton agent.

"I beg your pardon?"

"I come to you with the proper paperwork, a handwritten request from the president of the company and you refuse. Are you completely incompetent?" Cass moved to the door leading to the women's work area. The supervisor stood up to block him.

"How dare you!" the supervisor yelled.

"I demand to see your paperwork," Cass said.

"What?"

"Reports, ledgers, time logs. I want to see them. I want to see what you've been doing up here."

"We don't keep those kinds of records."

"Then you do *nothing* up here. That's even worse."

"We do plenty up here."

"If you don't keep paperwork, it didn't happen. I'll just have to interrupt the president and inform him of your blatant refusal." Cass snatched the letter and turned towards the door.

"No!" the supervisor yelled. "She's unavailable."

"What does that mean?"

"I'm afraid I had to terminate her yesterday," Mrs. Sappington said.

"Terminate? Did you file the correct paperwork?"

"No."

"Then she isn't terminated, is she?"

"I don't know how to reach her. Mrs. Sappington, do you know where she is?"

"No one knows where she lives?" Cass asked.

"I'm afraid not," Mrs. Sappington said with a pleased smile. Cass had hit a wall; if no one could tell him where Whitsett lived, she would be impossible to find. The supervisor and Sappington had beaten him.

"The single woman's boarding house on eleventh," came a voice from the other room.

"Who said that?" Sappington demanded, thrusting the door open. The young women blinked at her calmly. They looked as though they had heard nothing. Sappington went to her desk and pulled out her Bible, slamming it on the desk. "You, Miss Schlitz. You come up here first."

"I am running out of patience," Mr. Cass interrupted. "Send a messenger boy to collect her, this instant."

The messenger boy climbed the office stairs with Whitsett. She had to grab her skirt up in her fists to keep from tripping. Everyone stared at her. She was exhausted, a little dizzy, and the heat from the top floor almost made her pass out.

"Ah, Miss Whitsett, I have another special assignment for you," Cass said.

"I was fired yesterday."

"That was an error on their part. Wasn't it?" Cass turned towards Sappington and the supervisor with his letter. "They didn't fill out any of the proper paperwork. So, it didn't happen. Not only is their paperwork awful but it calls into question-"

"Terrific!" she interrupted. She smiled and gave Cass a rough hug to the shock of everyone.

"Good day," Mr. Cass said to the supervisor. "Miss Whitsett, would you please accompany me?"

Whitsett grabbed the Bible from the table and followed Cass to the door. Whitsett turned to Mrs. Sappington and threw the bible at her, hitting her in her chest. "See you in hell, you bearded cow."

They descended the stairs and walked out onto the street. "That felt so good," she said.

"How was that? Was I firm and tough?" Cass asked, letting all the air out of his chest.

"Much better, inspector. Very tough."

"Do you have your materials?"

"Yes, I do, inspector! What's going on?"

"I too was almost terminated yesterday for sneaking off and interviewing Mrs. Pitezel. But then I was given authority to pursue this case further."

"I told you! That's great. I told you!" Mrs. Jacobs won't be very happy, she thought. I'll have to think of something to tell her.

Whitsett had only lived with Mrs. Jacobs for a day but was already regretting her decision. She couldn't take her proposal acceptance back though. She was living with Mrs. Jacobs and they had already spent money on the engagement. She would figure out something to tell her. She would figure out what to do later.

"Whitsett and Inspector the Kid strike again. Are we getting bonuses? What did the president say? What did Mrs. Sappington say? Oh, thanks for gettin' my job back." She was one more thought away from crying but she was beyond relieved.

"I didn't just get your job back. We are working on the Pitezel case now as well."

"How exciting! Where are we going now? Not the prison again? You can't keep taking a lady to prisons."

"No, the morgue."

Morgue

Cass and Whitsett entered the narrow, four-story brick building. They passed three orderlies who were stumbling about and breathing hard as they lifted a gurney covered with a sheet onto a carriage by the curb. When they entered, the halls were dark and cold. Only a few windows were open, and the large curtains cast heavy shadows and cloaked the halls in hazy rectangles.

"Excuse me, sir," Cass said. "Is the doctor in today?"

"I don't know where he is at the moment," the orderly replied. "Let me try and find him."

"Are we talking to another of his doctor schoolmates?" Whitsett asked.

"No. I want to hear from a doctor that doesn't know him. Let's see if any of his claims are true."

After several minutes of waiting outside an office, Miss Whitsett grew bored and wandered down a hall. Mr. Cass followed after her, trying to catch up. She pushed her way through a heavy door into a cool room with blinding white light streaming down from an opening in the ceiling. There were tiers of viewing benches descending onto a small stage where a doctor was performing surgery. Dozens of bearded men were intently viewing the operation.

The patient was a young man strapped down with leather bands to an elevated chair. Two large orderlies held the patient's shoulders and chest secure as he writhed and struggled to escape. The doctor had blood and pus down the front of his black butcher's apron as he shifted his body to get leverage for his large polished knife.

The doctor wrapped his arm around the damaged leg just above the knee. In one fast motion, the knife had sliced bone-deep into the flesh. The doctor brought the knife all the way around the leg, cutting through muscle, tissue, tendons and nerves.

The gurgling screams of the patient shattered the silence of the room. The pleading and crying were so loud, the orderly had to put his arm around the boy's neck. The patient was unmistakably suffering louder than any person they had ever heard. Yet the onlookers just calmly and clinically observed.

In a quick hand off, the doctor was given a thick bone saw. He began to push and pull. The heavy exertion made the doctor's wispy hair flip wildly. The cries of the patient were so loud and ear piercing that no one heard Whitsett and Cass enter.

The saw motion was obstructed by the patient struggling and screaming. Blood and pus ran down the doctor's hands and instruments. Within ninety excruciating long seconds, the doctor had cut through the bone and used the knife to cut away any remaining attachments. The blood and fluid collected in a small box under the patient, the overflow absorbed by mounds of sawdust.

Before the leg could be sewn up, the patient stopped screaming. The doctor leaned over with his ear. The boy had died.

"Bring in the next patient," the surgeon said.

Cass and Whitsett froze. Their skin had turned a pale green and their ears rang. Cass fled the surgery but then returned to grab Whitsett and force her to leave with him.

Cass pulled Whitsett outside and heaved by the side of the building, next to the street.

"Are you okay, inspector?" Whitsett asked.

"Is there something I can help you with?" an orderly asked. He was loading another gurney onto the carriage with the help of his colleague.

"I'm with Fidelity Mutual Insurance. I have some questions regarding a case," he said, trying to compose himself.

The orderlies loaded the long gurney securely in the back of the black carriage. Miss Whitsett poked her head around to see what it was. She lifted the cloth and saw the blue dead face of a young man.

"I don't know if the doctor will be available today," the orderly said. "I could leave word."

"What did this one die from?" Whitsett asked, poking the body on the nose with her pencil.

"Madam!" The attendants jumped and herded her away from the cart like a small child. They covered the body and closed the door.

"Are you okay?" they asked her.

"I'm fine. Are you taking him to the graveyard?"

"No, ma'am. This one's goin' to the medical school."

"School? Why?"

"Doctor students learn on 'em."

"You deliver bodies frequently to the school?" Cass asked.

"Yes sir."

Whitsett looked up at the driver of the carriage. "Can we ride along?"

After negotiating a small cartage fee, the investigators were delivered to the St. Louis Medical School. Whitsett and Cass rode up top with the driver. They were so tightly packed on the seat that Whitsett draped her legs over Cass's knee. She was too busy talking to the driver about dead bodies and horses that she didn't notice Cass's face turn bright red. He had never touched a woman before and didn't know where to set his hands. He looked off into the distance trying to ignore the situation. He held up his hands at right angles, away from her legs, for the entire trip.

For a medical school, it was surprisingly difficult to find. They wandered inside the cavernous halls, looking for anyone who would speak to them. The male students that passed in the halls were slightly uncomfortable about seeing a young woman in their institution. They stared and gawked at her, sometimes coming to a complete and abrupt stop.

"Move along, boys," she said while waving her hand.

Cass felt uncomfortable for her and himself. Whitsett didn't notice the men hatefully staring at her; she was looking at the large oil paintings of alumni and Greek gods hanging from dusty frames on the walls.

They were eventually directed into Dr. Pauling's office. As they sat in the uncomfortable wooden chairs, Miss Whitsett couldn't help but focus her attention on a life-size skeleton suspended from a bolt that was protruding from the top of its skull. She wasn't frightened by the bones, just curious. She grabbed a long, wooden pointer from the desk and used it to push and poke the skeleton. The bones dangled and swayed as she prodded them.

Dr. Pauling entered and shook Mr. Cass's hand. He was shocked to find a young lady in his office.

"Umm, hello?"

Miss Whitsett quickly grabbed his hand and shook it.

"Miss Whitsett works for Fidelity as well, sir. She'll be recording our conversation."

"Oh, well, um," Dr. Pauling sat behind his desk. "What can I do for you?"

"Well, sir. I'm here regarding the Pitezel case. I need to know if it's possible to take a dead body from New York, fold it into a trunk, then several days later set it on fire, and get the body described in this report." Cass handed him the coroner's notes and reports.

Dr. Pauling was unnerved to have a young lady present while talking about such matters.

"How long had the body been dead?"

"Two days. Maybe three."

"In what conditions was it kept?" Dr. Pauling noticed his pointer was out of place and returned it to the proper spot on his desk.

"Let's see, folded in a trunk in the baggage car for a day. Then a house?"

"I don't believe this could be the body you described to me."

"Why?"

"Ambient temperature affects rigor mortis. The hotter it is, the faster the process. The body in this report was still in rigor mortis. The bladder had relieved itself and there was regurgitation. That also implies the death had happened much sooner than three days."

"Thank you very much, sir," Cass said.

"I need a body. Can I get one?" Whitsett asked.

The doctor was stunned. "What do you mean by that?"

"I need a body. How do I procure one? Hypothetically."

"What do you plan to do with it?"

"Scam an insurance company," Whitsett said.

"Oh, I see." The doctor caught on to Whitsett's meaning. "You could dig one up from the cemetery."

"No good. Has to be fresh. Still going through rigor mortis," Whitsett said, pleasantly blinking at him. The doctor's eyes were held open as far as they could go. *How inappropriate*, he thought. *Is this woman afflicted with some illness?* "Are you feeling well?" he asked Miss Whitsett.

"I'm just fine," she said, scribbling with her pen.

Suddenly the doctor noticed the scars along her wrists. "Where did you get those scars? Were you injured?"

Whitsett began to pull her sleeves over her wrists. "Where did you get that face, were you injured?" she asked.

"Doctor? The body?" Cass asked, hoping to keep the conversation focused.

"Well, they're something of a scarce commodity," the doctor said, trying to avoid looking in Whitsett's direction.

"What do you mean by that?"

"There are many people who need bodies, Mr. Cass. Researchers, medical students, the entire medical community can't procure enough of them. Demand far exceeds supply, to borrow an economist's concept, 'invisible hand' and all that."

"Why do you need so many dead bodies?" Whitsett asked.

"Medical students need them in their studies. Dissection...I'm sorry, miss," the doctor said. He had hoped to save her ears from such harsh realities.

"Sorry for what?" she said.

"Dissection specimens," the doctor whispered.

"Why are you whispering?" she whispered back.

"Students in their second year must dissect a corpse as part of their studies. Researchers need them to examine what happens to certain tissues or bones with procedures and chemistry. Even this one here." He pointed to the skeleton. "This one is made from a corpse. An invaluable tool in the teaching of anatomy." He began to touch it tenderly. "This was a female. Late 20s. I expect she was a beautiful woman. She must have been very fit and healthy. Six feet tall. I've never seen a six-foot-tall woman. I wonder what could have killed such a young, healthy, beautiful woman."

"Should we leave you two alone?" Whitsett asked.

"You will find one of these in most classrooms around the country. Students use them as a reference tool and aid."

"Did you?" she asked.

"Oh yes, three formal lectures a week, and every day we would study the cadavers. Twenty to forty hours over the table every week."

"Where do they get them?"

Dr. Pauling looked at Miss Whitsett's pencil and hesitated. *Women aren't supposed to ask questions*, he thought. "From the dead room."

"What's the dead room?" she asked.

"It's a department in our establishment that procures the materials for our research. The university itself doesn't obtain them. There is a liaison officer who supplies the anatomy suites. What's going on here? Who is she?"

"That's Miss Whitsett. She's a stenographer for Fidelity Mutual."

"Then why is she asking questions? Ladies shouldn't ask questions."

"I like knowing things," she said.

"It is very unnatural for a woman to discuss such things so freely. I think she must be suffering from some disease of the brain. Perhaps some brain anemia."

"How does the liaison officer supply all these corpses?" Cass asked.

"I'm sure I don't know and wouldn't want to know," the doctor said.

"Right. As long as you get to make money from them?" Whitsett said.

"The value of any art or science should be determined by the tendency it has to increase the happiness, or to diminish the misery, of mankind. Before, medicine was nothing more than folk remedies. Now it is a science. And the world is better for it. With better-trained doctors, we can provide people with a better quality of life. But as a woman with brain anemia, I wouldn't expect you to understand such concepts."

"How does a dead body in your office increase quality of life?" Whitsett asked.

"This isn't a 'dead body.' It's a teaching aid."

"Then why is it in your office, instead of a classroom?" she asked.

"They further our medical knowledge—"

"Fondling a skeleton furthers medical knowledge?"

"How dare you!" Dr. Pauling yelled. I will not be interrupted by a woman with brain anemia, he thought.

"Quite right. Miss Whitsett." Cass pointed to her pencil. She began recording again. "You don't think it's worth looking into how your school obtains all these dead bodies?"

"That isn't my job." Dr. Pauling went silent and turned his head like a stubborn mule.

"One last question. Where did you get this skeleton?"

"I don't know."

Dr. Pauling didn't see them to the door.

The Dead Room

Cass followed Whitsett as she wandered the halls of the medical building.

"What a pompous ass," Whitsett said. "Does he think he's the Duke of Buckingham?"

"Did you see his face when you asked him about the skeleton? I thought his eyes were going to bulge out of his head," Cass said.

"Okay, calm down, inspector," she said, trying to force back a smile.

"It's like when you nailed Holmes with the question about rigor mortis."

"That doctor knows where the bodies come from," Whitsett said.

"He said he didn't."

"He lied." She pointed at some stairs and said, "What's down there?"

As they descended the winding stairs, they noticed it was much cooler with a very low ceiling.

"I don't think we're supposed to be down here," Cass said.

Whitsett walked down the hall, knocking on every door she came across. Cass was mortified at her boldness, trying to convince her to stop. Then one of the doors opened and an older, short man with a door-knocker beard answered. With one look, Miss Whitsett knew this son of a bitch was a biter.

"Can I help you?" He was in the middle of winding his watch.

"Dr. Pauling said you know how to get dead bodies," Whitsett said.

"Sure. Sure," he said with a sniff. "That's me, Mr. Ellis. I'm in charge of the dead room." He was hooked on spicy snuff from Turkey that made his nose run.

"Is this the dead room?" Whitsett asked, poking her head in.

"It isn't for the eyes of young ladies," he said, closing the door behind him. "It's full of unsightly things. Who are you?"

"We're investigators for Fidelity Insurance," Cass said.

Whitsett enjoyed being referred to as an investigator. "Dr. Pauling sent us down here for information," she said.

"Sure, sure." Mr. Ellis took Whitsett's hand delicately after removing his hat. "What kind of information do you need?"

"What's the dead room?" she asked.

Cass was still fidgeting; he was terrible at lying and knew he would get in trouble.

"This is where we keep the cadavers that the students use in their studies."

"Where do you get the bodies?"

"I don't get bodies, my dear. I'm in the business of anatomical procurement. I deal with a liaison officer who supplies us."

"What about the one in Dr. Pauling's office?"

"Ah, the six-footer. Sure, everyone's very interested in her. Paid a pretty penny for her. Two hundred dollars."

"That's a fortune!" she yelled. Her voice echoed along the halls.

"Yes, but she's worth it. There aren't that many skeletons of young women. Plus, whoever prepared it, did a wonderful job. Who did you say you were again?" Mr. Ellis gave Cass a closer looking over.

While Mr. Ellis was distracted with Cass, Whitsett opened the door and peeked her head inside. There were rows of tables lining the long room. Each table was covered with a dirty blanket, which covered a dead body. The room smelled like bleach and salt. Large blocks of ice packed the floors making it very chilly and wet.

Mr. Ellis felt the chill and closed the door. "Miss!" he said in shock.

"That's a lot of bodies. Do you know all their names?"

"They don't have names. They're dead."

"Where did she come from?" Cass asked, pointing upstairs.

"The skeleton? I purchased it from a liaison officer some time ago."

"Perhaps if you look at your records, we can trace the sale," Cass said, eager to get his hands on some ledgers.

"Oh, we don't keep records of that, sir," Mr. Ellis said, laughing in amusement.

"You don't keep records?" Cass was appalled. His face turned red and he looked as though he would cry in frustration. "That is ridiculous, sir. All associations keep detailed records. The fact that you don't, calls into question the very institution. Why bother doing anything at all?"

Whitsett was forced to grab onto Cass's arm to calm him down.

"My dear!" Ellis said, taking her hand. "You have terrible scars on your wrists. How did you get those?"

She pulled her hand back quickly. "Is there anything more you can tell us?" Whitsett asked. She was jabbing Cass repeatedly in the side with her elbow.

"Why are you doing that?" Cass asked.

"Give him a tip," Whitsett whispered.

"How much?" Cass whispered back, reaching into his pockets.

"A few bits."

"How much is a few?"

She grabbed the coins from his hand and placed them in Mr. Ellis's hand.

"Sure, sure," Ellis said. "Should we get some air?"

He brought them outside for a walk around the block. The bright sun caused them to squint painfully. "Off the record?" Mr. Ellis asked. He put out his arm for Whitsett to hold onto as he escorted her. He was very happy to have the attention of a young lady.

"Of course," Whitsett said. She put her pencil and paper away.

"I believe that particular piece came from the LaSalle Medical School."

"Where do you get dead bodies?" Whitsett asked again. "Dr. Pauling upstairs acted like he didn't know."

"It's very much a don't ask, don't tell situation," Mr. Ellis said. "I would guess that about twenty percent are obtained legally. The rest are obtained on a grey market."

"How much are they?"

"I wouldn't know. I don't deal in grey markets."

"True, but if ya had to guess, how much? Hypothetically?" Whitsett asked.

"Hypothetically. Very good. $20 to $30 per body, hypothetically."

"That's what I earn in a month," Miss Whitsett said. "That's what a life's worth to medical people?"

"I'm afraid so, my pet. A dirty business."

"Why don't the cops stop it?"

"Too busy. And cops don't arrest doctors. They only arrest criminals. Doctors can't be criminals, they're doctors," Mr. Ellis said.

"Could you get a body to order?" Cass asked. He was forced to walk behind them.

"To order?" Mr. Ellis laughed. "What do you mean by that?"

"If I gave you a list of features that I needed a body to have, could you provide it?"

"There are no belles of the ball in this business, my boy. You take what you can get. Why is the Fidelity Insurance company so interested in anatomical procurement?"

Whitsett told him the story of how Holmes procured a corpse to collect a life insurance claim. Mr. Ellis was endlessly amused.

"This Holmes person seems very endearing," Mr. Ellis said as he laughed.

"Where do you get them?" Cass was frustrated and almost shouting. "And where are we going? Do you realize we're walking into the rough part of town?"

"I'm gonna tell you what the doctors tell the students. Learn by doing."

They continued down the street. Mr. Ellis grinned with delight as he was enjoying his walk with the attentive Miss Whitsett.

"What's it like looking at all those skeletons?" she asked.

"They're just parts. I don't really think about it."

"Do you imagine people as skeletons when you walk around every day?"

"No. Why are you asking these strange questions?"

"I like knowing things. What do you think happens when you die?"

"I'm sure I don't know."

"Are we going to meet a body snatcher?" Whitsett asked. She was excited, having read all about them.

"No. And they prefer to be called resurrectionists. Since you two are so interested in the trade, I am giving you the opportunity to help me procure a specimen."

"What an adventure! I'm so glad you don't smell. I expected you to smell. Where do you get them? Graveyards?"

"Graveyards? No. You have to get the fresh graves. Otherwise the dirt is too hard. But it isn't worth going to the graveyards anymore. There are hardly any bodies left in the graveyards." He laughed. "The only thing left in graveyards are tombstones and weeds."

"That can't be," Cass said. "Don't you think people would notice if their loved ones' graves had been dug up?"

"They don't go in that way, my boy. You go behind the tombstone. And extract the body from the head end of the coffin. Much less digging. Hypothetically."

"How many bodies are you using?" Whitsett asked.

"Thousands? The new graveyards have police guards and special coffins to deter resurrectionists. It's too expensive to use the graveyards anymore. Sure. Only amateurs do that. Decomposition has already set in and the doctors don't like that. They prefer them clean. Digging is too much work anyway."

"That is horrible," Whitsett said.

"That is supply and demand, my dear. Supply and demand."

"I don't think it's appropriate to take a lady on such an errand," Cass said, following them at their heels. Whitsett enjoyed knowing that Cass thought of her as a lady.

"Could you please stand further back as we walk?" Mr. Ellis demanded of Cass.

"Why?"

"I don't like you being a part of this conversation."

"Why?"

"You bother me, Mr. Cass."

Whitsett gave him a nod and Cass walked a few paces behind them.

"Sure, it might be grizzly," Mr. Ellis continued, "but resurrectionists and anatomical procurement are an essential service to society. It's like mucking the horse manure. Sure, it's not a pretty job, but it must be done."

"You're desecrating graves," she said.

"They're just holes in the ground. Most of these bastards will be of more use to society as anatomical subjects than they ever were as living people."

"And you get to decide who's worthless?" Whitsett said.

"No. I don't do anything but procure specimens for the betterment of mankind. If it was not for this trade, what would the doctors learn on? How would doctors learn about how the body works?"

"People don't want their loved ones stolen and mutilated. Especially if it's on some black market sustained on the misery of others. You have no right to these bodies," Cass said, interjecting again.

"They would just rot away, and our doctors would be ignorant. Think of all the treatments and medicines that have saved countless lives thanks to my profession."

"People deserve respect and dignity, in both life and death," Cass said.

"Dignity, sure. Once we give dignity to the living, then we can worry about giving it to the dead."

"I can see how that would be a good thing. What if they can cure an illness because of this? It helps more people than it hurts," Whitsett said.

"Here we are." Mr. Ellis stopped. They stood outside the poorhouse. It was a run-down building with rotted wood and broken windows.

"What is this?" Cass asked.

"It's a poorhouse, Mr. Cass. Where the unfortunates are cared for at the expense of our taxes. Now come along, my dear."

Whitsett couldn't get her feet to move.

"Here we go," Mr. Ellis said, pulling her along.

"I thought you got them from doctors."

"I have a deal with the city morgue and most doctors. They send product my way, but they could never fill up my anatomy suites. Too damaged. There has also been a shortage of deaths. We've had some good weather lately, so the prices have shot up. Fewer people die in good weather. I've gone over budget. Can you cry?" Ellis asked Whitsett.

"Cry?" Whitsett said in a slight panic.

"Sure, sure, can you cry on demand?"

"You mean as a con? A hustle?" Whitsett asked.

"Sure. You will go inside very weepy and upset saying you're looking for your husband. Say he was a man about 22 years old with dark hair. That's vague enough. If they ask for more details, just cry and scream. They'll take you to their morgue. You point at the best specimen and say, that's my husband. After a small tip, we can take the body away, no questions asked; and we have another victory for society."

"You want me to steal a body for you?"

"No. Remember, you aren't stealing them. Legally, the dead bodies don't belong to anyone. You are appropriating them for the betterment of the community. But you will have to remove their clothing. Stealing clothes from a dead body is a crime."

Ellis dragged Whitsett into the dilapidated building and they were immediately stopped by a tall skinny man who tipped his hat. Ellis smiled, as though they knew each other. They spoke to each other like actors reading their lines to the back of the audience.

"Can I help you?"

"Yes, we are here searching for this poor creature's lost husband."

"I see. What does he look like?"

Whitsett was overwhelmed by the state of the poor house. It was bare and dank. It smelled like sewage and she could hear moaning in the distance.

"Miss?" the man said.

"Umm, he has dark hair," she said. She was distracted by an open door where she could see dirty mounds of bodies forced to sleep in huddled bunches to keep warm.

"I think we may have your husband in the morgue. Please come this way."

It's a prison for being poor, she thought. She hated this place. If you were caught begging, drunk, or just being poor, they snatched you away and put you in these institutions where you were abused and tortured and raped and sold out for work or sex. It's where the city sent undesirables to die. The garbage can for unwanted people. Undesirables such as the poor, single women, blacks, immigrants and people with disabilities. They slowly starved them to death by stealing the money the government sent for food. *I'm never ending up here*, Whitsett thought. She swore she would never be this close to one.

"This way," Mr. Ellis said, trying to pull her along. The two men led her into the morgue. It was a small room with three tables lined against the wall. The bodies were divided into two groups. One group, where the bodies were entitled to respect as they were likely to be claimed, were properly laid out on the tables. The other bodies lined the floor like discarded trash. Their arms and legs intertwined with each other like in a dirty mass grave.

"Now you're going to want to pick out a young one, preferably 25 to 35 years old. Make sure they have all their parts and aren't mangled," Ellis whispered. "That one."

"I can't do that," Whitsett said. "I can't choose like that. I can't make them stand the line."

"Stand the line? What is that? I don't know what that means and it's not a problem, my dear. This is more of a formality. They know you're not the wife. But we have to keep up appearances, don't we? You won't get in trouble, nobody cares about these people."

"I was wrong, you do stink," she said.

"I'm sorry?"

"I'm not crying like that for you."

Whitsett ripped her arm away from Mr. Ellis and grasped Cass's arm. It might have been a useful misery for the betterment of the community, but it was dirty and horrible. She wanted no part in that misery.

Mr. Ellis watched them disappear around the street. He grabbed a servant woman running an errand off the street. "Hello, my dear. Can you cry on demand?"

Cass was relieved to be walking away. "When we get back to the office, I shall search for LaSalle Medical School."

"Holmes could've easily got his body here. He didn't need to go all the way to New York," Whitsett said. She forced herself to forget the poor house. *I'm never going to end up there so I didn't need to think about it ever again.*

"But the body couldn't be any old body," Cass said. "It would have to look exactly like Mr. Pitezel. Same height, same teeth, same wart on the back of the neck. No matter where he got it, my guess is that it would be extremely difficult to find a dead man, within sixty hours, that was identical to the subject being substituted."

"Unless that person wasn't dead until they were discovered to be identical," Mrs. Whitsett said.

"Very clever! And gruesome," Cass said. "Let's go through the facts we have discovered about the crime scene. Dr. Pauling said that the body was recently deceased due to the effects of rigor mortis. The bladder had emptied and there was regurgitation. Therefore, the man died in that room a day or so before the body was found.

"We know that chloroform was used on the man. Heavy traces were found in the corpse's stomach. That much chloroform would render a man unconscious. His face and clothes were burned, so there was an explosion. The man is exactly the same size and weight as Pitezel and has the same wart and injuries."

"What caused the explosion?"

"Apparently he was lighting his pipe and there was an explosion."

"How do they know that?"

"They found a pipe next to him."

"If there was an explosion, how is the pipe still intact?"

"Oh my goodness, you're right," Cass said. He began to flip through his notes. "The pipe was untouched. No damage. What does all of that information tell us, Miss Whitsett?"

"It tells us that Mr. Holmes is full of shit," she said.

"Yes! We are onto something, Miss Whitsett. Wait until Mr. Fouse hears about this. Still want to move to Holmes's Hotel in Chicago?" Cass asked, gloating.

"Oh please, you admired him so much more. You wanted to go into business with him," she said.

"Damnit!" Cass yelped.

"What?"

"The company won't reimburse me for what I paid Mr. Ellis."

"Why not?"

"Because the company doesn't reimburse for that kind of thing."

"Why not?"

"Because I'm not sure they know how to allocate 'bribes to body snatchers' on the ledger."

"They're called resurrectionists."

"Plus, I didn't get a receipt."

"It wasn't that much money," Whitsett said.

"You didn't even count it."

Second Confession

Cass and Whitsett drudged through the outskirts of the city to find the LaSalle Medical School. They wanted to find the source of the six-foot-tall woman skeleton in Dr. Pauling's office. The school was as cagey about their activities as Dr. Pauling, but they were able to discover the skeleton was bought from Hahnemann Medical School in Chicago.

Cass escorted Whitsett to the lobby of the Fidelity Mutual office building and told her to meet him in one hour. He disappeared into the filing room and searched through state registers and company information for any information on the LaSalle Medical School or the Hahnemann Medical School in Chicago. Unable to find anything useful, he dutifully filled out the forms to request information from other offices. It would take a few days for the information to get back to him.

Cass brushed off his jacket and made his way downstairs to the president's office. He was excited to tell Mr. Fouse of their discoveries. Mr. Holmes was lying.

"Mr. Cass, I'm glad you're here," the president said.

"We have a break in the Pitezel case, sir," Cass said.

"That can wait. The prisoner, Mr. Holmes, has asked for a stenographer to come to his cell so he can dictate a statement. He has asked for Miss Whitsett personally. Is this the same woman you requested to work with?"

"Miss Whitsett? Yes, sir. He met her during the Boston interview."

"Why would he ask for her by name?"

"I have no idea, sir."

"This is very improper. You will go to take his statement. But leave the woman. A prison is no place for a young woman."

"If you insist," Cass said. "But we've been through the evidence and we believe—"

"Yes, yes, we will discuss it when you get back. First, go speak to Holmes. And tell him how improper this entire thing is."

Whitsett was waiting impatiently by the side entrance.

"Mr. Holmes has requested a stenographer to record a statement. And he asked for you by name," Cass reported.

"That's a bit unsettling," she said.

"Extremely. So, I'm going down there to get his new statement."

"Great, let's go," she said.

"President Fouse has asked you to remain here. He doesn't think it's proper for a young girl to be in a prison. And the fact that Holmes asked for you by name is very improper."

"To hell with that. I'm going."

"Miss Whitsett, he's right, we can't have young girls at the call of prisoners."

Without another word, she climbed into the carriage Cass had summoned and waited. She tapped on the cushion beside her.

Holmes's cell was six feet across. The damp bricks rose to an arch in the ceiling. A surplus civil war era wooden cot was pushed against either wall. Holmes occupied the cell by himself.

"Miss Whitsett, Mr. Cass, thank you for coming," Holmes said. He pulled his cot closer to the iron bars and sat down. "Please sit."

"I am Inspector Cass interviewing Mr. Holmes. Recording is Miss Whitsett."

Holmes watched them very closely for a moment. His blue eyes glowed in the dark cell. He kept his fresh appearance even while in prison.

"I am very sorry I was so untruthful in my former statements when I declared that Pitezel was in South America and that the children were with him. I am now prepared to tell the truth. I've been reading about my case in the papers and can't be silent any longer," Holmes said. He flattened out his shirt. "Mr. Pitezel is not alive, but dead. It was really Pitezel's body which had been identified as Pitezel."

The investigators were disconcerted by his casual manner.

"If Pitezel is dead, where are the children?" Whitsett asked.

"With Miss Williams in London."

"Who is Miss Williams?" Cass asked.

"She's the woman who owned the property in Fort Worth."

Cass rubbed his eyes and sighed. "Why don't you just start from the beginning?"

"I contemplated defrauding the insurance company in August or September 1893. No one else was part of the plot until July 1894. About

1st August, I was released from jail and outlined the conspiracy to the lawyer Howe and showed him how I intended to raise money to liberate Mr. Hedgepeth, the Handsome Bandit, from jail.

"I got some $300 there to help him out, then I went to Chicago to raise some money, then I went to New York and got $600 from Minnie Williams. Then I arranged with Pitezel that he should provide a retreat to stop at after the conspiracy was consummated and also to get his teeth altered.

"Three days later Pitezel came and took the house. I think I visited the house four times besides the day he died. I found that he had been drinking and I took him to task for it. He remarked that he wanted to kill himself. He borrowed $15 from me and left about four o'clock. I next saw him the following Saturday, 1st September at the Mercantile Library. Then he came to my home and said his baby was sick and he had to go home. I raised no objection. He said he would have to have some money to go with. I asked him where the $15 was, which he had a few days ago, he said 'well, I haven't got it.' I had none to give him.

"The next morning, Sunday, I went to his office. I found no one there. No one on the first or the second floor. The second floor had a sleeping area with a cot made up. I checked the library, went over to Broad Street, then came back to the house. I went upstairs and laid down on the cot and read the paper for about half an hour. Then I went to his desk to leave a note.

"There was a scrap of paper written in cipher that said, 'get letter out bottle in cupboard.' I got the letter. He left a message for me in cipher. It told me that he was going to get out of it and that I should find him upstairs, if he could manage to kill himself."

Whitsett was having difficulty recording at the same speed Holmes spoke. There were also horrible screams of men being brutalized and broken from some hidden part of the prison. The yelling made Whitsett's hand jerk. Holmes kept on speaking as though there were no sounds at all, taking no notice of them.

"Kill himself? Do you still have this paper?" Cass asked.

"No, I destroyed it. I kept it until Toronto, where I used it in sending a cipher to Mrs. Pitezel. I went upstairs to the third floor and found him on the floor apparently dead. I felt his pulse and laid my hand on his and found it was cold. His eyes were partially closed. I had to leave the room on account of the fumes of chloroform being so strong.

"I went back and opened the window. I found that he was lying on his back with his left hand folded over his abdomen and his right hand lying at his side. I did not keep the letter which was in the bottle. I removed the furniture from the third story room and took it to the second story. I brought the body down to the second story and arranged it in the way it was found.

"I had arranged with Pitezel, that when he placed the substitute body, a bottle should be broken which he supposedly had in his hand when the explosion occurred, and that the fragments should be scattered around the room. I held the bottle up and broke it with a blow of a hammer, an old rusty one, upon the side. That bottle contained benzene, chloroform and ammonia, which was to be used for burning the floor to indicate that an explosion had occurred. I took some of this fluid and put it upon his right hand and side, and on the right side of his face, and then set fire to it. I then arranged the articles that he had taken from his pocket, putting them back again, and hung his vest in the second-story bedroom, and the coat on the first story where he had been in the habit of keeping it. I gathered together the rubber tube, towel and a bottle of chloroform and left the house as soon as I could, probably at a quarter to four.

"Then I left for St. Louis. I think I threw away the key I had for his home and left the door open. I got to my house about 5 o'clock. My wife was not well, and I went to work and straightened things and got the packing done before it was dark. When I found the body, the pockets of the pants were turned out, and his knife and the house key were lying on the chair.

"I went immediately to Howe's office, having made up my mind, that as he knew of it, I had better let him settle up the insurance. I found Mrs. Pitezel and we talked everything over. We found Howe and explained what had to be done. We didn't tell Mrs. Pitezel that her husband was dead. She just assumed that it was the substitute body.

"At the time of the discovery of the body, a towel was over his face. The tube was fastened to the bottle by a cork with a quill; then he had tied around a string to keep the chloroform from running too fast. I think the rubber tube was four or five feet long. I took the tube with me. But not the towel."

Cass and Whitsett were overwhelmed by his enthusiastic and confusing narrative. It was a flood of details with seemingly no measure of coherence that left them exhausted.

"The children are with Miss Minnie Williams?" Whitsett asked.

"Yes."

"Why didn't you just call the police?" Cass asked.

"Are you married, ma'am?" Holmes asked.

"Yes," Miss Whitsett said without looking up.

"You weren't wearing a ring on the train. But now you're wearing a ring. And Mr. Cass stated you for the record as being Miss. Are you two trying to confuse me? That isn't very nice. I don't appreciate being made a fool. Especially when I'm trying to voluntarily confess the truth."

"Oh, no," Cass said, stumbling over his words. "We're not trying to be deceptive, Mr. Holmes. It's just that—"

"Mr. Holmes? Why didn't you just call the police?" Whitsett said firmly, repeating the question. She wasn't going to let him change the subject so easily.

"The insurance would not have been paid if he killed himself."

"How do you keep all this information straight without writing it down?" Cass asked.

"I keep it all in my head, Mr. Cass. If you want to be an industrialist, you'll have to keep dozens of things in your head at once."

"Is there a way to teach yourself how to do that?" Cass asked.

"You just have to get out there and do it."

After Holmes's new statement, District Attorney Graham had to change the indictment. He issued a new indictment charging H.H. Holmes, Marion Hedgepeth and Jeptha D. Howe, with having conspired to cheat the insurance company by alleging that one B.F. Pitezel, who had been insured in said company, had died *as the result of an accident.*

During the court proceedings, Cass and Whitsett sat in the back of the courtroom. The maximum sentence for this was two years and if he pleaded guilty, he might get less.

"Look at him," Miss Whitsett whispered to Cass. "He's grinning. Why is he so pleased with himself?"

"I don't know. Two years in prison sounds awful. From the men I've seen, two years sounds like absolute torture."

When the judge said he would not sentence him then, but would consider his case at a later date, Holmes's grin turned into a smile.

The mystery of Holmes was solved. Holmes had confessed. The conspirators were in jail. Cass received a firm handshake from Mr. Fouse. No bonuses were given.

Case closed.

Mrs. Pitezel.

Whitsett hated Holmes's smile now. It made her kick chairs when she thought he was smiling in his cell. *Why the hell is that smug prick smiling?* she thought. She told Cass that people who go to jail shouldn't be smiling. *Why's he smiling? Where are the children?* She wasn't satisfied at all.

Whitsett led Cass up the steps of the prison by his hand like a child. They were, again, on their way to perform another unsanctioned interview.

"I'm in so much trouble," Cass said.

"Don't be silly. We've been right three times in a row. They'll be excited with what we come up with."

"It doesn't work like that. Bosses don't like being wrong. We've told him he was wrong three times in a row. He won't have any patience for us. Especially if all we have is how much you don't like his smile."

"I hate that goddamn smile."

"You were the one who said how handsome he was, ready to move into his hotel in Chicago."

"No, I didn't. You were the one who said he had the spirit of J.P. Morgan."

"You were the one saving up your bonus money for your ticket."

"Where's our bonus money, by the way?"

"Don't hold your breath."

The police officers were very cold to Whitsett and Cass. They didn't appreciate being lied to. Their annoyance was compounded when Cass produced a hand-written note from the district attorney, telling them that the insurance investigators should be allowed interviews with prisoners. They didn't care for people in ties telling them their business.

"This note was issued before the latest confession by Holmes; but they don't know that," Whitsett told Cass.

Mrs. Pitezel was haggard and rough. She had stopped eating and her face was turning inside out. Cass stated the date and attendees for the record.

"Mrs. Pitezel, I know this is difficult for you," Cass said. "But I want to thank you for coming forward and telling the truth. I know in your position it must seem very scary. But be assured, all we want to do is get your children back."

She nodded her head silently.

"Do you know where your children are?" Cass asked his questions very delicately and calmly.

"Canada?"

"When was the last time you saw your children?"

She struggled to push out the answers.

"I understand you weren't truthful before because you were concerned that your testimony would get your husband in trouble with the law. No one blames you for that. But I'm afraid your husband has committed suicide, so we need to try and find your children."

"They got no interest in you," Whitsett said. "They ain't trying to trap you or send you away. They just want to find your kids. You ain't gonna be in trouble. Stop acting like a blubbering fool. Just tell us what we want to know."

"If I'm sent away, my children will be institutionalized," Mrs. Pitezel finally said. "I won't send my children to those places."

"Good. And god damn you if you let that happen. Now just tell this inspector what he wants to know," Whitsett said.

Mrs. Pitezel nodded. Cass was shocked at Whitsett's hard-handed treatment towards the grieving Mrs. Pitezel.

"Mrs. Pitezel, this is very important," Cass said. "When was the last time you saw your children?"

"September 28th. Holmes took them."

"Have you ever met anyone named Minnie Williams?"

"No."

"Holmes didn't introduce you to another woman around the age of 26, maybe by another name?"

"He never introduced me to any women," she said. "Apart from Emily. Emily Cigrand."

"Tell me about her."

"She was Holmes's secretary. She was in her early twenties, a tiny little thing. I normally didn't acquaint myself with Holmes's young women. She was the most beautiful girl I have ever seen though."

"How did Holmes meet her?"

"Through my husband. She was working at the Golden Cure as a stenographer."

"Your husband was an alcoholic?"

"Holmes sent my husband to the Golden Cure to rid him of his alcoholism. Keeley Cure it's called. It cost $100 a week. He was sober at first, but eventually he strayed back to the bottle. Mr. Holmes was furious. He was kicking and screaming."

"Did he really have that much affection for Mr. Pitezel?" Cass asked.

"I don't know. I think he was upset about being swindled. Mr. Holmes can't stand to be taken advantage of."

"But he spent $100 a week on his health. Sounds like he was fond of your husband," Whitsett said.

"He was fond of all the things my husband did for him," she said.

"And what did he do?" Cass asked.

"All manner of things."

"Like what?"

"My husband had a variety of work experience. He was a janitor, lumber worker, circus hand, railroad worker. He is good with his hands and his fists."

"But what did he do for Mr. Holmes that made him worth $100 a week?" Whitsett asked.

"Well...he brought back Emily Cigrand for him."

"For him?"

"My husband was bewitched by her at the Cure. He is enchanted with blondes. When he returned and the cure didn't work, Mr. Holmes was furious. My husband told Holmes about this girl that worked there that was the most beautiful thing in the world. He hoped it would ease the loss of all that money. Holmes wrote her a letter offering her a job and board in Chicago as a secretary. She was young enough to jump at the opportunity. Then she and Holmes became very friendly. Pretty girls are nothing but slags. Flipping their blonde hair everywhere. Nothing but trouble for men with families."

Whitsett remembered Holmes had offered her a place to live and work. I was so silly to get excited over the prospect. I would have just been the latest girl to do so. That was a good con, she thought bitterly. Now she really hated him.

"Where's she now?" Whitsett asked.

"I don't know. Gone to the devil hopefully. Away from my husband and children."

"And where *are* your children, ma'am?" Whitsett asked.

"I don't know."

"Why would you send your small children away with a strange man?" Whitsett asked.

"He wasn't strange. I knew him."

"As a fraudster and philanderer," Whitsett said.

"I thought he was taking them to their father. I couldn't so Alice had to go identify the body. I think she might have been sick, but she never let on. She's like that, you know. Always trying to act so strong and firm. But then she giggles with her sister like a fool and forgets her act.

"She was so pretty and ladylike in her dress and hat the day she left. She looked so small. She must have been so scared, going off to another city with a strange man. Then seeing her father like that. I couldn't do it. I couldn't do it, I was so sick and the baby was sick. I couldn't do it. Oh God, she must have hated me. Making her see her father like that. She's just a child. She was all alone. My poor Alice."

"Did they take anything with them?" Cass asked.

"Yes, the trunk, it's missing. It was the same trunk Holmes borrowed from me in Detroit."

"Why did he borrow it?"

"He said he was going to use it to smuggle my husband out."

"Do you remember what kind of trunk it was?"

"Yes."

"Can you describe all the things that they took with them when they left your care?"

"It will take me a moment to remember—when I'm not so cloudy in my head."

"You can write it down later if you like."

Mrs. Pitezel was tenderly led out of the room by the officer, weeping. Whitsett rolled her eyes and sighed.

"Why were you so rough with Mrs. Pitezel?"

"She sent her children off with some strange man. That's terrible."

"You were ready to move to Chicago with him," Cass said.

"I was not!"

"Yes, you were. The least you can do is have some sympathy for that poor creature."

"Why should I? No one had any sympathy for me," Whitsett said. "Oh, I forgot, all mothers are saints. Well, that saint handed her children over to Holmes without blinking, and now they're gone. Poor Alice, all alone. I was alone and worse. How come no one's falling over me?"

Mrs. Howard

Georgiana Howard was brought in with a guard. She was unhappy to see Cass and Whitsett waiting for her. She tried to move her chair away from Whitsett, but Whitsett scooted her seat closer, causing a loud creak.

"Good afternoon, Mrs. Howard," Cass said.

"Yes," she said. She was no longer wearing her expensive dress with a tailored jacket, but a state-issued dirty dress with a belt. She did her best to appear lady-like, rolling the sleeves and pulling the hem down, but she still looked like a prisoner. The color matched Whitsett's dress.

"I have a few more questions for you if that's alright?"

"I don't really have a choice, do I?"

"I suppose not. After your honeymoon in Fort Worth, didn't you find it odd that your husband was arrested?"

"It was a ridiculous farce," she said harshly. "Jealous competitors of my husband using the corrupt legal system to their advantage. My husband is a gentleman. Something you would know nothing about."

"That's not true," Cass said.

Whitsett saw the insult cut Cass deep. She felt her face flush and get hot.

"Did your husband ever introduce you to a woman named Minnie Williams?"

"No."

"Any woman?"

"No. My husband doesn't keep the company of strange women."

Whitsett grinned.

"Mr. Howard seems to have brought you on the same route as the children. Did you ever see any children or hear him speak about children?" Cass asked.

"What children? I never saw any children. I was mostly in our room. I would read, or rest, or tend to personal matters."

Miss Whitsett felt a pang of jealousy. This pompous woman is living my dream of traveling and reading.

"What about when you were in Philadelphia. Did he seem nervous or preoccupied?"

"No, he was in rather a good mood. He had received many orders for a special machine that copies business documents. You and your kind might be out of a job."

"My kind?" Whitsett said.

"One of his customers is the owner of the Pennsylvania railroad," she said.

Miss Whitsett snorted derisively causing Mrs. Howard to become outraged.

"You will show my husband respect! I don't know where a piece of trash from the gutter like you gets off speaking about my husband," she said, looking straight at Whitsett.

Miss Whitsett became dizzy with anger.

"Alright, alright," Whitsett said, rolling up her sleeves. She was going to enjoy this. "We've some bad news for you, Mrs. Howard." Whitsett smiled and put her pencil down. "Your husband is already married. Two times over."

"What nonsense."

"He's also a fraud, doing insurance cons all over the country."

"Such terrible lies. You're just propagating the lies of his competitors, you slut."

"He admitted to the frauds," Cass joined in. He wouldn't stand for any insults directed towards Whitsett. "The Pinkertons discovered one of his other marriages. We met his second wife."

Mrs. Howard's proper and stone-like exterior began to melt away. "I don't believe a single word of it."

Miss Whitsett produced a document from her bag. It was a statement signed by Holmes, confessing to his frauds. Mrs. Howard immediately recognized the handwriting. She involuntarily brushed away some dust from the paper and returned it to Whitsett. She looked away, hoping to hold back the humiliation and tears.

"He didn't love me?" she asked, weeping.

"Holmes never permitted you to discover that he was a swindler. He evidently desired to hold your respect for him until the very last," Cass said, trying to be nice.

"Or he didn't want her as a witness," Whitsett said to him.

"So, I'm nothing more than little Georgiana Yoke?" she asked.

Miss Whitsett suddenly hated herself for bringing the truth down on her so harshly. She felt terrible that she wanted to do it and was embarrassed that she did do it. She had torn down this woman's world like a brute. It wasn't very proper, but it did feel good.

"No, you're Miss Georgiana Yoke," Cass said, handing her a handkerchief. "And you have your entire life in front of you."

Miss Yoke dabbed her eyes and tried to regain her composure. Whitsett felt her face grow hot again when she saw that terrible woman take Cass's handkerchief. She wanted to rip it from her. *Don't give her a handkerchief!*

"You never ventured out with him?" Cass asked.

"Only a few times. Most of the time I was in our room."

"No children? No woman named Minnie Williams?"

"No."

"Did you ever hear or see anything odd?"

"No," she said. Then she paused. "There was a key."

"What kind of key?"

"I found it in one of our trunks while I was unpacking."

"What does it open?" Mr. Cass asked.

"I have no idea."

They sent a police officer to collect her bag from downstairs. She fished through the contents and pulled out a small key. She handed Cass the key and a cop escorted her back to her cell. She kept the handkerchief.

"What do you suppose it opens, Miss Whitsett?" Cass asked, inspecting the key.

"I don't know. She's got her whole life ahead of her apparently. Perhaps you could marry her and then you could find out together on your honeymoon." Whitsett stormed out of the room leaving Cass drowning in his confusion.

Detective Frank Geyer

"You wanted to see me, sir?" Cass asked, entering the conference room. He felt like he was being escorted to the firing squad without a blindfold.

President Fouse and the district attorney were sitting at a conference table drinking whiskey in a very serious and manly way. They looked at Cass as though they wanted to turn him inside out. Standing by the window was a large man chewing a cigar. Smoke lingered around him like mist.

"Yes, Mr. Cass. I know you have been working very hard on this Pitezel case, but the district attorney and I have been going over the paperwork and reports you keep turning in and we have a question for you. Why?"

Cass tried to say something but could only manage a squeak.

"The district attorney says that you're still interviewing people in the Pitezel case. I want to know why. We already have the criminal. He has confessed and is in jail serving his sentence. Case closed."

Cass squeaked again.

"Please say something, Mr. Cass."

"May I be excused for just one moment?" Cass asked.

"Excused?"

"Yes, I feel I'm going to be sick."

"Hurry back," Mr. Fouse said.

Cass ran out of the room and down the stairs to the side entrance of the building. He found Miss Whitsett standing next to a small boy who was selling newspapers. She was asking the boy a series of probing and awkward questions about his profession.

"Mr. Cass, back from your honeymoon with Georgiana Yoke?" she asked.

He was panting and sweating. He couldn't catch his breath. "President Fouse...district attorney...big problem."

"Calm down, what's the problem?"

"Case closed…why are we still looking?" Cass felt his chest was about to explode.

"Because Holmes is lying."

"Right...Holmes is lying." Cass ran back up the stairs into the conference room.

"Are you alright, Mr. Cass?" Fouse asked.

"Yes, thank you. We are continuing to investigate because Holmes is lying. It couldn't have happened the way he said it happened." Cass was still struggling to get his wind.

"I see." Fouse gestured towards the man by the window. "This is Detective Geyer. We thought it would be best if a real inspector were here to tell you."

Real inspector? I'm a real inspector, Cass thought.

"Mr. Cass," Geyer said with his thick, gravely, deep voice. Geyer was a big, serious-looking man with a thick walrus mustache. He was 41 years old but appeared 65. "Here's the way investigations go. We have a crime, we find the criminal, we put 'em in jail. We don't go to the jail, find the criminal and then look for the crime."

"Yes. That makes sense."

"This isn't a mystery, it's clear cut. We have an insurance fraud, we found the fraudster, he's in jail. Crime, criminal, jail."

"Yes," Cass said, trying not to breathe hard.

"Now we have you. You go to the jail, talk with the prisoner, look for, whatever it is you're lookin' for. Jail, criminal, crime. You're doing it backward. It can't be done that way. Understand?"

"Yes."

"What is it exactly you're looking for?" the district attorney asked. "Why would Holmes confess to a crime that's worse than the one we charged him for in the first place?"

"May I be excused again?"

Cass didn't wait for an answer and ran down the stairs to Miss Whitsett.

"What did they say?" she asked. Cass was breathing hard again and was beginning to feel dizzy. He could only puff out a word at a time.

"Jail, criminal, crime."

"Are you having a stroke?"

"No."

"Why are you talking like that? What's wrong with you?" she asked.

Detective Geyer appeared behind them. "Who is this? What are you doin'?"

"This...Miss Whitsett," Cass said, rattled and still short of breath. He fidgeted as though he had been caught doing something inappropriate.

"I'm the stenographer," Miss Whitsett said. "I've been working on this case with Inspector Cass." She giggled to herself. "Case with Cass."

Geyer was slightly unnerved at a woman young enough to be his daughter working at Fidelity Mutual. She was just standing in the street where any harm could come to her.

"Working on what? The case is closed."

"The case isn't closed," she said, snorting derisively.

"How do ya figure, woman?"

"Where are the children?"

Geyer's eyes wandered off to the side. She was right, where were the children? This little woman had asked a question that should have been obvious to everyone in the conference room.

"Do you have gloves?" Geyer asked Whitsett.

"For what?"

"So you can be presentable in public. You have a stenographer kit, you're a stenographer; you can write everything people say in that chicken scratch shorthand?"

"Yes, detective."

"Good, so I don't need to. Let's go. Get out of the street before you get run over."

Geyer lifted his hand and let Miss Whitsett walk in front of him. Geyer grabbed the newspaper boy from the street and gave him a message to deliver to the district attorney and Fouse upstairs. He wanted them to wait while he interviewed Mr. Holmes. It cost him a penny.

He hailed a carriage. A four-wheeled calash drawn by a pair of horses pulled up and Geyer helped Miss Whitsett inside.

"You'll need to wear gloves while we're out interviewing people. We got to look respectable. And don't talk unless I ask you a question. I don't want no woman yapping her mouth while I'm trying to work."

"I don't have gloves."

"We'll stop and buy you some. We can't be seen in an official setting with a lady without any gloves. Then we'll get to Holmes."

"I can't afford gloves."

"Then I'll buy you some."

Cass's head was beginning to clear. Miss Whitsett helped him into the coach.

"Feeling better, Inspector Cass?" she asked.

"Yes, it's going away."

Geyer had put Whitsett in a bad mood. She didn't want to wear any goddamn gloves. She hated wearing those white gloves. And now she hated Geyer.

"What a charming new friend you found, Cass," she said, under her breath. "Who is this mule?"

"A real investigator, apparently. Will you scoot over a bit?"

"No," she said.

Cass leaned his body against the side of the coach and thrust the tiny Whitsett into the side of the carriage. The horses pulled away. Cass saw that Geyer was cringing as he adjusted himself to the small seat across from him.

"I notice your back is hurting," Cass said.

"Old back issues. Don't affect my work," Geyer said.

"I have a special tonic that will help the pain."

Geyer laughed with a cough. "Oh please, you have a medicine con too?"

"No, it's not a con. We spent months on the formula and—"

"Save your con for the feeble-minded men and hysterical women."

Whitsett didn't like how the detective was treating Cass. She took the bottle of tonic that Cass had given her out of her bag and took a long slow drink in front of the detective, causing him to smirk hatefully.

Another Interview

The cells were nice and cool; a relief from the hot, uncomfortable summer weather. They approached Holmes's cell and sat in chairs that had been left out for them. Screams and cries echoed through the cavernous jail halls. The reverberations and echoes blended together until the screams were indistinguishable, like the flowing sound of the ocean.

Inside the damp cell, Holmes had pushed the two cots together to make himself a larger bed. When he saw his visitors, he pulled one of the cots closer to the iron bars.

"Good morning, everyone," Holmes said as though he were holding court. "Please sit." His bright eyes were smiling; he loved company.

Geyer kicked his chair away with his boot and continued to stand with an intense frown. The old detective seemed to be twice the size of the petite Holmes. Whitsett assumed Geyer wanted to stand in hopes of intimidating him.

"Good morning, Mr. Holmes. This is Detective Geyer. He's going to join our interview today."

"That will be fine." Holmes stuck his small hand through the bars, but Geyer wouldn't shake it.

"We are very anxious to find the Pitezel children and restore them to their mother. We have decided to abandon the case against Mrs. Pitezel. She's suffered quite enough. An immediate recovery of the children would remove a growing suspicion that they had been foully dealt with," Cass said.

"Yes, the papers can be such sensationalists. Lies; just printed lies, aren't they?" he said.

"The best way to prove them to be lies is to produce the children at once. Where are they? Where can we find them?" Cass said as firmly as someone like him could manage. Holmes didn't even blink.

"You were arrested in November," Cass continued, "and you said the children were with their father in South America. It is now May, and we've heard nothing of them. We know your November statement to be untrue. Their father died on the second day of September. You then said that you gave the children to Miss Williams in Detroit, and you have furthermore given several variations from this last statement. I am almost persuaded that your word cannot be depended upon, yet I am not averse to giving you an opportunity to assist me. Where are the children?"

Holmes sat still and remained in attentive silence.

"I'm glad of the opportunity to assist in the restoration of the children to their mother. The last time I saw Howard," Holmes said, "was in Detroit, Michigan. There I gave him to Miss Williams, who took him to Buffalo, New York, from which point she proceeded to Niagara Falls.

"I took Alice and Nellie to Toronto, Canada, where they remained for several days. In Toronto, I purchased railroad tickets for them for Niagara Falls, put them on the train, and rode out of Toronto with them a few miles so that they would be assured that they were on the right train. Before their departure, I prepared a telegram which they were to send me from the falls if they failed to meet Miss Williams and Howard, and I also carefully pinned in Alice's dress $400 in large bills so Miss Williams would be in the funds to defray their expenses.

"They joined Miss Williams and Howard at Niagara Falls, from which point they went to New York City. At the latter place, Miss Williams dressed Nellie as a boy and took a steamer to Liverpool, whence they went to London. If you search among the steamship offices in New York, you must search for a woman and a girl and two boys.

"Mrs. Williams opened a massage establishment at No. 80 Vender or Vadar street, London. We had agreed upon a cipher, which they were to use in communicating with each other in the personal column of the *New York Herald*, and that if an advertisement were prepared in accordance with this cipher, very doubtless she would be heard from in a very short time."

"What about the trunk? Mrs. Pitezel claims that you took a trunk when you left her in St. Louis."

"The trunk held the effects of the children, I had to take it," Holmes said.

"Is that in No. 80 Vender street as well?"

"Oh no, it was not fit for such a journey. I believe I left it in a hotel on West Madison Street, about 50 feet from the corner of Ashland Avenue in Chicago."

"Chicago? Do you remember the date?" Cass asked.

"Yes, it was Septem—"

"Did you kill Pitezel and the children?" Geyer interjected. The large man's voice boomed off the walls. He spoke with a firmness and resolution that caught Holmes off guard.

"No. Why would I kill innocent children?" Holmes asked. He went through his beloved and exaggerated indignation pantomime.

"Give me the name of one respectable person in Detroit, Buffalo, Toronto, Niagara Falls or New York who'll say that they saw Miss Williams and the three children together!" Geyer yelled, shoving his thick hand against the bars, causing them to ring.

This question staggered Holmes for a moment, but he quickly recovered himself and said in an injured tone, "I don't know everyone in the world's name. You act as though you don't believe me. I'm a gentleman, sir. I'm offended that you don't believe me."

"You're a damned liar. This entire story is bullshit," Geyer said. "Is there anyone in the entire fucking Midwest who can speak to this story?"

"Well, I—"

"Is there anyone who can attest to anything you've ever stated? I ought to come in there and beat the hell out of you, you little shit." Geyer was screaming and spitting. Holmes never changed the expression on his face. He acted as calm and indifferent as though they were speaking about the weather or the ocean.

"Mr. Plummer of Chicago," Holmes said, "he's an attorney and has represented me in some business ventures in the past. He took dinner with me and the children at the hotel. The children were stopping on West Madison Street. Does that satisfy you, detective?"

"No. I believe everything you utter to be nothin' but a goddamn lie. Even your greeting of good morning. It's not a good morning, sir. It's not a good morning because I'm in a prison listening to a degenerate runt prattle on about cities and ridiculous ciphers. And if these bars weren't here, I'd be all over you."

Holmes stood up from his cot indignantly.

"I will be more than happy to furnish a cipher, with which an advertisement in *The Herald* should be made up, and by means of which the children would be recovered."

"When you're done, send it to the district attorney," Geyer said as he started down the cell block. Cass and Whitsett quickly followed. As they walked down the corridor, the ocean of screams faded away.

They emerged onto the street and were immediately struck by the heat.

"Excuse me, detective, but I was conducting that interview," Cass said.

"No, you were lettin' a bored criminal waste all our time."

"He didn't even get flustered when you pushed him," Whitsett said.

"That's right. Didn't really bother him, did it?" Geyer was impressed she had picked up on his gambit to catch Holmes by surprise.

"What are you two talking about?" Cass asked.

"Most people become outraged when accused of a crime they didn't commit and get rattled by threats. He was going toe to toe with me and was as calm as a Sunday afternoon," Geyer said. "Who the hell is this Mr. Holmes?"

Cipher

Inspector Cass was back in the conference room with District Attorney Graham, Fidelity's President Foust and Detective Geyer. Cass had spent the last few hours discussing the case and filling in gaps of information for the detective and district attorney. He was sweating as he was watched intently by these fat men who drank and smoked cigars. The thick smoke hung in the air, stinging the back of Cass's throat. Geyer was at the window trying to stretch out his back with the cigar gripped between his teeth.

"He has very strong penmanship," Cass said. "This means he has a character that—"

"Let's hear the cipher," Graham said.

Cass began to read.

District Attorney Graham

Dear Sir:

The adv. should appear in the New York Sunday Herald and if some comment upon the case can also be put in body of paper stating absence of children and if that adv. concerning this appears in this paper, etc. it would be an advantage. Any word you may see fit to use in adv. will do and if a long one, only one sentence need be in cipher as she will know by this that it must come from me as no one else, unless I told them, could have same.

Perhaps the first sentence should be –Important to hear before 10th. Cable. Also write to Mr. Massie. AplbenRun-nb-CBRc-etc.

The New York Herald is (or was a year ago) to be found at only a few places regularly in London.

Very Respectfully,

H.H. Holmes."

"Is he confusing to anyone else?" Fouse asked.

"He's doin' it on purpose," Geyer said. "He's filling you with nonsense to distract you from his lies."

"He attached the cipher code. It appears to be nonsense. The *New York Herald* published it in the personal column of the Sunday edition."

"This message would supposedly convey to Miss Williams to return the children?" District Attorney Graham asked.

"The following is the cipher and its decoded message." Cass began to read.

"MINNIE WILLIAMS, ADELE COVELLE, GERALDINE WANDA-AplebenRun nb CBRc EBLbrB 10th PREeB ABnucn PCAeUcBuRubuPB. Also write pk PRaaAB CBepBA. Address, GEORGE S. GRAHAM, City Hall, Philadelphia, Penn., U.S.A."

IMPORTANT TO HEAR BEFORE 10th
CABLE RETURN CHILDREN AT ONCE. ALSO AplbenRun nb CBRc EBLbrB 10th PREeb ABnucu PCAeUeBu Ru buPB. Also Write MR. Massie. Holmes
Write pk PRaaAB. Cbepba.

"And what of this Miss Williams in London?" Graham asked.

"There is no Veder or Vadar street in London," Geyer said.

"Is there a Miss Williams?"

"Yes," Cass said. "I contacted the Fort Worth office and asked for any information on Minnie Williams. She was raised by her uncle in Dallas, Texas. She has a younger sister named Nannie Williams who was raised by another uncle. She studied at the Boston Conservatory of music and elocution. The uncle died and bequeathed her property in Fort Worth. The land was valued at around $40,000."

"Do we know where she is?" the district attorney asked.

"We don't know. We've sent our requests to different offices to find her. It doesn't make sense why a woman with so much money would take the children to London, or anywhere for that matter," Geyer said. "His cipher is nonsense. Everything he says is nonsense."

"What do we know?"

"We know that Mr. Pitezel is dead, and the children were last seen in the company and under the protection of Holmes," Geyer said. "I'm concerned no one's heard from those children."

"They are with Minnie Williams in London," Cass said.

"That confession you obtained is garbage."

Cass was offended. *Miss Whitsett was correct*, he thought, *he's a mule*. "Why would he confess to a greater crime than he was being accused of? Crime, criminal, jail?" Cass asked.

"By reading the newspapers, he knew you were snoopin' around and askin' questions. He used that garbage confession to get ahead of you," Geyer said.

"You don't think he's brought injury to them?" the district attorney asked.

"No. I don't. It doesn't bring him anything. Money, hate and love. Killing the children won't satisfy any of these. Who would harm children for no reason?"

"Excuse me, but I don't understand the great rush?" Mr. Foust asked. "He's caught. He's in prison, we won. Case closed."

"We've won nothing. He's in jail for insurance fraud, not kidnapping. We have to find more evidence, and the children," the district attorney added. "The longer we wait, the less likely we will be able to find any evidence. Then Holmes is released and doesn't have to pay for his crimes against the Pitezel family."

"May I suggest the Pinkerton's, sir," Foust said.

"No Pinkertons," the district attorney said. "They're expensive and I don't want this city to fund the personal army of bankers and railroad owners. I want a detective, not some union-busting bully. I want someone who represents the city and can be held accountable. The Pinkertons aren't detectives, they're a bunch of capitalists; they'll just keep looking and looking. They never sleep so they can bill you around the clock."

"And, due to the Pinkerton act that passed last year, no one in government can hire the Pinkerton's for any purpose," Geyer said.

"Precisely, detective. I would like Detective Geyer to lead this investigation. I want those children found. You have full authority in this matter, detective. You may spare no expense. Poor, blessed little things. We must make one final effort, for the mother's sake."

"Sir, I appreciate what you're sayin'. But I think your expectations are too high. It'll cost a fortune and most likely end in failure," Geyer said. "I know there's a lot of pressure to find these missing children from the press. But, as much as I hate to say it, to find three children that went missing almost a year ago is an impossible task. They could be anywhere. Even in England as Holmes claims. Holmes is too astute and wily a criminal to have left a track behind him. You should unbind yourself from the expectation of ever finding them. And remember, we already have him locked up."

"I understand, detective. But we have moved beyond concern at this point. Twice a day the papers are filled with this story. Now the public demands to know where the children are. We have a year to find these children or Holmes goes free. If we don't find the children, we can't charge him. I will not be the district attorney that let Holmes just walk away with a slap on the wrist."

"Two years in prison ain't a slap on the wrist, sir," Geyer said. "You don't come out of prison the same you went in. I can ask the men at the prison to make his stay extra uncomfortable. They can make it so he pays for any crimes he might have done."

"An investigation, detective. That is final."

"Yes, sir."

"And with your permission, Mr. Graham, and yours, detective, I would like to offer my investigator Cass to assist you in the search for the Pitezel children. He's been working very hard on this case for months and could be very helpful."

"I have no objection," the district attorney said.

Geyer thought for a moment. He was loath to take some pencil-neck insurance agent with him. "I don't know if that's such a great idea," he said.

"I think it will be of great help to you to have some support on this investigation," Fouse said. "He has intimate knowledge of all the details and will be happy to help you in any capacity." Fouse was also excited about the free publicity his firm would receive from its continued involvement in a highly-publicized investigation.

"I don't know if having someone with no experience or skill set is appropriate."

"I defer to your judgment," the district attorney said.

"This is utterly base!" Cass exploded. "I have been working on this case for almost a year. I know all the facts and have amazing record-keeping skills. I have worked as the lead investigator on three medium-term assignments with three people as support staff. I am also quite known for being able to differentiate a person from their footsteps alone."

"You can't find any use for him?" the district attorney pleaded.

Geyer reluctantly agreed with a nod of his head.

The Metal Box

Cass followed Geyer out of the conference room to the crowded lobby where they collected their coats and hats from a series of hooks by the wall that resembled gallows for clothing.

"I'm very excited to get to work with you, detective," Cass said. "This assignment has gone from an insurance fraud to a missing person's case."

"Just stay out of my way or I'll wring you out like a wet bar towel, you understand me?" Geyer asked. Geyer stomped out into the street without another word. Miss Whitsett noticed them and called out as she ran towards them.

"Inspector!" She trotted up to them like a curious child. "Inspector! What happened? What did they say? Did we get bonuses?"

"Well, there's a slight problem," Cass whispered to her. "I've been assigned to work under the detective."

"So?"

"What if he doesn't let you work with us? What if he tells the president that you should go back to Mrs. Sappington?" Cass asked in a panic.

"Calm down," Whitsett said.

"It seems Mr. Cass is to assist me in finding the children," Geyer announced to Whitsett. "Which, I assume, means that you think you'll be tagging along as well?"

"You bet your damn life I'm coming along."

"Language, Miss Whitsett," the detective said, gasping as though correcting his daughter. He took her hand and slapped it. She struggled to keep from laughing in his face. Then he saw the scars on her wrist. The detective instantly knew what they were; they were scars from wrist manacles. Geyer had never seen them on a young woman, only prisoners.

Whitsett pulled her shirt cuff over her hand, hoping he would forget what he saw.

"I can't be lookin' after a woman while I work," Geyer told her.

"If you don't let me come, I'll lay you out in front of all these people." She held her fists tight and leaned into the large man. The detective looked down at the tiny woman who seemed like she was ready to fight him at the drop of a hat. He couldn't hold back his smile; she was like a fluffy, little bunny growling at him.

"Alright," Geyer said with a slow nod of his head. "Alright."

"Where do you want to start?" Cass asked.

"Don't you have a proper straw hat, man? You look like a street sweeper," Geyer said.

"This is the same hat the Handsome Bandit wears."

"Jesus Christ," he said with a long sigh. "Show me his personal effects."

"They're being held at the county jail," Cass said.

The detective nodded, putting his hat on.

Cass saw Whitsett had a big smile. "Why are you so happy?" he asked.

"Isn't this exciting?"

"Exciting? To be some mule-faced detective's valet? Does that sound exciting?"

"Yes!" she yelped.

"Maybe to you, but not to me."

"Don't think of it as being a valet. Think of it as being a posse on a round ups." She made fake guns with her fingers.

"It's called a roundup."

"That's the spirit."

A posse, thought Cass, is not so humiliating after all.

The detective held the coach door open for Whitsett but she hesitated. She didn't know what Geyer had made of her wrists.

"Where are your white gloves?" Geyer asked her.

They arrived in the storeroom of the county jail. Miss Whitsett opened the window while the gentlemen removed their coats. The dust from the window left black streaks on the stupid white gloves she was forced to wear.

"Damn it," she said to herself.

Every surface was covered in dust and webs. Both sides of the long room were lined with a row of open shelves that held personal items taken from prisoners. The shelves were numbered individually, and each item had a small paper tag tied to it with the prisoner's name and number written in black ink.

Geyer, Whitsett and Cass began searching through the tags one by one.

"Why is the district attorney so interested in these children all of a sudden?"

"It isn't all of a sudden, Miss Whitsett, these are children in distress, who have met with a cruel hand of fate," Cass said.

"There are hundreds of children rotting away in institutions, lining the streets across the city. Why doesn't he spare no expense on those poor bastard's cruel hand?"

"Language, Miss Whitsett," Geyer said. "He cares because people see it in the headlines and want to know why. No one cares about the children in the streets and institutions because they don't see them, but they see headlines."

"Amen," she said.

"In my day, the newspapers couldn't write just anything. They had to watch what they printed. The world is falling apart."

"Detective! It's impolite to talk politics in front of a lady," Cass said.

"You took me to a prison," Whitsett said to Cass.

"That was a special circumstance."

"Twice," Whitsett said. "And the morgue. Found it!" Whitsett presented a tag with the crooked letters of 'Holmes' printed on it. Cass dragged out a mid-size trunk and a suitcase onto the open floor by the light from the window.

Geyer unlocked the trunk and suitcase with the keys he picked up at the police desk. The suitcase was filled with shirts, hairbrushes and a syringe kit. The trunk held more clothes, pipes, a hat box and a leather pouch of surgeon knives.

The sun from the window reflected a shiny tin box.

"What's this?" Geyer asked.

"I don't know. I was never given permission to look through his effects," Cass said.

"It's locked," Geyer said. He shook it and tried to pry it open.

"Wait! Didn't Georgina Yoke give you a key?" Whitsett asked. "A key that she didn't know what it opened?"

Cass produced the key from his pocket and gave it to Geyer.

The box unlocked with a dull snap.

Geyer opened the box and found it was filled with yellowed papers. He thumbed through them, stepping closer to the window. There were titles, deeds and private memoranda. There were pages and pages of banking and creditor information.

Among the papers were letters from the missing children, Alice and Nellie Pitezel, written to their mother and grandparents from Cincinnati, Indianapolis and Detroit. They had evidently been given to Holmes to mail. A number of letters written by Mrs. Pitezel were also found in the box.

"Take a look at these. Letters, written by the children. Holmes never mailed them," Cass said.

"Open one. Read it," Geyer said.

Cass opened the first one. It was dated September 20th. The writing was large and crooked. It was obviously the hand of a child.

Philadelphia, PA.,
Cor. Filbert & 11 sts., Sept 20, 1894
Dear Momma and the Rest:

Just arrived in Philadelphia this morning and I wrote you yesterday of this. Mr. Howe and I have each a room at the above address. I am going to the Morgue after awhile. Yesterday I had to sit with someone. It was Mr. Holmes. I don't like him to call me babe and child and dear and all such trash. How I wish I could see you all and hug the baby. I hope you are better. Mr. H. says that I will have a ride on the ocean. I have seen more scenery than I have seen since I was born. Mr. H says that I may be off tomorrow. If you are worse wire me good-bye kisses to all and two big ones for you and babe. Love to all.

E. Alice Pitezel.

"This letter was written the day before she first met the insurance agents at Fidelity Mutual," Cass said, looking up from the letter. "She must have given the letters to Holmes, hoping he would post them. And he just kept them. He kept all of them."

"Why wouldn't he mail them?" Whitsett asked. "Do they say something wicked?"

"Read the next one," Geyer demanded.

Imperial Hotel,
Eleventh, above Market Street,
Hendricks & Scott, Propr's.,
Philadelphia, PA., Sept 21, 1894
Dear Mama:

I was over to the insurance office this afternoon and Mr. Howe thinks there will be no trouble about getting it. They asked me almost a thousand questions, of course not quite so many. Is his nose broken or has he a Roman nose. I said it was broken. Good bye love to all with kisses to all. Your loving daughter,

E. Alice Pitezel.

Geyer was struck after hearing Cass read the letter. Hearing the little girl's own words reminded him of his daughter and wife. His eyes fogged over and he stood up slowly, clutching his back. "We need to get these copied before we leave," Geyer said.

"Leave? Where're we going?" Cass asked.

"To find the missin' children."

"I thought you said it was impossible to find them. When did you change your mind?" Whitsett asked.

"I want to talk to Holmes again," Geyer said.

Third Confession

"We're goin' to look for the children, you bastard," Geyer said to Holmes. His voice echoed across the cell. "Our train leaves tomorrow. I wanna give you this opportunity to come clean and tell us their whereabouts. It'll look a lot better for you with the judge and the jury."

"You're right. You're right." Holmes put his head into his hands and began to sigh in exaggerated heaves. He rose up and spoke in a repentant tone. "I do have some information for you."

"Remember, Mrs. Pitezel has come forward and told us a lot of interesting things. Some of them don't necessarily reconcile with what you've been sayin'," Geyer said.

"What has Mrs. Pitezel told you?"

"Don't worry about what she said. You just worry about speakin' the truth. Where are the children?"

"Aren't you going to write this down, Mrs. Whitsett? Oh, no ring, I guess it's Miss today."

Whitsett had removed her white gloves to record the interview. She had forgotten to switch the ring to the other finger.

"No need for her to write until you start tellin' the truth," Geyer said.

"Why do you have the letters?" Whitsett asked.

Geyer was outraged that she would speak without any prompting from him. He pointed at her and, with his shaking hand, signaled for her to be silent.

"What letters?"

"The children's letters," Geyer said. He hated that Whitsett had given Holmes a clue to what they had discovered.

"I never had any letters."

"We found them in your trunk," Cass said.

"No, there were no letters in that trunk."

"We pulled them out of there this morning."

"I don't know anything about any letters in my trunk. I did have Edward Hatch carry my trunk. He must have inserted them to cover his tracks. I gave the children to a man named Edward Hatch, a bricklayer and odd-chore man around the block. Ask Dr. Robinson, he knows him too."

"And what about Miss Williams?" Geyer asked.

"She doesn't have the children and I'm afraid she is not a real person," Holmes said.

Geyer turned to Cass for confirmation who shook his head.

"Why did she sign over her Fort Worth properties to you? Seems odd for an imaginary person to have an inheritance," Geyer said.

"Impressive, Mr. Cass. You have done your work. She was a rather fragile person and had no idea what to do. The paperwork and the due diligence; she was going mad. She asked if I would help. I told her I couldn't do anything with it because it was hers. She signed them over to me so I could help her manage it. But she disappeared before I could speak with her and arrange the property the way she wanted."

"Our office in Chicago sent me a report. The Williams sisters, Minnie and Nannie, were last seen traveling with you."

"Yes, I was hoping to spare them. What happened to them is so sad. I didn't want to destroy their names. I met Minnie Williams in Boston in 1889. At that time, I was forced to do business under the name of Howard Gordon. Minnie and I got along rather well; I was teaching her about business as she recently had come into an inheritance.

"She was a nice girl, but I believe she was quite infatuated with me and hoped to engage in an affair. I, of course, was married. After some months, she moved to Chicago along with her sister. Nannie, her sister, also became very fond of me as well. She had an uncommon fascination with old flutes.

"One night I returned home to discover that Minnie, in a moment of jealous rage over me, had killed Nannie. I could see she was very upset. I hoped to shield her from any humiliation by taking Nettie's body out on the lake at Chicago and quietly sinking it."

"You sunk the body in the lake? What did you do with Minnie?" Cass asked.

"I tried to help her as much as I could, but I had my own wife to think about. Once her love grew so strong for me, the only thing I could do was commit her to an institution."

Geyer snorted a mocking laugh. "You're sayin' that these women were so infatuated with you that they killed each other over it?" Geyer turned to Whitsett and said, "Don't write any of that down."

Whitsett tore the piece of paper from her lap and crumpled it up.

The investigators left the prison and emerged into the city heat.

"Holmes seems to have taken the children all over the Midwest. He uses so many different aliases that a lesser researcher would have trouble keeping track of them," Cass said.

"We start from the identification of the body. We know that Mr. Holmes and Alice were here in Philadelphia looking at the body at the end of September. We know the other two children were in St. Louis with Mrs. Pitezel, their sick mother," Geyer said.

"Correct," Cass said.

"Then what?"

"Then Holmes sends Alice to Indianapolis. He goes to St. Louis and collects the other two children, along with $6,700 of the $7,000 insurance claim payout that the lawyer didn't take. In return, Holmes gives her a worthless banknote for $16,000."

"So, he has the money. Then he takes two of Mrs. Pitezel's children with him. Why?" Geyer asked.

"Holmes claims that detectives will be looking for them and if Mrs. Pitezel traveled with so many children it would cause suspicion."

"Where do they go next?"

"Holmes takes the children to Cincinnati. Alice meets them there."

"And from there they go on a very strange wandering, yes?"

"I was able to trace them from Cincinnati to Indianapolis, Chicago, Detroit, Toronto and Burlington from the girl's letters he kept," Cass said.

"I think the best thing to do is to go over the route taken by Holmes in company with the children. Starting from Cincinnati."

"We're going to Cincinnati?" Whitsett asked with excitement.

"And don't ever speak during an interview again. You two idiots gave away valuable information to the prisoner. Do you understand me?" Geyer told Whitsett, "Put your gloves back on."

"It's hot," Whitsett said.

"Put 'em on! Or I'll see you off without ceremony of any kind."

Cincinnati

Geyer, Cass and Whitsett stepped off the train in Cincinnati and took a coach to the Palace Hotel. The city was only willing to pay for modest accommodation. Absolutely no frills. The city had nothing to worry about. The floors creaked and the windows were stained. Cass inquired with the clerk about renting three rooms.

"Where are your bags, sir?" The clerk took one look at the odd trio and squinted his eyes. A strange group to be traveling together.

"Nice try. They're outside. I have a boy watching them. Just charge us the goin' rate." Geyer had experience traveling for work. He knew that the prices the hotel clerk charged were based on the bag. The nicer the bag, the higher the rate. That was why he was so interested in finding the missing children's trunk. The clerks may or may not remember the children, but they would definitely remember the trunk.

"I see." The clerk darted his eyes around the travelers, looking for anything that would give away what they could afford.

"And is this woman with you, gentleman?" the clerk asked.

"Yes," Cass said.

"Is this your wife, sir?"

"No," he replied.

"Your daughter?"

"No," Geyer said.

"Three rooms then? We don't allow unmarried men and women to lodge together. We aren't that kind of hotel."

"It's alright, I'm a detective with the Philadelphia police."

"Oh yes, of course you are, so am I," the clerk said.

Geyer was exhausted from the journey and wanted to get to bed. "We need three single rooms."

"I'm afraid we only have two doubles available," the clerk said.

"Right, very good con," Whitsett said with a smile.

"Now look here, you son of a bitch." Geyer grabbed the clerk and squeezed his collar. "You better look at that board and find another room or you and I are gonna have words," Geyer said, raising his voice.

"I'm sorry, sir. We only have the wedding suite."

"I'm a detective of the Philadelphia police department. I'll have you for this."

"You can't do this," Cass said to the clerk.

"Look guys, do you wanna spend another few hours walking to another hotel, or do you wanna just have dinner and rest?"

"You're lucky the city is paying our way," Geyer said to the clerk.

"Yes, sir," the clerk said.

"There are plenty of keys there. This is ridiculous," Cass said. "This hotel is nowhere near filled to capacity."

"It's a hustle," Whitsett whispered to Cass. "He wants to rent out the more expensive double rooms rather than the cheap single rooms."

"Nonsense, we'll just go to another hotel." Cass was indignant. "We'll not stand here and be swindled."

"I don't want to spend all goddamn night walking, so just shut up." Geyer entered his name into the register. "I want dinner ready for us soon. It better be hot. No soup or sausages." Geyer was certain that those particular meals were filled out respectively with water and dead rats.

Cass carried Miss Whitsett's bags up to her room under the watchful eye of the hotel manager. Whitsett thanked him and closed the door behind him.

Whitsett's hotel room was twice the size of her apartment at the boarding house. She poked her head out of the door and saw a maid walking down the hall.

"Pardon me. Do you know how much the lamps are?"

"Lamps?" the maid asked with her thick German accent.

"Yes, the gas lamps in the room. How much to use them?"

"It's complimentary."

"Complimentary?"

"Yes. It is included in your stay."

"So, I'll be able to see when the sun goes down?"

"Of course."

Whitsett entered her room and smiled. The bed had been freshly made, although the sheets were old and threadbare. She took a corner of the sheets and shook it. No bugs. She sprawled out on the bed, relishing the cool softness.

She removed her hat and itchy white gloves. She unfastened her collar and the buttons around her waist. Instead of unpacking, she stretched out on the bed like a cat and began to read.

Cass knocked on her door. She looked up. The sun was setting. How long had she been reading? To her, it only felt like a short time.

"Yes?" she called through the door.

"Miss Whitsett. We're meeting downstairs for a meal."

Whitsett stood up from the bed and jumped towards the door.

"Umm, Mr. Cass?" she whispered through the door. She had not thought about how she would eat until now. "I can't afford a meal," she said. She was lacerated with shame.

"Oh, no. You don't have to worry about that. The city is paying for our meals. It's called a per diem."

"Just a moment." She buttoned up, put on her hat and collar hastily, and opened the door. "We'll need to stop by a bookstore after our per diem," she said as she passed him. She walked out of her room as though she were floating on a cloud. She felt so fancy to be called to a meal. She held her hands out and took small steps in an exaggerated effort to walk with grace and fluidity.

"Miss Whitsett, your gloves. Geyer told me you had better wear your gloves."

She looked down at her hands and noticed she had forgotten them.

"Shit, just don't look." She put her hands behind her back. No one would notice.

Cass escorted her down the stairs to the dining room. Whitsett was so thrilled to be getting a good meal, she squeaked with excitement.

Geyer stood as she approached the table.

"Detective Geyer, thank you so much for the food." She stopped to correct herself. "I mean, for the per diem." She carefully enunciated every word; her interpretation of how an elegant lady would speak.

"That's quite alright," he said.

"The detective didn't buy it," Cass said. "The city is paying for all of us."

"Well, thank you anyway." She was so happy, her smile made her face hot. "And thank you, inspector."

"You're welcome," Cass said.

"Why aren't you wearing your gloves?" Geyer demanded.

"They're itchy," she said, hiding her hands under the table. Geyer wouldn't allow dinner to be served until she went back upstairs and put on her gloves.

The table. The first line of defense in a respectable home. The apex of everything that properly separates us from them. Whitsett had never had a meal at a dining table as a member of 'us' before. She ate at troughs in the orphanage when she was a child and at her workstation as an adult. There was a small table in her apartment, but not a dining table. She had eaten food, but never a meal.

Cass helped her into her seat and Geyer led the prayer. When he was finished, Geyer braced himself for the descent into his chair. His back had grown worse from the train ride.

Whitsett saw bread and butter and chicken and potatoes. A respectable meal at a respectable table. She reached for the bread.

"No! Napkin, young lady," Geyer said.

Cass pointed to the napkin in front of her and whispered, "This goes on your lap." He handed her the bread plate. She took a slice and offered the plate back to Cass.

"We pass to the right at the table, young lady," Geyer said.

"Sorry," Whitsett said to Cass as she passed the plate to Geyer.

"Shouldn't we carry guns?" Cass asked.

"Guns? What for?"

"He wants to be 'Inspector the Kid,'" Whitsett said.

"No guns. The fork goes in the left hand, young lady," Geyer said.

"I'm worried about meeting brigands," Cass said.

"Brigands?" Whitsett asked. She thought she might like to meet a brigand.

"There won't be any brigands."

"You carry a gun," Cass said.

"I would also like a gun," Miss Whitsett stated.

"No one's getting a gun. Don't butter the entire slice. Cut a small bite-sized piece and butter that. No, Mr. Cass, our feet will be our guns."

"What does that mean?" Cass asked.

Geyer yelled at Whitsett for not using the silverware properly. *Pass to the right. No elbows. Small bites. Don't ever reach!* There were so many rules for eating. Her 'meal' was more stressful than she had anticipated. She felt she stood out as someone who wasn't one of them.

"When was the first child separated from Mrs. Pitezel?" Geyer asked.

"Alice left her home with the lawyer Howe on September 19th."

"And when was she last seen?"

"She signed an affidavit at our office on September 23rd."

"Don't look at me while I eat," Whitsett said to Cass, smiling.

"And when did Holmes take the other two children from their mother?" Geyer demanded.

"September 28th," Cass said.

"So that's our start date. What day was Holmes arrested?"

"November 17th."

"From September 23rd to November 17th. That's our window. For this time, we got no account of the children. We gotta fill in the gaps. Miss Yoke, the second wife of Holmes, never saw any children while they were traveling together. This means that Holmes had the children stay in a separate place."

"How do we fill in the gaps?" Whitsett asked.

"Mr. Cass has worked out a rough outline of cities they were in. We go from city to city and check the hotel registers. From there, we follow the trail to our missin' children."

"Which hotels?" Cass asked.

"All of 'em."

"All the hotels in all those cities? Are you mad? There're hundreds of hotels in each city," Cass said.

"We gotta look at where they've been, don't we?"

Miss Whitsett smiled. She realized she was going to be staying in hotels for months, eating free meals and reading on clean beds. She put some butter on her potatoes and calmly ate. They could be searching for years. Years of butter and complementary reading. She hoped they never found the children.

"The fork goes in the left hand, Miss Whitsett!" Geyer yelled.

"Let me live!" she exclaimed.

"You're gonna be respectable. Or you can go back to Philadelphia."

"We all might as well go back. This will take us 100 years," Cass said. "There won't be any fresh clues."

"Through hard work and the grace of God, we may find them. And if you two don't change your attitude, I'll send you both back to your outhouse insurance company."

Whitsett couldn't take any more of Detective Geyer's respectability. "I have finished my per diem and would like to go buy a book now." She affected her speech, this time mocking their respectability. She stood up and Cass immediately scrambled to his feet to follow her.

Find the Lady

Cass escorted Whitsett to the corner newsstand. Evening editions were being called out as people walked home or waited for the trolley. Newsboys were yelling out headlines and wives were calling for their husbands. Hundreds of people with hats and walking sticks pushed through the streets and walkways, racing to get home before the sun set.

A small crowd gathered around a man seated on a small box. In front of him was a large crate covered with a green cloth. He was manipulating and rearranging three cards in a row.

"Find the lady. Find the lady. You find the lady, you win. You can't win if you don't play. You can't play if you don't step up. If you don't step up, you'll never find the lady," the dealer barked. He rearranged the cards so fast, the crowd began to mumble.

"How do you play?" a man with a crate of hardware goods asked.

The dealer flipped over the cards to reveal the jack of clubs, the jack of spades, and the queen of hearts. He pointed to the queen. "That's the lady. Isn't she pretty?" He flipped the cards face down and began to rearrange them. "If you can point to the lady, you win. You can't win if you don't play."

"What do you win?" the hardware man asked.

"Place a bet on the card you think is the lady. You win, you get paid. Step up and play once for free as a demonstration, sir."

The hardware man slowly stepped forward. The dealer showed him the queen and then turned the card over. He began to rearrange them on the cloth. "Find the lady, find the lady. You find the lady, you win."

The hardware man pointed.

The crowd let out a collective sigh.

"I'm sorry, sir. That's not the lady. There she is, look how pretty she is. One more time, sir. One more time. Find the lady. Find the lady.

You did it, sir. You found the lady! See, anyone can play. But you can't play if you don't step up. If you don't step up, you'll never find the lady. Who wants to play? You, sir? Find the lady. Find the lady. Place your bids to find the lady. Betting has no limit. You, sir, yes thank you. Find the lady, find the lady. A winner! You found the lady! Isn't she pretty? Here is your money, sir. Congratulations. Who's next to find the lady? Place your bid, sir. Find the lady. Find the lady. I'm sorry sir, that's not the lady."

"It's the one in the middle," Cass whispered to Whitsett.

"No, it isn't," she whispered back.

"I'm pretty sure."

"No, there is no lady," she said.

"What do you mean?"

"It's a con; a hustle. You'll never find the lady because he's using sleight of hand. You can't win because it ain't a game, it's a con."

"I just saw someone win," Cass said.

"Those are the dealer's shills, his partners. The dealer lets them win to draw in the crowd."

"He looked normal to me."

"That's the point. Some dealers use street children as the shill to show how easy it is to win. It's so easy a child can do it. Bastards," she said.

"How do you know so much about this?"

"How do you not know this hustle? You haven't seen this on the street? Don't you go out?"

"Out for what?" Cass asked.

"What do you do at night?"

"Night is when I do my filing at the office."

"What do you do after work?"

"Read."

"What do you read? Books about filing?"

"No, cowboys and treasure hunters."

"You read about adventures but don't want to go on your own," she said, musing the thought to herself.

"I go on adventures!" he protested.

"Name one."

"I go on plenty of adventures."

They approached a newsstand. The names of Holmes and the children filled every headline. Cass bought an edition and thought he might keep it as a memento. Whitsett was disappointed to learn the book stores were closed. The newsman however offered her a dime magazine. It was cheap but entertaining and would be enough for tonight. The bright color of the cover caught her attention and she immediately bought one. She was so excited to get to read in her room.

"We have to go back now so I can read it," she said.

"This paper has some shocking theories on Holmes," Cass said. "They say here that the reason he stole was because he was Catholic; that being Catholic inclines a person to kill or steal. What rubbish."

"What do you think makes people kill or steal, Mr. Cass?"

"Weakness of character, something only Jesus Christ and a firm hand can cure. Someone who grows up low or away from Christ has the propensity to steal and kill. The degenerates in the institutions and orphanages. They need the fear of God beaten into them or they will grow up to be degenerates. Their hideous acts come from devils and low character."

"So, the situation has nothing to do with it?" Whitsett asked.

"For example. You live in a boarding house for low women, away from the good people of society. That is why you were prone to lie about where you lived."

"How do you know where I live?!"

"One of the women you work with told me. You don't live with your family on the edge of town, you live in a boarding house for women without families. Oh! That's how you knew about the card hustles on the street," Cass said, suddenly realizing.

Whitsett ripped her arm away from Cass and ran ahead.

Geyer was drinking coffee and smoking when he saw Whitsett run past him and up to her room.

"Miss Whitsett?"

"Get the hell out of my way!" she said, running past him.

"Language, young lady!"

When Cass returned to the hotel, Geyer asked why Whitsett was so upset. Cass retold the conversation to Geyer. "I can't, for the life of me, understand why she gets so mad," Cass said.

"You're not very observant, inspector," Geyer said. He took a drink of coffee. "Perhaps you should pay more attention. Why are you here, Mr. Cass?"

"To find the children."

"You couldn't find your ass with both hands. You're a pansy little pencil pusher. What are you really hoping to accomplish?"

"Why are *you* here, detective? You said how futile this search is, then you hear the letter Alice wrote and you're suddenly willing to roam the wilderness for 40 years to find them."

The two men spent the next ten minutes staring at each other awkwardly. Detective Geyer took the paper Cass bought and retired upstairs.

Cass slowly walked to Miss Whitsett's room and knocked.

"Miss Whitsett, I'm sorry if anything I said offended you."

"Go away."

"Could you at least tell me what I did to upset you?"

"No! Go away. I hope you fall in a well. You call yourself a gentleman. You didn't use the right fork either. Your superior character didn't help you with the fork, did it?"

"I don't understand."

"You wouldn't! Raised with your silver forks!"

"Okay? Goodnight." Cass was confused and tipped his hat to the closed door before heading to his room.

Whitsett sat on the end of her bed trying to calm down. She hated what Cass would think of her if he knew she was raised in an orphanage. Her skin ached all over and she thought of his disgusted face. She was surprised that he could make her feel like that. *No one makes me feel like that*, she thought to herself.

She struck a match, lit the gas lamp, and began to read. She was too angry to concentrate. She sat up all night thinking and grinding her teeth. An entire night was wasted not reading.

The honeymoon suite was the same size as the regular rooms, except it had a metal tub and paper partitions. There were two beds, in adherence to all modesty and propriety. The last line of defense in the respectable home.

By the time Mr. Cass entered their room, detective Geyer was asleep. He had taken the pillows from Cass's bed and used them to support his lower back. Cass made himself a pillow from his coat and went to sleep.

The Search Begins

They had their breakfast in heavy silence. Whitsett stared hatefully at Cass, who was too nervous to eat. Cass's neck was sore, and he didn't understand why Miss Whitsett was so upset.

"How was your evening?" he asked.

"No. I hate you," she said.

When Geyer was finished eating, he left the annoying insurance people at the hotel and went to the Cincinnati Police Station to meet with the superintendent to inform him of the situation and get the credentials and papers of authority straightened out.

Geyer entered the police station to talk to his old acquaintance Detective Schnooks and Superintendent Dietch. Geyer told the story of Holmes and the children. He showed them the photographs of Holmes, Pitezel, Alice, Nellie and Howard. And that of Mrs. Pitezel's trunk. The two Cincinnati men were fascinated by the elaborate nature of the story.

"Do you have any leads?" the superintendent asked.

Geyer showed him the letters.

"That's your only lead?"

"Not a lot, is it?" Geyer agreed.

"I don't envy you. You must be receiving terrible pressure from your city. An impossible task. If you don't find them, you shall take the blame for it all. And if you do find them, the mayor will take the credit for you. It's a bad hand, inspector. But all my hopes and prayers go with you."

"Thank you." Geyer felt heavy with the weight of his task.

"And, detective, I was very sorry to hear about your wife and little girl. Terrible thing. I prayed for you."

"Thank you." Geyer tried to fight his eyes from turning glassy in front of the other men.

Geyer returned to the hotel to find one of the annoying insurance people, Cass, alone in the lobby.

"Where's Miss Whitsett?" he asked.

"In her room."

"Well, go collect her, we have work to do. When did Holmes leave for St. Louis?"

"September 28th, with two children, Nellie and Howard."

"I suggest we first search the hotels around the depots to see whether a man registered there on that day, who had three children with him, a boy and two girls. Go get Miss Whitsett."

"I suggest you do. She won't answer me at her door."

"What are you writing there?"

"This is a ledger I have come up with to help us. It lists all the days we need to account for from Sept 23rd to November 16th."

"I see, very thorough."

The trio of investigators called at several hotels during the day. Hotel after hotel of the same questions and speeches. They checked the registers and showed the clerks and porters the photographs. *Oh yes, that's him. I can't remember. He had bright blue eyes. Those might be the children.*

After every register check, Geyer interrogated the staff about the missing trunk. Whitsett recorded every interview and conversation. Cass meanwhile dutifully logged the information into his ledger.

Atlantic House. Entry for Alex. E. Cook and three children. Sept 28th through Sept 29th.

Intrepid House. Entry for A.E. Cook and three children. Sept 29th through Sept 30th.

With a small victory, they were invigorated and continued their search well into the night.

"We can account for the children up to September 30th. Just 52 more days to account for," Cass said.

Back at their own hotel, they had a small dinner prepared for them. It was late and the clerk had to make special preparations for them. Before the meal, Geyer was able to sneak a few large sips from his little silver flask with the dent on the side.

"I must say, all and all, it wasn't a bad first day." He turned to Whitsett. "How are we feeling, little one? Feet sore?"

"No, detective."

Geyer used the back of his hand to feel the forehead of Miss Whitsett to check for a fever.

"Good girl. Finish up now, you'll need your strength."

Whitsett wanted to punch the detective in the ear.

"I'm fine as well, detective, thank you. Other than the terrible pain in my neck," Cass chirped.

"Well, now you know how I feel," Geyer said, laughing to himself. "Settle down, Mr. Cass. It was merely a joke." The silver flask always helped his humor.

"Inspector, if you please. I prefer to be called inspector," Cass said.

"I'm hesitant to call you inspector because it might give people we're interviewing the impression that you're in the police department."

"You could still call me inspector in private settings, such as a dinner. Like the one we're having now."

"I'll try to remember."

"Why would you forget?"

"Okay, *inspector*, what is the most important thing we learned today about Mr. Holmes and his tendencies regarding lodging?"

Cass froze after being put on the spot. "I don't know."

"Miss Whitsett, what is the most important thing we learned today about Mr. Holmes and his tendencies regarding lodging?"

"He doesn't just stay in hotels," she said.

"Correct," Geyer said. "We'll expand our inquiries to include real estate agents for rental houses. Very good, Inspector Whitsett."

Whitsett was very pleased with her new title. *What a great trip this has turned out to be.* She tried not to smile like a fool but just couldn't help herself.

I'm an inspector, Cass thought. *I can differentiate a person from their footsteps alone.* Cass took a moment to calm down before he could finish his meal.

After visiting many real estate agents, the trio came to the office of J.C. Thomas, No 15 East 3rd Street. Mr. Thomas immediately recognized Holmes and suggested they call on Miss Hill, who lived at No 303 Poplar Street next door.

"Cass, go find us a coach to take us to Poplar Street."

"Very well. Miss Whitsett and I will leave right now," Cass said.

"I'm not going with you, *Mr.* Cass," she said.

"Oh." Cass felt as though he shrank three feet. He excused himself to hail a carriage.

"You hurt his feelings," Geyer said.

"Good."

Geyer knocked at the door at No 303 Poplar Street and a pleasant middle-aged woman answered. She was in the middle of cleaning and held a broom.

"Hello, my name is Detective Geyer. This is Mr. Cass and Miss Whitsett. I have here a letter of authority from the Superintendent of the Cincinnati Police giving me the authority to question you in the matter of the Pitezel children." Geyer presented his credentials. "Could you please tell me about the man who rented this house on Friday, September 28th, 1894?"

"There's very little to tell," Miss Hill said. "The first I noticed of him was on Saturday morning, September 29th, when a furniture wagon was driven in front of the house and a man and a small boy arrived. The man took a large, iron cylinder stove, such as is used in barrooms or a large hall, out of the wagon and carried it into the house. It was odd that the stove was the only furniture taken in. I spoke with several neighbors about it and they were as confused as I was.

"The next morning, Sunday, September 30th, he rang my bell and told me he was not going to occupy the house and that I could have the stove. I suppose he saw me watching him and thought I should know. He seemed very put out, as though I had ruined something."

"Did he say why he needed that big of a stove?" Geyer asked.

"No, I thought it was very peculiar. The house already had a stove."

Geyer thanked the woman and they loaded back into the carriage.

"Not bad for our first day. We've been able to fill in two days on the ledger," Cass said.

"Where to next?" Whitsett asked.

"Indianapolis," Geyer answered.

"Another city? Fantastic! Why there?" Whitsett asked.

"Because that is where several of the children's letters were sent from," Cass said.

"I wasn't talking to you!" Whitsett said childishly.

No 303 Poplar St. Entry for A.C. Hayes & little boy (paid in advance. Stove?). Sept 29th through Sept 30th.

Indianapolis

After a full, grueling day of traveling on the inhumane express train, the searchers arrived in Indianapolis and registered at the Spencer Boarding House. Again, through some strange coincidence, the clerk said the hotel was full. They had the same sleeping arrangements as in Cincinnati. Whitsett got her own room and Cass and Geyer shared a room with only one bed; Cass slept on the floor.

While Cass and Whitsett made a list of hotels around and near the Union Depot, Geyer took off his boots and poked at an abscess that had developed on the side of his foot. The infection had been developing since Cincinnati and now the skin was red and purple. After a quick swig, Geyer poured some of the contents of his flask onto his pocketknife. He prodded the abscess with the tip to find the thinnest area and pushed in. With his thumbs, Geyer worked out as much of the pus as he could bear into a discarded coffee can he'd found in an alley. When he finished, he went to the police headquarters on Alabama Street, south of Washington Street.

Geyer explained the story of Holmes to the captain of the detective corps and the superintendent.

"You're never going to find 'em," the captain said.

"We'll find 'em," Geyer responded.

"You don't really believe that, do you?"

Geyer sat in silence.

"It isn't a slur on your abilities," the superintendent said. "Everyone knows you're a great detective. But searching the entire Midwest for three children? Like trying to find a milkman in a snowstorm."

A police officer burst into the office, skidding across the wooden floor.

"Sir! There's been a murder. A man's been shot and killed in the northern part of the city. The murderer escaped."

"Care to come along, detective? We could use an extra pair of feet," the captain said.

"I guess I'll have to," Geyer said.

"You can help us with our own exercise in futility."

The entire station grabbed their hats and rushed out the door.

At the murder scene, a large crowd had gathered and surrounded the street. A uniformed officer approached the captain.

"The man ain't dead, tough bastard. Pistol shot in the neck."

"Description of the suspect, lieutenant."

"Short. Dark hair. Missing one of his front teeth."

The captain gathered all the men around him. He divided them into teams and assigned them different parts of the neighborhood. Geyer followed the captain. He could feel the open abscess with each step.

The police searched for the better part of the afternoon and evening. They stopped everyone they saw and asked if they had seen a man with a missing tooth. Geyer hated these kinds of useless dragnets. All they accomplished was to make his knees sore. They checked alleys and side streets. They asked person after person on the street but as usual, no one had seen a damn thing.

"Have you seen a man with brown hair and a missing tooth?"

"That could be hundreds of people in this neighborhood."

"He would have been running, possibly in a panic." The streets were filled with hundreds of people moving about their lives. *They wouldn't notice a dragon made of fire and gold*, Geyer thought. "No one will ever find him."

"Sometimes we get lucky," the captain said.

"Twenty years ago, an attempted murderer couldn't get ten miles without being noticed. Now he could be standing next to us and we wouldn't see him," Geyer said.

"Twenty years ago, this country was all villages and small towns. Now everyone moves to the city."

"It's the damn factories," Geyer said. "Everyone moves into the cities for those damn factory jobs. Twenty years ago, I knew everyone's business and their dog's name. Now, I barely know who lives next door. We live in a world of strangers now."

"This will be another nameless man who disappears into the crowd."

"The city has grown so much; more shadows to hide in. This country's going to hell," Geyer said. "Just find some Catholic or immigrant to pin it on and be done with it. They're all criminals anyway."

"Sir! Sir, we found someone."

They entered the small shop of a family grocer. The walls were stuffed with food and cooking supplies. Spoiling greens and old tubers made the air thick and wet. A man in a white apron was sitting in a chair surrounded by burly cops.

"Report," the captain said.

"This one's got a reputation in the neighborhood. And he's a damn Italian." The cops were slapping him and twisting his ear. No bruises. Never leave any bruises when you question a suspect.

"Where is he?" the cop yelled.

"I don't know what you're talking about," the Italian said in his slight accent.

They kept screaming and slapping him. The Italian's wife and children were watching from a separation in the door frame. The mother quickly grabbed their children and pulled them away.

"Let me try," Geyer said, strutting up to the weeping man. His back was hurting so he was eager to wrap the investigation up. "If you just tell us where he is, we'll leave."

"I don't know!"

Geyer punched him in the stomach. The man gasped and began to cough. Each punch sent a pulse of pain down the old detective's back and into his abscess.

"Which way did he go?"

"I don't know."

Punch.

Cough.

They spent almost an hour working him over. Geyer grabbed a towel and buried his face in it. "He don't know nothing." His hand ached from his punches and his knuckles began to bruise over.

Geyer and the captain exited the shop.

"I don't know what this damn country is coming to," Geyer said with disgust. "The whole world's going to hell."

"Oh, detective, I almost forgot. I'm sorry about your loss."

"Thank you."

With the sun set, and lamps on the street being lit, the captain finally threw up his hands.

"Alright, that's enough for today. Appreciate your help, detective. Better come back tomorrow. Hopefully we won't make you join the search party," said the captain.

"That's the job," Geyer said, rubbing his knuckles.

"Let me walk you to your hotel. Give the boys time to get back to the station."

Arriving at the hotel, Geyer and the captain found Cass and Whitsett going through the paperwork. Geyer could feel his foot was wet from walking so much on his open abscess.

"Captain, this is my posse," Geyer said, "We got Mr. Cass and Miss Whitsett. They work for Fidelity Mutual."

"Keeping your powder dry, are ya?" the captain asked.

"What powder?" Cass said.

"It's an expression, you… What are you reading?" Geyer asked.

"This is the next letter written by the missing child," Whitsett said.

"I told you not to waste your time reading those anymore," Geyer said. We have all the information from them, there's no need. Use your time to go through real estate ledgers."

"Oh, could I hear it?" the captain asked. "The papers never mentioned letters."

"Child, will you read out loud for the captain?" Geyer asked Whitsett.

Stubbins' European Hotel, One square north of Union Depot on Illinois Street.

Indianapolis, Ind.,

Sep. 24, 1894

Dear Ones at Home,

I am glad to hear that you are all well and that you are up. I guess you will not have any trouble in getting the money. 4, 18, 8 is going to get two of you and fetch you here with me and then I won't be so lonesome at the above address. I am not going to Miss Williams until I see where you are going to live and then see you all again because 4, 18, 8 is afraid that I will get two lonesome then he will send me on and go to school. I wish I had a silk dress. I have seen more since I have been away then I ever saw before in my life. I have another picture for your album. I will have to close for this time now so good bye love and kisses and squesses to all.

Yours daughter, Etta Pitezel.

P.O. I go by Etta here 4, 18, 8 told me to O Howard O Dessa O mamma, O Baby. Nell you & Howard will come with 4, 18, 8 & Mamma and Dessa later on won't you or as Mamma says.

Etta Pitezel.

"Haunting. What is that 4, 18, 8 business?" the captain asked.

"It's a code for Mr. Holmes, I think," Whitsett answered.

"Why would the poor child write in code?"

"Maybe she thought Holmes would read them."

"I'm sure he read them," the captain said. "But why keep them?"

"We don't know," Geyer said. "From our searching, so far, we know Holmes took Alice from viewing the dead body to the Stubbins House. Then he went to steal the other children and checked them into the other hotel we found in Cincinnati. While they were staying there, he took the young boy to No. 305 Poplar Street, a house he rented in Cincinnati. And at that house, he bought a big stove."

"Why a stove?"

"We don't know. The house already had a working furnace."

The next day, the search of the hotels resumed. They went from hotel to hotel to hotel. Some were in the red-light district and Miss Whitsett had to remain in her room. She happily sat on her bed and read. Cass had been buying her a book every day, hoping she wouldn't be mad at him anymore.

Stubbins House. Entry for E.A. Cook and one child. Room 34. Sept 24th through Sept 28th.

Hotel English. Entry for Mr. Cook and three children. Room 79. Sept 30th through Oct 1st.

They spent the following days searching every hotel and lodging house in Indianapolis. They were exhausted. They all limped from blisters on their feet that were the size of half-dollar coins. Their clothes were yellow with sweat. The children couldn't be located, only a ghostly record of where they had slept.

"We still have no account for them after October 1st. Maybe they went to another city," Geyer said.

"No, we have letters addressed to home on October 6th, 7th and 8th," Cass said.

"Perhaps we missed a hotel," Geyer said.

"That is a list of all the registered hotels in the city from town hall records," Cass said.

"I don't know," Geyer said, rubbing his hands over his eyes. They were exhausted. Geyer had to sneak more sips from his silver flask. "Alright, let's go over the list of hotels in the area again."

Whitsett took out some scratch paper and began to make a list of the hotels they had visited in order. "What about hotels that have closed down?" Whitsett asked. "It's been over six months. Maybe there's a hotel that burned down."

"Excellent, little one!" Geyer said. He grabbed her and patted the top of her head.

The Circle

Geyer hired a coach to take them back downtown to the area known as The Circle. They asked the clerks if there were any hotels in the area that had closed down in the past year. They were immediately directed to an abandoned hotel called The Circle House on Meridian Street, just a couple of blocks away.

"The Circle House that's not located in the Circle. How did we miss it?" Whitsett mused.

"We're going around in circles," Cass said.

There was a large building that had been boarded up along Meridian Street. *This is an obvious insurance job*, Cass thought. The burn pattern on the side of the building was too uniform, too deliberate.

"Okay, Mr. Cass, you take Miss Whitsett and ask everyone you see on that side of the street if they know anything about who owned this hotel. I'll take this side of the street. Go door to door."

"Door to door?" Cass asked. "That'll take all night."

"It very well might, Mr. Cass. Now get to it, you little shit." Geyer dug his finger into the side of Mr. Cass's stomach.

Geyer walked on his heels to try and keep the pressure off his abscess. It had been a few days since he had drained it and it was digging into the side of his old, worn boots. The constant walking in the heat was causing it to throb.

For hours, they searched the streets and shops. They repeated the same questions so many times their ears rang. Eventually, they were able to learn the name of the proprietor, Mr. Herman Ackelow. No one in the area knew where to locate him. He had apparently moved to West Indianapolis.

One porter remembered the name of the old clerk of the hotel, Mr. Reisner, who they found hours later, working in a hotel south of the depot. He said the register and records were at the office of an attorney named Everett. Geyer bullied him until he agreed to meet them at the lawyer's office the next day.

After another stressful meal at the dining table, Whitsett spent the rest of the night reading on her bed. She had finished her book and wished she had picked something up while they were out. She went through her stenographer's case and found the letters the little girls wrote to their mother from Indianapolis. She reread them, even though Geyer had told her not to waste her time with them.

Indianapolis, Ind.,
Oct 1st, 1894.
Dear Mamma.

We was in Cincinnati Yesterday and we got here last night getting that telegram from Mr. Howe yesterday afternoon.

Mr. H. is going to-night for you and he will take this letter. We went us three over to the zoological Garden in Cincinnati yesterday afternoon and we saw all the different kinds of animals. We saw the ostrich it is about a head taller than I am so you know about how hight it is. And the giraffe you have to look up in the sky to see it. I like it lots better here than in Cincinnati. It is such a dirty town CIn.

good bye love to all & Kisses. Hope you are all well.
Your loving daughter,
Etta Pitezel.

Indianapolis, Ind.,
Oc. 1st, 1894
Dear Mamma, Baby, and D.

We are all well here. Mr. H. is going on a late train to-night. He is not here now I just saw him go by the Hotel.

I haveto wear this warm dress becaus my close an't ironet. We ate dinner over to the Stibbins Hotel where Alice staid and they knew her to. We are not staying there we are at the English H.

We have a room right in front of a monument and I think it was A. Lincolns. I don't think you would like it in Cincinnati either but Mr. H. sais he likes it there.

Good bye your dau.
Nellie Pitezel.

Whitsett wanted to go to the zoo. She had never seen a giraffe. She also wanted to see the monument of Lincoln. She imagined how nice it must have been for the little girls to be on a journey and see all the different wonders. *What a bunch of spoiled children*, she thought. *And now, we are going to spare no expense to search the world and make sure they are okay; these three children.*

I would have given anything to have been one of these children when I was their age, she thought. *This would have been my heaven; it* is *my heaven. What a great adventure.* She realized she was doing exactly what the girls did. She was living in her idea of heaven. A swell of happiness filled her before she was sickened by the sudden thought of Mrs. Jacobs and her cousin's son. How could she break off the engagement?

The clerk arrived at the attorney's office three hours late.

"You are late, sir!" Cass pointed out.

"Yes, I know, so sorry."

"Let's get to it," Geyer said.

The lawyer produced the register for The Circle House and the clerk began to thumb through the thin white paper of the October listings. He found an entry for three Canning children from Galva Illinois, Room 24.

"Canning, those are the children. Just like in Hotel English. When did they stay?"

"I'm not sure, we didn't keep dates here in this register."

"You didn't keep dates?" Cass said. He was appalled at their record keeping. "Check the cash flow statement, man."

The attorney brought out another register and the clerk thumbed through it.

"I say they arrived on October 1st and left on October 6th."

"Are you sure of these dates?" Geyer asked.

"Oh yes, I have a memory like an elephant."

"You were late today, sir," Cass said.

"That wasn't my fault."

"You keep the worst records I have ever seen," Cass snapped. "It is almost as if you didn't keep any records at all."

Miss Whitsett wrapped her arms around Cass's arm and tried to pull him away. "Calm down, Mr. Cass. Calm down."

"No! He needs to hear this," Cass exclaimed, pointing his finger. "Your records are almost criminal. And your penmanship is unreadable."

"He isn't worth it," Whitsett said. "He isn't worth it."

Cass stormed out of the office and slammed the door.

Circle House. Entry for Mr. Cook and three children. Oct 1st through Oct 6th.

Geyer and Whitsett finished the interview and went to look for Mr. Cass. When they found Cass, he stood up straight in front of them.

"I would like to apologize to you and detective Geyer. I'm sorry you had to see that. And I apologize for letting my anger get the best of me." He walked ahead, hoping to put everything behind him.

Geyer leaned over to Whitsett. "What the hell's he talkin' about?"

"When he was scolding the clerk for having bad paperwork."

"Who cares?"

"That's the worst thing that Mr. Cass can say to someone," she said.

Cass stopped as if he had been yanked by a rope. He bent to the ground and took out one of his ledgers from his briefcase. He flipped through the pages violently.

"Detective," Cass said.

"We know, Mr. Cass, his paperwork was horrible," Whitsett said.

"No. Not that. Holmes had his wife registered at the Circle Park Hotel under the name of Mrs. Georgia Howard. He stayed there while the children stayed here at the The Circle House. Circle Park Hotel is only down the street from here. It's probably less than 100 feet from The Circle House. *That* is how you keep paperwork," Cass emphasized.

"Holmes seems to be playing his own game of 'find the lady'," Whitsett added.

"Now we know that he likes to keep his interests close to each other," Geyer said.

"This isn't as dangerous as I thought it was gonna be," she said.

"No. The only danger is yourself. You're more likely to kill yourself than get killed," Geyer said. Whitsett was fascinated with Geyer's grim comments.

"I still think I should get a gun," Whitsett said. "Or a sword."

Saloon

They rode all day on the crowded train to West Indianapolis to speak to Mr. Herman Ackelow, owner of The Circle House. He was running a beer saloon operating right next door to a new factory; supply and demand.

Geyer stopped them at the door.

"We're going to a saloon!" Whitsett said with a squeal.

"Miss Whitsett can't go in," Geyer said.

"We can't leave her outside."

"We can take her to a store and maybe the shop owner will watch her while we go in." There were no stores on the street. Just the factory and the saloon.

"I'm going in with you. I have to record the interview. No one can read either of your handwriting."

"I have terrific penmanship!" Cass protested. "My handwriting shows me to be industrious and virtuous."

"This is a beerhouse, Miss Whitsett. You can't be in a place like this."

"I'm not going in to drink. I'm going in to find three missing children. Now open the door for me, Mr. Cass."

"Miss Whitsett. Listen, you can't go in here. Now, if you don't obey me, I shall be forced to lay hands on you," Cass said.

"I beg your pardon?"

"I'm afraid so."

"Very well," Whitsett said as she lifted her arm chest high for Cass to grab. Cass didn't think he would actually have to force her. He stared at her arm.

"Well? Go on," she said.

"Don't rush me!" Cass said.

Geyer, impressed with her grit, held open one of the batwing doors for her. "I guess we should mosey on in here."

Whitsett had always wanted to know what a saloon was like. She had heard married women complain for hours about their husbands wasting their lives and weeks' wages inside them. There were tables of men drinking and playing cards. A man was playing a lively song on an out-of-tune piano. Men were arguing and laughing and carrying on. It didn't look nearly as scandalous as the other girls had made it out to be. It was bright and colorful and actually looked fun, other than the dirty floors and the smell of rotting death.

Geyer strutted into the middle of the room, which caused his back to throb. He stood still and stared at each man, making them uncomfortable.

"What are you doing?" Whitsett whispered.

"Making sure the criminals can see me," he said, puffing out his chest. "I can tell if a person is guilty of something by their eyes. It's always in the eyes. There's always one of them in these places. You have to show them who's boss."

"Like how Mr. Cass can tell someone's personality by their penmanship?"

"No, that's stupid," Geyer said. "I use experience and my gut."

"You certainly have a lot of it," Whitsett said, laughing. "Your gut that is."

Geyer sneered at her before moving towards a man sitting at the bar.

"What are you doing?" Geyer demanded of the young man. "I'm a police detective. Why are you here?"

"Just having a drink, boss." The young man spoke with a thick accent. Geyer grabbed him by his collar.

"I knew it, a goddamn immigrant. Come on with you."

"What for?"

"You know what you did."

"I didn't do anything."

"A likely story."

"Let him go," Whitsett said. "We have enough to do without you hauling in men who you don't like the look of. Let's have a drink."

"No fighting in here," the bartender called out. "Take it outside."

"It's okay. Detective Geyer was showing us his gut."

"What seems to be the problem here?"

The detective let the young man go and followed Whitsett and Cass to the smooth mahogany bar. The bartender looked up and almost dropped a bottle of cheap whiskey at seeing Miss Whitsett stare back at him with her smiling face and stenographer's bag.

"I'm sorry, ma'am, but you can't be in here."

"Oh?"

"I'm afraid we don't allow ladies here. You'll have to leave."

"Don't be ridiculous. She's here." Whitsett pointed to a lady in the corner baring her shoulders.

"That's different. She's working," the bartender said.

"So am I."

The bartender turned his head in confusion.

"She's working for me, sir. I'm Detective Geyer. This is Mr. Cass and Miss Whitsett. I have here a letter from the superintendent of the Indianapolis police giving me the authority to question you in the matter of the Pitezel children. I'm sure you've read the papers. Is there a Mr. Herman Ackelow employed here?"

"Yes. Let me get 'im."

"Why is she allowed to work but I'm not?"

"That, Miss Whitsett, is a lady of sin," Geyer said.

"That's a prostitute? I've never seen a prostitute working inside before. She looks like a normal woman to me. Her dress isn't covered with mud on the bottom. That's nice, for her."

"Please try to keep from staring, Miss Whitsett," Cass said.

"Oh wow, look at her shoulders!"

The bartender returned from the back office with Mr. Ackelow. He was a cowboy from the top of his hat to the heel of his boot.

"Would y'all care to join me in my office?"

Whitsett took out her writing materials and sat in the chair next to Geyer. Cass stood in the back.

"You don't mind if Miss Whitsett records this interview?" Geyer asked.

"No, sir," Mr. Ackelow said.

"Do you recognize these children? They may have stayed at your hotel at the beginning of October last year." Geyer showed him the sketches.

"I have a distant recollection of three children staying by themselves at the hotel. I think those are them."

"Was this the man that brought them in and took them away?" Geyer asked, showing the picture of Holmes.

"Yes. He said he was their uncle, and their mother, who was a widow, was his sister, and that she would be with them in a few days."

"Did you notice anything that stood out to you? Anything that seemed odd?"

"The man said that the little boy was a very bad boy and that he was trying to place him in some institution or bind him out to some farmer. He wanted to get rid of the responsibility of looking after 'em."

"But he left with the little boy?" Geyer asked.

"Yes. Also, I would send my oldest son up to the children's room to call them for their meals. He told me he found the children crying, heartbroken and homesick to see their mother."

"Do you remember what days they stayed?"

"No, sir. I don't."

"Do you remember if they had a trunk?"

"I didn't deal with luggage."

"Thank you very much for your time."

Geyer stood up, shook his hand and left abruptly, eager to sneak a sip from his flask.

"You might be able to get some more information from the chambermaid, Caroline Klausemann. She was in charge of that room in The Circle House," he told Cass.

"Where might we find her?"

"She's working in Detroit now, I think."

Cass shook his hand and waited for Miss Whitsett. She stood and leaned over the desk to speak to Mr. Ackelow frankly.

"How much does a prostitute make here?" she whispered.

Cass quickly grabbed her and pulled her to the door. "Come along, Miss Whitsett."

"I'm just curious. Can I talk to them?" she asked. "Why are they lined up like that?"

Four women stood on a small platform beside the bar. They were winking and smiling at the men walking by.

"That's where you pick 'em out," Geyer said.

"What?" She was outraged. "They have to stand the line?"

"What does that mean? Stand the line? Why do you always say that?" Cass asked.

"You wouldn't understand because you were raised with a silk blindfold," she yelled.

Cass pulled Whitsett out onto the street. The batwing doors flapped violently behind them.

"Behave, Miss Whitsett. And why are you so bothered, detective?" Cass asked.

"We must now search the institutions and orphanages to discover if he had the children committed. Holmes may have put them in an institution as orphans to get rid of 'em," Geyer said. "Jesus Christ. This is why you don't look for a crime. You look for criminals. You have the crime and look for the criminal. You don't find the criminal and look for the crime. Crime, criminal, jail," Geyer said, taking a sip from his flask.

Whitsett turned red hot. The mention of institutions filled her with rage. "I would rather they be dead in the street than alive in an institution. That pecker!"

"Miss Whitsett!" Geyer said. He took her hand and lightly slapped it. "You mustn't use that kind of language, young lady."

"Stop hitting my hand!"

A drunk stammered past Geyer, stepping on his boot, causing pus to leak from his abscess. He could feel it ooze down his foot as his head spun from the pain. The drunk was running from his wife, trying to stumble into the saloon. His wife had tracked him down and was yelling and slapping him as he struggled to stand.

"You spent all the money in the damn saloon. What am I supposed to buy food with tomorrow?"

"My back hurts and I can't stand to come home to a shithole every night."

"What are your children going to eat, Friedrich?!"

"I break my back 15 hours a day at the mill. All I want is one night to spend where I don't want to kill myself."

Geyer stomped over to the drunk and grabbed him by his collar. The drunk rolled his head back to see what had ahold of him.

"Go home, son, take care of your family," Geyer told him, looking into his eyes. The drunk was no more than 25 years old, but he looked to be 50. Fifteen years working in the mill had aged him at twice the rate. Long days and hard work had destroyed his body, and he was still a boy. Geyer had seen it before, young men drinking to ease the aches and pains of the hard labor and sadness. *Eventually, the drink consumes them and destroys the family. They just give up.*

"I grew up in a small farming town. I knew all my neighbors and the names of their dogs. Things didn't use to be like this. The world's goin' to hell," Geyer said.

Geyer helped the drunk home and into his bed. He saw the dirty, hungry little children in the home. They must be around five or six years old, Geyer thought. They only have a couple more years before they'll be forced to get their own jobs in the mill. A life sentence of painful work and poverty. A life of new industry. Welcome to the 20th century.

They loaded onto the carriage and rode back to town. It was a long, quiet ride back to the hotel.

Detroit

When they arrived at the hotel, Cass went straight up to the room. He had been working on his ledger during the entire trip and was exhausted. He had to sleep on the floor again. Geyer and Whitsett remained in the lobby drinking coffee and thinking. Geyer mostly drank his coffee from his silver flask.

"Could I have some of that? It's whiskey, right?"

"Women shouldn't drink whiskey." Geyer was cranky from the battering the train ride gave him.

"You know, men aren't supposed to drink either. But damned if you all don't drink to beat the band."

"Is your hand alright, Miss Whitsett?" Geyer asked.

She looked down and noticed her cuffs had slid up and her scars were showing. "If you wore your gloves, no one would see your scars."

She smiled at his attempt to get under her skin. She couldn't decide if he was better or worse after he snuck his drinks from his silver flask. "Why don't you tell me about your daughter?" she asked, going back at him.

He flinched and cleared his throat. He took another sip from his silver flask. "Tomorrow we find the maid. Maybe she can give us a lead on the trunk. I wanna find the children's trunk. We can account for the children up to October 6th."

While Geyer was nodding off in the lobby, Whitsett quietly reached into her bag and pulled out the letters written by the Pitezel children. She hid them behind one of her books so Geyer wouldn't see them and yell at her for wasting her time.

Indianapolis, Ind,
October 6, 1894.
Dear Mamma, Grandma and Grandpa:-

We are all well here. There is so many buggies go by that you cant hear yourself think. I am in a hustle because Mr. H. has to go at 3 o'clock I don't know where. Mr. H. went to T. H. Indiana last night again. The patrols are lots different here than they are in St. Louis & Chicago. We haft get up early if we get breakfast. Their is more bicycles go by here in one day than goes by in a month in St. Louis. I saw two great big ostriges alive. Is the baby were and does he like coco I want you to all write. Why don't you write mama. I will close for this time goodby write.

Yours truly,
Nellie Pitezel
over
Alice eyes hurts so she won't write this time.

Indianapolis Ind.
Oct. 6th 1894
Dear Mamma.

We are all well except I have got a bad cold and I have read so much in Uncle Tom's book that I could not see to write yesterday when Nell and Howard did. Last Sunday we was at the Zoological Garden in Cincinnati, O. And I expect this Sunday will pass away slower than I dont know what and Howard is two dirty to be seen out on the street to-day. Why don't you write to me. I have not got a letter from you since I have been away? This letter is for you all because I cant write to so many of you I guess I have told all the news so good bye love to all and kisses

Your loving daughter
E. Alice Pitezel.

Whitsett read the children's letters over and over. There was something unsettling about them. She was following the children's path and began to think they weren't so lucky after all. They were cut off from their family and were forced to spend day in and day out in a hotel room. Something was very unsettling.

The three searchers checked into the Hotel Normandie.

Geyer spoke with Superintendent Starkweather and obtained his credentials.

"I was sorry to hear about your wife and daughter."

"Yes, thank you."

They spent the rest of the morning tracking down the chambermaid from The Circle House in Indianapolis. They went from hotel to hotel to hotel. They eventually found a woman who said Miss

Klausmann worked at the Hotel Swiss on Wells Street between Ohio and Indiana Avenue.

"Is there a Miss Klausmann employed here?" Geyer asked.

"Yes, detective, just a moment." The clerk set his pen down and went into the back. He returned with a middle-aged German woman with broad shoulders.

"Hello, my name is Detective Geyer."

"She doesn't speak English," the clerk said.

"Great," Whitsett said, rubbing her eyes in exasperation.

Detective Geyer began speaking to her in German. He explained why they were there and showed her the sketches of the children. When she saw the children's faces, her eyes bolted open.

"She says she recognizes them," Geyer translated

"How do you know German?" Whitsett asked.

"It doesn't matter."

"For someone who blames everything on immigrants, you have a strong command of the German language," Whitsett said with a wry smile.

"Mind your business," Geyer snapped. He continued to translate. "They were always kept in the room. She said the children were always drawing pictures of houses or engaged in writing or reading a book. She frequently went into their room and found them crying. She never saw any adults with them and assumed they were alone at the hotel, she says she believed they were orphans, crying over their lost parents. She couldn't speak to them because she doesn't know English. She says the children arrived with a trunk. One day Holmes took the boy and she never saw him again."

The chambermaid began to cry.

"She says if she had known English, she could have spoken to them and learned about their abduction. The children were cold because they didn't have proper clothing for the weather. They were cold and alone and kept in that small room."

The chambermaid could no longer speak.

"That's enough," Geyer said. "She says she doesn't know where they went. What a waste of time."

Miss Whitsett set her writing instruments on the floor. For the first time, she felt as though the children were children. She remembered what it was like to be cold and alone as a child. She no longer felt bitterness and jealousy about their 'great adventure.' They suffered, just as she suffered.

Geyer gathered the chambermaid and gently brought her to a chair. He offered her his handkerchief and placed his hand on her shoulder.

Whitsett suddenly hated the chambermaid. Why does everyone give every other woman a handkerchief but me? No one has ever given me their handkerchief, she thought. The chambermaid is never cold or hungry or alone, why does she get the handkerchief? God damn all the chambermaids. She angrily packed up her writing materials and stormed out.

Geyer stopped and turned back to the maid. "What about the trunk? Do you know where he sent the trunk?"

House on West Madison Street

The investigators turned their attention to a lodging house on West Madison Street and Ashland Avenue to find the missing trunk. The chambermaid said she was tipped a rather handsome sum to ship it there. The trunk was one of the few pieces of evidence that could corroborate an account of the winding journey Holmes had taken. They found the lodging house about 50 feet from the corner.

"Oh yes, I remember him. Harry Gordon," the lodging house owner said. She was a hard-working woman with a thick apron and dirty boots.

"Did he have a trunk with him?" Geyer showed the picture of the trunk.

"No."

"Did he have any children with him?"

"No, just the lady who he called Miss Gordon."

"He called?"

"That wasn't her real name."

"Was she about 25 years old? Dark hair, round face?" Geyer asked, describing Georgiana Yoke, Holmes's second wife.

"Oh no. She was early twenties, but she had blonde hair. This woman was the most beautiful woman I have ever seen. She told everyone in the neighborhood that Gordon was the son of an English lord. They were going to travel through Europe for their honeymoon. The poor child couldn't keep a secret to save her life. We discovered that she was really someone named Emily Cigrand. She was his secretary."

"How'd you know it was her?"

"Everyone knew it. It was a big scandal. She mysteriously disappeared from his care."

"What do you mean disappeared?"

"One day she was here, the next day she was gone. No one has heard from her since."

Emily Cigrand was the woman that Mr. Pitezel brought back from the out-of-state alcohol treatment center. Holmes had been there with her, but not with the children and the trunk.

They began their search outside the house, looking for any clues. There was nothing but overgrown grass.

"Why is he always lookin' for houses on the outskirts of town?" Geyer asked. "Is the house empty?"

"Oh yes, other than some furniture. What part of the house would you like to see first?"

"The cellar."

They descended the dusty wooden stairs from the kitchen into the dark cellar.

"Didn't you think his behavior was odd?"

"Yes, it was a little peculiar, but the gentleman seemed sincere. It would have been improper to ask. It really wasn't any of my business, was it?"

"No, I guess it wasn't," Geyer said.

"Aren't you coming?" Cass asked Whitsett.

"No."

"Why not?"

"I don't like cellars."

The cellar was divided into three parts. The front ran along the length of the entire house. It was paved with a cement floor and contained a wood and coal bin next to a large portable heater about four feet in diameter.

Geyer and Cass examined the heater. Geyer thought Holmes may have tried to burn some of the children's possessions to cover his tracks. They opened the metal side door and brushed around. Cass, worried about getting his suit dirty, tried to angle his body in a different direction while he stoked the ashes.

"Get in there, man!" Geyer said. "To hell with your suit."

Cass fumed with embarrassment, then copied Geyer's rigor in the examination. They were covered in ash and surrounded by plumes of smoke.

The part to the rear of the west side of the house had a large stationary washtub and a board floor, used as a washroom. The east part was used for storage.

"Has anything been changed? Rooms added or removed?" Geyer asked.

"Everything is as it was, detective," she called from above.

Geyer and Cass examined every part of the cement and wood floor looking for disturbances.

"What are you looking for?" the owner asked from the top of the stairs.

"I'd rather not say, ma'am," Geyer called out.

"A trunk," Whitsett said. "Or, hypothetically, a dead body."

Mrs. Moore covered her gasp with her hand. Feeling nauseous, she retreated to the kitchen.

"Was that necessary?" Geyer asked. He stood up straight with his hands on his hips.

"I said, hypothetically." Whitsett enjoyed seeing the shock on people's faces. She had been telling everyone they interviewed behind Geyer's back.

"They're not dead. Hate, love or money. That's why people kill. Understand?"

"Then why are you checking for holes in the ground?" Whitsett snapped. "It's her house, I think she has a right to know," Whitsett said.

"It's the man's house. And you can't tell women everything they want to know," Geyer said. He broke off his search to stand up straight. "And I'm looking for the trunk."

"If you say so, detective," she said.

Geyer saw Cass start for the stairs. "Where are you going?"

"She looked sick. I am going to show her my headache tonic," Cass said.

"Not now! Peddle your con later," Geyer screamed.

The men reluctantly resumed their search as they bent over, glaring hatefully at each other.

"Nothing has been tampered with here," Geyer said.

There was a door that led out of the washroom, up a stairway to the backyard. The stairway was enclosed by a red brick wall. This brick was used as a foundation for the rear porch.

"Why have we stopped?" Cass asked looking at Geyer at the top of the stairs.

"I found something," Geyer said.

There was about six feet of clearance under the porch. Cass was conscripted to climb under it and investigate. A hole had been dug towards the back of the wall facing the steps. It was about four feet long, three feet wide and three feet deep.

"It's empty," Cass said.

Cass emerged from under the porch covered in thick dirt. Miss Whitsett helped dust off his clothes as best she could.

"Easy, Miss Whitsett. You don't need to hit so hard," Cass said.

"Don't be a baby," she said.

"Was that hole there before Holmes rented?" Geyer asked the owner.

"I don't think so. But I don't really know. I don't ever look under the porch."

"They must be alive," Geyer said firmly. "I believe it was for hiding the trunk. It's the exact same dimension of the trunk."

"Or a grave for a child," Whitsett said. "Are we still getting guns? Did we decide if we were getting guns?"

They continued their search of the hotels near the depot, hoping to pick up the trail of the trunk. Hotel after hotel after hotel.

No 60 Monroe Street. Holmes rents a house.

New Western Hotel. Entry for Etta and Nellie Canning. Room 5. Oct 10th.

Normandie Hotel. Entry for G. Howell and wife, Adrian (Holmes's handwriting). 2nd floor. Oct 12th

No 241. E. Forest Avenue. House rental for a widowed sister with three children. Oct 13th.

Gies's Hotel. Entry for Mrs. C.A. Adams and daughter. No 33. October 14th.

No 54 Park Place. Entry for husband and wife. Room 21. Oct 13th through Oct 18th.

No 91 Congress Street. Entry for two girls. Corner room, 3rd floor. Oct 13th through 19th.

"Why is he going to all this trouble at all? He's keeping the children in a hotel, less than 100 feet from the hotel of the mother. This is overly complicated," Whitsett said. "Why is he keeping the children at all?"

"Even Holmes's wife is in total ignorance of the careful management. She thinks he's traveling from city to city selling leases for a patent copier or some foolish thing. Holmes is lying to at least three different parties and keeping them in walking distance all over the country a few weeks at a time. How does he keep all that in his head?" Cass asked. "I would have to write everything down to keep track of it."

"That's the problem with these modern cities," Geyer said. "You can sleep down the street from your own children and not know it. No one to help you. We'll never be able to catch criminals anymore. The more people that move into these cities, the more difficult it is to find someone. The entire world is falling apart."

There were so many houses. Each filled with dozens of names of guests, tended to by unobservant staff. They searched house after house after house. Ringing bells, showing pictures and telling the story. They all identified their occupant as Holmes from the picture. Sometimes he was a doctor, sometimes he was an actor. He was always polite, and he never left a trail of that damn trunk.

They searched for days, showing pictures and interviewing expressmen, visiting freight depots, omnibus companies and express offices. The interviewed hackmen and liverymen, but they found no clues.

"Why is the trunk so important?" Miss Whitsett asked.

"Because that's what these hotel and house people notice. That's how these bastards know how much to charge you; if you have nice trunks, you get a higher rate. A couple of kids aren't important to remember, but a trunk is. It's probably with the children," Geyer said, sneaking sips from his silver flask.

Side Show

Whitsett and Cass pushed their way through the crowded street. The gravel crunched beneath their shoes. They had left Geyer alone with his flask to rest his back. Whitsett assumed he would find a saloon to mosey on into.

"Why don't you like cellars?" Cass asked.

"I told you, they aren't ladylike."

"I don't think that's true. Lots of ladies-"

Whitsett stopped abruptly. She was entranced by a wall of posters and playbills for a sideshow.

"Look!" she said. "Let's go see one. We can't go see the World's Fair in Chicago because it burned down. I think they burned it down just to piss me off. I can't believe they lied to us about the marble. What a shit pot Chicago was. I hope this show is fun."

"We can't go to a show, we have to meet Geyer, he'll be waiting for us."

"Trust me, the longer we make him wait, the more agreeable he'll be."

"Why?"

"He's at the nearest saloon. This way, he'll get a couple more drinks under his belt. He'll be slightly more pleasant to be around."

"Really?" he asked as Whitsett led him towards the sideshow. "How do you know that?"

"When we get back, look at his face. It'll be bright red."

"I'm known for being able to distinguish people by their footsteps alone," he said, pouting.

"I know," she said.

They turned the corner and were assaulted with screaming children and the smell of popcorn. The sideshow posters and flags stretched off into the distance, hundreds of bright, colorful ads vanishing on the horizon. Adults and children wandered up and down the rickety promenade. They were captivated by the dingy novelties.

The talker wore a stovepipe hat and a red and white striped jacket.

"Ladies and gentlemen, step right up, step right up. Inside this tent, you'll see wonders that defy explanation. Curiosity killed the cat and the answer brought him back. The line starts behind me, entry is only 12 cents. Twelves cents for the most amazing sights you are legally allowed to see. Alive, alive, alive. Hurry ladies and gentlemen. Everything is real, from the good Lord himself. See the hat, the hat of Abraham Lincoln. See a human mocking bird. See a two-headed baby, a baby with two heads. See a real mermaid, caught off the shores of Fiji. Alive, alive, alive."

Whitsett wanted to see this one.

"If we go, you can't be mad at me anymore," Cass demanded.

"We'll see," she said.

Cass paid with a few coins and waited for his change.

"You owe me two cents," Cass said to the ticket taker.

"I'm sorry, sir. There you are." The man slid the coins over with his pinky.

"Good catch," Whitsett said.

"I think he did that on purpose."

They entered the tent and their eyes struggled to adjust to the darkness. The tent fermented the smell of grass and salt into a potent aroma. There was a long walkway with four compartments on each side. It was a grindhouse. People were entering and exiting the compartment through a heavy canvas drape over the door.

They entered the first room. The drape had a picture of a bird with a human head: the human mocking bird. Whitsett was excited and a little afraid of what she would find. She grabbed onto Cass's arm and used him as a shield as they inched their way past the other people.

A man in a suit was screaming insults at a bird in the cage. *The human mockingbird is a human mocking a bird*, Whitsett thought. She led Cass out of the tent laughing. She loved puns!

"We didn't pay 12 cents for this," Cass said angrily.

The human in the act quickly turned to the crowd. "Ladies and gentlemen, this is merely a joke, the rest of the attractions are very real. Ladies and gentlemen, prepare yourselves."

Two small children were quickly strafing the crowd, casually bumping into the gentlemen in the tent.

"Scuse me, sir," they would say. "Beg ya pardon, sir."

Whitsett smile. *What a great con*, she thought. Little pickpockets using the exhibits of the sideshow as a distraction for their lifts. She tested out the con by lifting Mr. Cass's wallet. Worked like a charm. *These poor kids are beaten by their boss if they don't make their quota.*

"Here you go," she said, handing Cass his wallet.

"What's this?"

"Your wallet. Keep it in your inner jacket pocket so no one takes it."

They went from tent to tent, looking at the different acts.

"That's Abraham Lincoln's hat?" Whitsett said excitedly. She told Cass everything that came to her mind as they went from act to act. "It looks just like a top hat. Ooh, I can see the bullet hole. That's chilling… Look, an actual octopus, I've only read about these in books. They don't have any bones…How do you think they shrink the heads like that? It says a shrunken head from deep in the Amazon, but how do they do it? Oh my, he actually put that sword all the way down his mouth. That's so disgusting…What animal is that? That can't be a rat, it's too big. I didn't know rats got that big, I hate this act."

"I think this is the last one. The mermaid," Cass said, exhausted from listening to Whitsett.

They entered the tent. The picture on the canvas was of a beautiful blonde woman with exposed breasts and a blue fishtail below the waist. The canvas kept the smell of dirt and fresh grass thick inside the enclosure. It was dark and smelled like the dead room at the university. Whitsett pushed her way to the back and found a glass case. The lid was open and a small group of people was struggling to see without getting too close.

According to the display, the mermaid had been caught by a fishing boat off the coast of the Fiji Islands. It was about five feet across. From the waist down, it was in the shape of a preserved cod-fish tail. From the waist up, it was a grotesque mummified human figure with a large mouth, sharpened teeth and sagging breasts. The eyes were black and bulging. The mouth was fixed open as though it were screaming. It was a dried-out monster.

Whitsett put her hands over her mouth. It was horrible and she couldn't stop smiling. Cass's arm was almost numb from Whitsett gripping on to it. She was instantly reminded of the corpses she had seen in the dead room. "Imagine how much we could get if we sold this body to the university?"

"Don't even say that, Miss Whitsett. We're not grave robbers."

"No, we're resurrectionists," she said, laughing. She began to think about what she said, which had started as a joke. *Are we resurrectionists?* she wondered. *Oh my, look at the mermaid's mouth. It's screaming,* she thought. *The mermaid is screaming.* Whitsett let her imagination run wild and she became dizzy. She let go of Cass's arm and ran out of the tent. Cass followed her but was stopped by an exotic woman with her head covered in a shawl.

"Hello, dear," she said with a vague European accent. "Where you going?"

"Outside," Cass said. He was so confused. He had never seen a girl with such dark lines under her eyes.

"Don't run far," she said, holding up a brass key. "Would you like to join me in my room?" she added with long, soft words.

"Your room? I don't understand."

"This is the key to my room. For five dollars, I sell to you."

"What do I do with it?"

"Whatever you want," she said.

Whitsett slapped the key out of the woman's hand and pulled Cass out of the tent.

"I can't leave you alone for a minute," Whitsett said.

"What was that lady saying? Something about her key?" Cass asked as Whitsett pulled him away from any danger.

"It's a con. She lures you to pay for the key for a night in bed with her, but the key doesn't open anything. She just takes your money. She's a hustler."

"Why would she think I'd buy a key?"

"You bought a ticket to see a mermaid," Whitsett said, laughing. "She knew her customer." Cass couldn't think of anything to say. "It's all a con, it's a hustle. These circuses and sideshows are all a hustle."

"Then why did you want to go inside?" Cass asked

"They're still fun," she said, leading Cass into another sideshow.

"Is everything a con?" Cass asked huffing and puffing in exasperation.

"Probably," Whitsett said, smiling at him. "Isn't that what makes it fun?"

The Night Off

They arrived early in the morning in Toronto and registered at the Rossin House. After Geyer checked in with the police department and collected his credentials, letters of introduction, conversations of futility, condolences for his wife and young daughter, and paperwork, they examined the registers of hotels.

"Those are the children," Jones, the chief clerk of one hotel said, "they were brought to the hotel by their porter on Friday evening October 19th. A gentleman called to see them. He would take them away for the day but come back before supper. On the morning of October 25th, he came, paid the bill and took them away."

"And you let this strange man take the children?" Cass asked.

"Yes, the children knew him."

"That didn't seem odd to you?"

"I didn't really think about it."

"Maybe you should have paid more attention," Cass snapped.

The Albion. Entry for Alice and Nellie Canning from Detroit. October 19th through 25th.

State House. Entry for G. Howell and wife. Room No 14. Oct 18th through 20th.

Union House. Entry for Mrs. C.A. Adams and daughter. October 18th.

The Palmer House. Entry for H. Howell and wife. Room 32. Oct 21st.

They had walked the streets exhaustively. More hotels seemed to grow up like weeds through the concrete overnight for them to search. They were hot and so tired.

"We know now he didn't leave until as late as the 25th," Cass said. "Holmes left the Walker House on the afternoon of October 20th. But we know he stayed until as late as the 25th. That is when he took the children from this house."

"Wait, slow down, Mr. Cass. Where was he until the 20th?" Whitsett asked. "Why do you walk so goddamn fast!"

"You never pay attention!" Cass said. He stomped off down the street.

"What's his problem?" Whitsett asked.

"You don't call him inspector anymore," Geyer said. "He liked it when you called him inspector."

Whitsett saw two children approach Geyer and ask him for money. She gave them each a nickel. She wanted to give them advice on how to avoid capture and where to go. Before she could think of anything, they had run away. She tried to think of some piece of advice to help them. Nothing. *Don't get caught and don't stand the line.* There was no advice, no special way, no magic word. Everything really was a con. She really didn't want to go back to her normal life. She didn't want to be like these little children again. *I hope we never find them*, she thought. Although she still meant it, it stung to think it this time.

Geyer had been through the Toronto directory and prepared a list of all the real estate agents. They interviewed every one of them, working their way through the list alphabetically. For days, they went from agent to agent.

"We could be doing this for the rest of our lives," Cass said. "We could take all this information we're learning about real estate and make some well-placed investments in property. I'll bet we could triple our money in a few years."

"You know you don't have to exploit and capitalize every situation!" Geyer said. "We're looking for missing children."

"I'm not exploiting anything," Cass said.

"He just wants to be J.P. Morgan, that's all," Whitsett said. "He doesn't mean anything by it."

"I'm tired of reminding him that we're here to find children, not help get him rich so he can live in a mansion and drink ice water. You don't have that kind of quality to be successful."

"I don't have to stand here and listen to this." Cass stormed off down the street.

"Why are you so agitated?" Whitsett asked.

"I'm tired of his nonsense, that's all," Geyer said.

"It isn't nonsense, he's just talking. Just harmless talk. Don't take your frustration out on him."

Geyer stopped and took a deep breath. He rubbed his exhausted eyes and sighed.

"You're right. I shouldn't swear in front of you."

"I don't care if you swear, detective. Just be nicer."

"The three of us can't interview every real estate agent in the midwest. It's impossible. This entire thing is impossible. We'll never be able to find 'em," Geyer said.

"Okay, we need to take a break. Tonight, we'll have our meal, rest and drink whiskey." She took Geyer by the arm and walked him towards their hotel.

"Ladies don't drink whiskey," he said.

Cass fumed while he stomped down the street. He was so angry that he only noticed the street was a dead end when he walked into the red bricks in front of him.

"Afternoon Daily!" A boy was selling newspapers in the streets. "Afternoon Daily!" he kept shouting. He was dirty and rough with a small frame from malnutrition. He'd set himself up at the corner once the evening began to buzz with people getting off work, hoping to get as many eyeballs on his edition as he could.

Cass was hit by a thought. What if they could use the papers to have the real estate agents come to them? If the real estate agents knew who and what they were looking for, they could read the paper and then contact the detective.

Cass grabbed the boy by his collar. "Where's your office located?"

Geyer sipped his silver flask.

"Can I have some of your whiskey?" Whitsett asked.

"It's not whiskey, it's a preparation from my doctor."

"Right. I need some preparation too." She pretended to cough and sneeze. She was very close to persuading him when they both heard a loud rumble coming from the lobby.

They were shocked to see Cass trying to corral an enormous gathering of newspapermen like he was driving cattle.

"What the hell's going on here?" Geyer asked.

"I have the solution to all our problems," Cass said. "I called all these paper men here to record the story of Holmes and what we're looking for. This way, they can print the story and have the real estate agents come to us!"

"You can't sell a story to the newspapers," Geyer said.

"No, not a story, an interview. And we don't get any money for it. What if every paper had the details of the lodging house and real estate agent we were looking for? Have the matter brought before the public for help. Then the agents could come to us!"

"That sounds unprofessional. I'm a detective, I'm not supposed to help sell newspapers."

"No, we're supposed to find the children," Cass said. "Right?"

Geyer reluctantly agreed and sat with the newsmen for hours. He gave them the whole story, and the pictures too. All the grizzly parts were withheld for the purposes of decorum. If there was one thing Geyer hated, it was pencil-pushing newsmen. He spent the entire night answering the hacks's questions. Whitsett knew not to bother him about his whiskey now.

In the morning, Geyer and Whitsett continued searching for real estate agents in the suburban towns Mimco and North Parkdale. Cass stayed behind in case there were any leads from the newspaper.

When they returned for lunch, they were met by Cass.

"How was it?" Cass was sitting down with his legs up. He looked so smug and could barely contain his smile.

Geyer refused to admit the newspaper was a good idea so he resolved to say nothing.

"Much faster, all the agents had read the paper and we were able to interview twice as many," Whitsett said. "What have you been doing all day?"

"I've been to the police station. We received word that a man giving the name Holmes rented a house on the outskirts of the city. A property that wasn't on our list."

"You got to be shitting me!" Geyer said.

"Welcome to the 20th century, detective."

Based on a handwritten tip from the police, the three searchers drove to Perth and Bloor Street. They came upon a house that stood in the middle of a field and was surrounded by a board fence six feet high. Geyer knocked on the door and was met by an aged couple with a son about 20 years old.

Geyer introduced himself and ran through his dull speech. "How long have you lived here?" Geyer asked.

"A few months," the old man said.

"Do you mind if we inspect the grounds of the house?"

"No, what are you looking for?"

"I'd rather not say," Geyer said.

"We believe Holmes, who rented this place, murdered some children and buried them under the house. Hypothetically," Whitsett said with wide eyes and a smile. The old couple gasped at the vulgarity of a young lady saying such awful things. Whitsett loved to see people's reactions; it never got old. Geyer rubbed his eyes with a long sigh.

"I apologize for that outburst," Geyer said. "She has an odd way about her. We're really looking for a trunk."

"That might account for that pile of loose dirt under the main building," said the old man.

"I beg your pardon?" Miss Whitsett asked. Her smile quickly disappeared and was replaced by concern.

"Get a shovel," Geyer said.

They were shown how to get under the house by the old couple's boy. Whitsett stayed upstairs. She didn't like going into cellars, she told them, it wasn't ladylike.

Cass and Geyer took off their coats. They crawled into a small hole underneath the floor of the main building. The floor was raised a little more than two feet above the earth. In the center of the space, they found a small mound of loose dirt. They called for the boy to bring them another shovel and several oil lamps.

Cass and Geyer spent all night digging like prisoners on a chain gang. The hole was waist-deep, and the dirt clung to their sweat to form a paste.

"Shh. Do you hear that?" Cass asked. "Footsteps. Above us." The boards above them creaked and flexed.

"And? It's probably the people who own the house."

"No, that's Whitsett. I can tell someone from their footsteps. She's right above us. I think she's pacing, she must be nervous."

"Keep digging, jackass. I am getting really tired of you and her and your nonsense."

It was getting late. The oil lamps were fading so they decided to stop digging until the next morning.

As they were leaving, Geyer showed the couple the picture of Holmes.

"Is this definitely the man who stayed here?" Geyer asked.

"No, that's not him."

"What? It's not? Are you sure?"

"That's not him," the man said. "The Mr. Holmes who rented before us was fat and had a large scar on his chin."

Geyer was so angry, he left without a word. Whitsett and Cass followed sheepishly.

"We spent all day digging a goddamn hole for nothing!" Geyer yelled.

"I suppose we should have shown the sketch to them before we started digging," Cass said.

"Incredible observation!" Geyer said. "Why don't we just start a venture selling tickets to our investigation. Would that make you happy?"

"Calm down!" Whitsett said.

"What are you even doing here?" Geyer asked. "You don't think we'll find anything. Why didn't you stay home?"

Cass was about to say something, but he could only manage to say "I" before Geyer had grabbed him by the collar.

"Calm down," Whitsett said to Geyer.

"I will not calm down. We wasted an entire day because of this fool and his damned newspapers."

"It wasn't his fault! He's just trying to help. And I seem to remember you were the one asking for a shovel."

"How dare you speak to me like that. I will not be spoken to like that by a woman. A vulgar, low woman. You need to learn your goddamn place." Geyer limped down the street, clutching his back. The digging had left sharp pains in his body.

Cass took off his hat and sat on the curb. Whitsett sat next to him, using his shoulder to steady herself.

"You boys love to storm off," Whitsett said. She rested her head on his shoulder. "Why *are* you here?"

"Because you wanted to be here." She didn't know what to make of what Cass had said. They sat in silence, listening to the footsteps of strangers. "I can tell people apart just by the sound of their footsteps."

"No, you can't," she said. She thought of Mrs. Jacobs and her cousin's son. She didn't want to go back to Philadelphia and marry him. But what could she do? It seemed her trip would be coming to an end soon, whether she liked it or not.

"What should we do now?" Cass asked.

"Whiskey?"

Cantina

Geyer spent the rest of the day stomping around the Grand Trunk Depot. He went from ticket agent to ticket agent, sneaking an ever-increasing number of sips from his flask in-between.

"Were there any half tickets sold on Oct 25th from Toronto to Niagara Falls?" Geyer asked.

"No, but there was a whole ticket sold for Niagara Falls."

"Would a conductor take a whole ticket for two children?"

"He would."

"So, we got no way of knowing if Holmes sent the girls to Niagara Falls to meet Minnie Williams, as he claims?"

"I'm sorry, sir?"

"Do you have any crimes around here?" he asked, rubbing the fatigue from his face.

"Crimes?"

"Crimes. I'm lookin' for a crime."

"Our city does have crime, if that's what you're asking, sir."

"No, I'm lookin' for a specific crime. Something that has to do with these children and this man."

"What is the nature of the crime?"

"Have no idea. But we already got the criminal in jail."

"I don't understand what you're asking?"

"We don't have victims, just Holmes. He's a dandy piece of work, but he don't look like a criminal. Where are the victims? Everyone seems to be a goddamn victim. Cons and factories and children. The children. The children are the victims, aren't they?"

"I'm afraid I don't understand, sir."

"Forget it, son."

Geyer passed a saloon and thought he should mosey on inside. The piano was harsh and piercing. He ordered his ale and waited for the alcohol to dull the pain in his back and calm the red in his face. He kicked the bar with the tip of his boot like a mule in a stall, hoping to knock away the throbbing pain of his abscess.

There was a factory worker next to him, humming along with the piano.

"Do you know why people kill?" Geyer asked him.

"Why's that, boss?" asked the haggard-looking young man.

"For money, for love or for hate."

"Is that right?"

"Simple as that. Money, love and hate. Now sometimes you get the mad man who kills, but even then, there's a reason."

"Catholics. Those bastards kill just to satisfy their blood rituals," the factory worker said.

"Even the immigrants kill for a reason. But Holmes, he got the money, he got no passion for these children, he don't need to bother with them. He's adding work and trouble for himself. What's the point of taking 'em all over the country? They wasn't witnesses to anything, they wasn't ransomed. The expense and trouble of keeping these children must have been enormous. Why go to that trouble? Don't make sense."

"What children?"

"Exactly. What children?" Geyer said. "Crime, criminal, jail. That's how you work a case. Locate the crime, find the criminal, put him in jail. You never start from the jail and go look for a crime. It's backward."

"Is this Holmes a Catholic?"

"I don't know. I don't think so. Why would he torture these children by keeping them cold and hungry and alone? He isn't mad. He's brilliant, industrious, clever. It don't make any sense. This country is going to shit. Even when there's no crime to see, it all looks criminal. The crimes and the not-crimes are gettin' worse."

A respectable-looking man approached Geyer wearing a nice suit. He was looking around and searching under the tables.

"Excuse me, sir," he said. "I wonder if you have seen a gold ring? It has a small inscription on it that reads Eleanor. It's worth hundreds of dollars."

"Take your con down the street, son," Geyer said.

"I beg your pardon?"

"You heard me, piss off."

The gentleman left the saloon, deflated.

"What did you mean by that?" his drinking partner asked.

"You're not part of that con, are you?" Geyer asked. He looked at him very carefully.

"No."

"Because I'll run your ass in if you're a con."

"I'm just askin'."

"He's straight," the bartender said as he refilled the detective's drink.

"It's a con. A hustle. There's always at least one in these kinds of places. That guy in a suit tells you a story about an expensive ring and how it's worth hundreds of dollars. Then a little while later another man shows up with the ring and offers to sell it to you for ten dollars. Then you buy the ring thinking you'll make a killing but the ring turns out to be brass."

"How do they know who to ask?"

"They pick the people who look the most desperate." Geyer froze in shock. *Am I the most desperate-looking man in the saloon?* he thought. *That can't be.*

A man sat next to Geyer and ordered a drink. He took out a gold ring and asked if Geyer knew anything about rings. Geyer was disgusted. It made him feel hollow. In this whole dingy saloon, Geyer was the most desperate looking. It shook the red-faced detective to the core. Geyer grabbed the man by his shoulder and punched him in the face.

"I have you, you bastard," Geyer said. "I'm taking you in."

"For what?" the man asked.

"I'm hauling you in for the murder of the Pitezel children."

"I didn't murder anyone!" the man screamed.

"Yes, you did. Were you born here? You murdered those kids. You look like a murderer." Geyer was losing his grip on the man's collar. Everyone around him was staring. They all looked like murderers. He could tell by looking into their eyes. He swung his fist towards the screaming man.

"No. I didn't. Help!"

Geyer slipped and fell to the floor. He released the man who then escaped into the street. Geyer grabbed his throbbing temple. *I don't need to pin it on someone, I already have the criminal in jail*, he thought. *I need to find the crime.*

The children are the crime, aren't they? he thought. Maybe not. The children could still be with their father. We don't know if he's dead or not. Or if he's the father or not. I hate these goddamn dragnets, he thought. They made his back hurt and his knees ache.

But where's the trunk? Forget the children, where's the trunk? The trunk is missing.

He finished his beers and wandered to the freight office. He wanted to know how much baggage was shipped to Prescott, Canada on the night of the 25th of October and morning of the 26th.

The poor children.

Just find the trunk, Geyer thought. Don't think about the children, just find the trunk.

What a ridiculous assignment this is, he thought. *I should just go home.* He missed his home. Then he remembered he had no home. The home he missed was a pile of ashes providing nitrogen to the soil.

He looked around the streets. He knew he could tell a criminal from their eyes. He felt disgusted because they all looked like criminals.

Just find the trunk, he thought. Don't think about home, just find the trunk. Thinking about missing trunks doesn't sting as much as thinking about missing children.

He continued to drink until he passed out.

Madam Eldora

Cass picked up the stack of notes and letters from a specially-marked milk crate kept behind the clerk's desk. The hotel clerk was irritated he had to act as a postman. *That's what you get for making me share a honeymoon suite with Geyer*, Cass thought.

"What are those?" Whitsett asked.

"Letters with tips about Holmes," Cass said.

"Ooh! Can I read some?"

"Sure, you can take half. Most of them are bad information."

They sat and began to read in the lobby. Cass fell asleep sitting up. Whitsett laughed at his awkward posture; he looked like the world's most boring marionette. She was throwing pencils at him when she came across a letter from someone named,

Madam Eldora Desmond Burlingham

Medium and Psychic

She tore open the letter.

In very elegant and elaborate handwriting, Madam Eldora offered to perform a séance to locate the missing children and commune with their spirits from the afterlife.

Whitsett was so excited she grabbed Cass's head and shook it.

"What are you doing?" Cass asked.

"Get your hat on!"

Before taking a coach to visit Madam Eldora, Whitsett decided she needed a change of clothes. She had been traipsing around the Midwest in her work clothes and felt like a used horse-blanket. Cass was dragged into the dress shop and made to wait while she was fitted with something more presentable.

"It will take me a few minutes to make these adjustments, madam. Can I get anything for you and your husband while you wait?"

"We're not married," Cass said.

"It's all so new for him, he's still getting used to the idea," Whitsett told the seamstress.

"Why did you tell her we were married?" Cass whispered.

"I thought it would be fun. So far, you're not being a very fun husband."

"Why are we even here? I thought you wanted to see the medium."

"I do. But my black dress and white shirt are so ragged, they wouldn't be fit for work clothes anymore. And I'm not going to have a sitting with Madam Eldora Desmond Burlingham dressed like a goddamn servant," she said. She had been saving her money for months in the hope of having a safety net when the investigation eventually ended and she was faced with hard reality. *However, since I need new clothes anyway, why not get something presentable?* she thought.

When the dress was finished, she tried it on and examined how it looked in the mirror. It was a red bell-shaped skirt that fit smoothly over her hips. She had it pulled out a little so it wouldn't be so cumbersome to walk in. She wanted sleeves that puffed out more but knew it would get in the way of her writing. She had a cream shirtwaist under a slim-fitting burgundy jacket with a respectable amount of puff around the shoulders.

It was the first time she had seen herself in something resembling the fashionable hourglass silhouette. Although it was a step up from her work clothes, she was still in the basement, which she hated. *I wish I could afford one of these hats*, she thought.

"You should get a new hat while we're here," she told Cass.

"There's nothing wrong with my hat," she said defensively. "What's wrong with my hat?"

"It's ugly."

Whitsett swayed down the street, exaggerating her hips so the new dress would flow back and forth. They found the address printed on the envelope. It was a modest brownstone in a sleepy neighborhood. The drapes were drawn and there didn't appear to be anyone at home. Whitsett knocked on the door.

"This is ridiculous. I don't want to participate in this fraud," Cass said.

"You just keep an open mind."

"This is nonsense."

"If you don't change your attitude, I'll have her cast you into another mystical realm," she said waving her hands.

"You can't read any more dime magazines."

The door opened and a middle-aged woman presented herself. She had grey hair and a black dress.

"May I help you?"

"Yes, we received this letter." Whitsett showed her the letter. She was glad she had her new dress; otherwise, she would have looked like the servant who answered the door.

"I see; you seek Madam Eldora."

"Yes," Whitsett said. "We seek Madam Eldora." Whitsett smiled with excitement.

"Follow me."

The woman took her candle and led them into a sitting room.

"May I present Madam Eldora Desmond Burlingham."

A woman in her late twenties stood up from her chair. She was dressed all in white. Her form was shapeless except for a waist pulled tight with a corset. She appeared as though she had just returned from the beyond herself. The dark room and candles made her white dress and pale skin glow. The lamps were covered in paper shades and the room was filled with Japanese-style furniture. Drawings of Asian trees and strange letters decorated paper partitions and blue vases.

"Hello, my name is-"

Lady Eldora put up her hand to silence Whitsett.

"I know who you are. You are the investigators searching for the Pitezel children."

"Yes!"

"You are Mr. Cass and Miss Whitsett from Philadelphia."

"Inspector Cass," Cass said. All this information could be read in the papers, he thought.

"I am so pleased you responded to my letter. I was born with a gift. I can see into another world. I do not believe I see heaven or hell. I see a place where spirits can dwell and communicate. It is through me that they can have access to our world. I learned the many secrets of the spirit realm on my travels through the orient, with all its mystical traditions. It is using these powers that I help people. I have held séances for many important people. On the desk next to you, you will see a letter from Frances Folsom Cleveland, the First Lady of the United States, thanking me for my intervention with her and her departed mother. And next to that is a lock of hair from Napoleon."

Cass examined the letter. It was very affectionate and grateful towards Madam Eldora. It was signed and written on, what appeared to be, presidential stationery.

"Can I offer you a drink?"

"We would love a glass of whiskey," Whitsett said.

Madam Eldora waved her hand and the middle-aged woman prepared them both a drink. The drinks were served in strange goblets made from clay.

"I appreciate your hospitality, madam," Cass said. "And I don't mean to insult you, but I'm having trouble believing all this."

"I understand. It is confusing and can be rather unsettling. It can be both natural and unnatural at the same time. Would you be comfortable with a demonstration?"

"A demonstration? Of your psychic abilities?"

"Yes, unless *you* have some ability you'd like to demonstrate," Lady Eldora said, smiling reassuringly.

"Yes, of course. A demonstration," Cass said, laughing nervously. Whitsett smiled at Cass's awkward response.

Lady Eldora closed her eyes and put her hand to her head and reached out, touching the top of Cass's palm. She rolled her head around slowly and began to mumble to herself.

"I see a woman, grey hair. She has a cane. She died recently. She wants me to say that that detective is just a cranky old man and doesn't see how smart you are."

Cass was unimpressed.

"She says you should tell Miss Whitsett how you really feel about her. She won't laugh at you."

Whitsett smiled. "Mr. Cass!"

"This is silly," Cass said, blushing. He wanted to pull his hand away, but Lady Eldora gripped it tight.

"It was very sad for you. You tried not to tell anyone. But it really hurt. Why did it hurt? You knew her. May? Is there a May?"

"Maybelle."

"Yes, Maybelle, your grandmother. She says it's okay, you don't have to be alone."

Mr. Cass pulled his hand away and became so pale, Miss Whitsett thought he was going to be ill. His eyes fogged and became distant.

"The spirit has left us," Madam Eldora said.

"Mr. Cass?" Whitsett asked. "Are you alright?"

"I'm sorry about that Mr. Cass. I didn't mean to upset you."

Cass remained still and silent.

"I can commune with the spirits of the children. Perhaps their tormented spirits can give you some clue that will lead you to them."

"That sounds neat. How do we start?" Whitsett said. She liked this much better than the mermaid show.

"You must sit down at this table."

Madam Eldora pointed to a small circular table in the middle of the room. Whitsett dragged Cass by the arm and made him sit. Madame Eldora sat with them and held out her hands. They grabbed each other's hands in a circle.

"You must put the name and faces of those you wish to commune in the front of your mind. You must concentrate on them very carefully."

Madam Eldora closed her eyes. The middle-aged assistant turned off all the lamps except for the candle on the table. They heard her leave the room and lock the door.

"You will notice there's a box under the table. It's full of implements that the spirits may want to use to communicate with us. Place a few of them on the table."

Whitsett let go of Cass's hand and reached for the box. She pulled out a tambourine, a bell and a mirror and put them on the table. She grabbed Cass's hand again and squeezed with nervous excitement.

"I will now attempt to contact the spirit world. No matter what happens, don't let go of my hands. Don't break the circle." Madam Eldora leaned forward and blew out the candle.

They sat in the complete darkness in silence.

Whitsett began to feel smoke. A warm, spicy mist gathered around her.

The table began to shake.

"I believe there are spirits with us now. Can you feel it?"

"It tastes like smoke," Cass said.

"That is ectoplasm."

Whitsett let out a short laugh. "Who are they?" Whitsett asked, trying to get back into the operation.

"Who are you, spirits? Tell us who you are!" Madam Eldora was unfazed.

The tambourine on the table began to rattle.

"If we are speaking to the spirits of the Pitezel children, please give us a sign!"

The smoke hit the back of Whitsett's throat. Though no one could see, her eyes were wide open and she was smiling.

The bell gave a small shake.

"Thank you, spirits!" Madam Eldora said. "Did you meet with a foul end?"

The bell rattled violently. Whitsett coughed; the smoke was beginning to tickle her throat.

"We wish to know where you are! Show me the location."

The table began to rumble. Whitsett felt the tabletop pushing up against her hands. It was lifting up. She used her knees and feet to search underneath and found no source of the levitation.

"Yes! I can almost see it! Just a bit more, spirits. Show me just a little more so we can find you."

A piercing scream rang in their ears. The smoke was bitter and chalky. The table was levitating up to Whitsett's neck. The tambourine and bell clanged violently.

"Don't break the circle. What is it, spirits? What is it?"

The table dropped. The room went silent. Whitsett looked up and saw a glow. In the glow, she saw a face. It was the face of a small child floating above them. The mouth was open as if gasping in pain. The eyes appeared to be blinking and rolling. Whitsett could hear herself panting.

The face vanished and they were left in the dark.

"The spirit has left us," Madam Eldora said with a deep exhale. She let go and lit the candle on the table.

Whitsett was exhilarated. She had never been through anything like that before. The smoke hung thick in the air.

They stood up and wandered aimlessly around the room. Madam Eldora gave them another drink. Mr. Cass was silent and distant. Whitsett was dizzy from the whiskey and smoke.

Madam Eldora grabbed Whitsett's hand. "You have the same gift as me. You don't want to live in man's material world," she whispered.

"Good con," Whitsett said with exultation.

"I must bid you goodnight. I am very weary from our experience," Madam Eldora said. She escorted them to the door. "We can try again another day. My door is always open to you."

"Thank you. It was very fun," Whitsett said like a little girl.

Whitsett was about to walk away when Madam Eldora grabbed her hand.

"When you see the mother, don't blame her. And don't be bitter. Not everyone will abandon you. Hypothetically."

Whitsett was broadsided. She didn't know how this hustler knew what she knew. She almost believed her. *That's pretty goddamn good*, she thought.

They said goodnight as Whitsett took Mr. Cass's arm and was led out into the street.

They walked back to the hotel.

"Nonsense," Cass said dismissively. He was noticeably shaken. "Ineffable nonsense."

"No, it was great."

"I didn't believe a moment of it."

"Yes, you did; you loved it."

"It's fake. There's no such thing as ectoplasm. It's fake."

"Of course it's fake! It's a con. That's not the point; it's supposed to be fun. We all know there is no lady in 'find the lady', no ectoplasm, no mermaid and no Pitezel children. We all know it's not real. But she was able to con us into thinking it was real, even just for a moment. That's to be admired in itself."

"A con isn't to be admired."

"Yes, it is. That's all life is—a con. She knew her customer and was able to get us to believe in the spirit world. You can't even get a person with a headache to buy your headache tonic."

Cass stopped. Whitsett could see she had hurt his feelings.

"I'm sorry, Mr. Cass. Inspector."

"No, you're right. No one takes my product seriously."

"You're trying to make them buy it. You have to make them want to buy it."

"How do you do that?"

"With a con."

"I don't think I can do that. Who am I kidding? I can't do any of this. You could do it; you can do anything."

Whitsett felt that in her chest. "You just need a little practice," she said.

Whitsett grabbed Cass and took him to a promenade.

"How do you know so much about cons?" Cass asked.

"I like knowing things. Okay, you're gonna practice. See that man there? The one standing next to that lady with the red scarf. Go and start a conversation with them. Try and get 'em to say something personal to you. Con men tell you what you want to hear. Everyone wants to be conned, except con men. Remember, you have to know your customer. He's rich and fancy. He wants to be admired. Get him to say something personal."

"What do you mean personal?"

"Hustling is all about making the other person feel comfortable. Try and make 'em feel comfortable enough with you to tell you something personal."

"What if they don't?"

"It doesn't matter; this is hypothetical."

"No, it isn't. Hypothetical means in theory. I'm actually doing this."

"Don't be an asshole. It's just practice. Now go."

Whitsett watched Cass approach the people. He stared at them awkwardly. After what seemed like an eternity, he tipped his hat and walked back to Miss Whitsett.

"That was good for a first time," Miss Whitsett said.

"I couldn't think of anything to say."

Whitsett heard a clanging sound behind her. She looked around to find small children digging through piles of trash for food. They had dirty little hands and dirty little faces. She remembered that feeling of hunger and desperation. She grabbed Cass by the arm, pulling him away. She wanted no part of it anymore. She would try and outrun it now.

"Okay. Let's not try that anymore. I know, let's get some whiskey."

Whitsett and Cass returned to the hotel with a bottle of whiskey.

"Your job is to try and convince the clerk to look the other way so you can come to my room."

Cass's eyes became wide and frightened.

"Remember to know your customer. He's uptight and a bit stuffy. So, you should have lots in common. Good luck."

Whitsett giggled as she walked up the stairs. Cass was about to follow Whitsett into her room when they were yelled at by the clerk.

"Excuse me, sir," the clerk said. He was yelling from the bottom of the stairs. "We don't allow single gentlemen callers in our ladies' rooms."

"It's okay, I'm not a caller, she works for me. I'm staying just across the way."

"I don't work for him. He followed me here, he's trying to rob me," she said laughing.

"If you wish to speak with the lady, you must do so in the lobby. That's what it's for."

They stayed in the lobby. Cass grabbed two teacups from the tray and began to pour the whiskey.

"Sir!" the clerk yelled. "This is not that kind of establishment."

"Listen," Cass said, trying his best to get control of the situation. "What's your name, sir?"

"We don't allow drinking and we certainly don't allow ladies to be drinking!"

"Okay. I apologize. We'll just go to our separate rooms," Cass said.

Whitsett couldn't control her laughter. When she got to her room, she left the door open slightly and sat on the floor. Cass's room was on the other side of the staircase and out of the clerk's view. Miss

Whitsett poured the whiskey into her water glass to the top. When no one was watching, she put the cork back on, kissed it, and laid it on its side. She gently rolled it across the wood panel floor. It rocked and swerved like a carriage with one wheel.

Cass reached out and retrieved the whiskey bottle, filling his glass. They began to drink, silently watching each other from across the chasm of the staircase. They made faces and communicated through drunken hand signals.

Whitsett was very entertained by Cass's rigid movements. He looked like a broken set of clock gears. She laughed and then quickly covered her mouth. Cass put his finger to his lips. It felt so good to not think about their dreadful assignment. They spent the rest of the night drinking and miming to each other across the gulf of respectability.

Another Tip

Geyer arrived back in Toronto with piercing back pain and dark circles under his eyes. He had been kicked out of every saloon in walking distance and had to sleep the rest of the night on a bench. The trunk was still in Toronto; it had to be. He decided he would visit the newspaper office to check the records of every advertised private renter. He would visit each and every one of them until he found that goddamn trunk.

Whitsett woke up on the floor of her room with a stiff neck and a sore arm. As she stood, her head began to throb and spin. She sat on the bed and waited for the nausea to pass. She slowly dressed herself in her new suit and went downstairs.

Geyer was drinking coffee and reading the paper, rubbing out the pain in his foot over the thin leather of his boot.

"Good morning, Miss Whitsett."

"Good morning, detective," she said, squinting her eyes. "Where's Mr. Cass?"

"He's upstairs, very much in the state you're in."

"Musta been something we ate."

"Yes," he said, chuckling, "or something you drank. That's why women shouldn't drink."

"I see you're back to your charming old self."

"Yes, would you like some coffee?"

"Enough. Either be a cranky old man or be a regular old man. You can't be an old mule and then give me coffee right after and make it all go away. Stop going back and forth."

"There was a message this morning. Report about a man who had rented a house on St. Vincent Street whose description corresponds with Holmes."

"I take it we aren't going to respond to it?"

"Haven't decided yet. Probably another wild goose chase. But we should mosey on over."

"Cass will be happy you think that way now. You really hurt his feelings."

"He's too sensitive. I'll go and raise him from the dead."

"Be gentle, detective," she said.

Geyer filled a glass with water and tossed it in Cass's face.

After a quick and disgusting breakfast, the searchers rode to meet Mr. Nudel, the agent who sent in the tip. Geyer showed him the picture of Holmes before he said anything.

"That's him."

They drove out to the St. Vincent Street house. The jumpy ride made Whitsett and Cass nauseous and tired. The sound of horse hooves flopping against the pavement amplified their splitting headaches. The small neighborhood was still and calm on the edge of the city. Smoke from the factory rose in the distance like a volcano.

The building was a quaint little two-story cottage of an old and simple style. Before going to the house, Geyer knocked on the door of the neighbor's house at No 18 Vincent Street. An old Scotsman answered.

"I suppose you're the police about the newspaper article," he said.

"Yes, sir." Geyer introduced himself and showed his credentials. "Are you the man who notified the police about the Pitezel children?"

"That's right. Name's Thomas William Ryves. I saw the pictures in the paper and wrote in directly."

"Can you tell me about the man who rented that house?"

"The man had rented it for a widowed sister, who was in Hamilton, Ontario, and who he expected in a few days."

"Is this the man you saw?" Geyer showed him a picture of Holmes.

"I'm not so sure about that. But the little girls. I got a good look at those ones. Horrible sight they was. Crying and thin, like mangy dogs. Horrible."

Geyer showed him Alice's picture.

"That's the one. Poor little dear," Ryves said.

"Did you ever talk to the children?"

"No, they was never outside. And that man that brought 'em never told a straight story. And the only furniture that he brought was an old bed and mattress, and a big trunk."

"A trunk!" Geyer said. His eyes caught fire. "Did you ever see him workin' about the house at all?"

"No. But the man did ask me to loan him a spade. Said he wanted to arrange a place in his cellar for his sister to put potatoes in. Borrowed it four in the afternoon and returned it at ten the next morning, handing it over the fence. Never saw the girls again. The day after I got my spade back, he came to the house and removed the trunk, and left the key with me. I went inside the next day to see the potatoes and found fresh earth scattered around the bottom of the cellar and some loose boards lying on top."

They rang the bell at Mrs. Nudel's house to get the keys. She lived in the house next to Mr. Ryves. Her daughter answered. She wasn't more than a few years younger than Miss Whitsett. She had on respectable afternoon clothing and perfume. Miss Whitsett's cheeks turned red and she stopped recording. *Why does she get perfume?* she thought.

"Is Mrs. Nudel home?" Geyer asked.

"Yes."

"Tell her we want to see her at once. It's very important." Geyer leaned into Whitsett. "Put your goddamn gloves on," he whispered harshly through his teeth.

The daughter took them through the house and into the parlor. Cass stepped aside to let Miss Whitsett go in front of him, putting his arm lightly on her back. Whitsett pushed Cass's hand away in one hard motion. It was an instinctive reaction and she felt bad the moment she did it.

"Please have a seat. Could I offer anyone tea or biscuits?" she asked.

Everyone sat down except Miss Whitsett. She jammed the insides of her fingers together to rub the itch from the gloves away. *What a great place to grow up*, she thought as she admired the house silently and hatefully. There was a bookshelf full of books. *A bookshelf full of goddamn books and I'll bet she never reads them, too busy with the bows on her stupid head.*

"Would you like to have a seat too?" the daughter asked Whitsett.

"No. I prefer to stand," Whitsett said.

Mrs. Nudel entered and helped her daughter serve everyone peppermint tea. The women of the house wore identical white shirtwaist dresses with open necks and short sleeves. The mother fussed over her daughter's clothes and made sure the bows in her hair fell the right way. Mr. Geyer introduced himself and explained the situation. He thanked the mother and daughter energetically for their hospitality.

The women wore tied, looped skirts with contrasting underskirts. Their low and tiny waists were embellished by corsets that supported a full bust. Their coiffures had French twists with bright pink bows. All

Whitsett had was a straight shirt, managed braids and dirty, white gloves that made her hands itch. Even in her new dress, she felt like a servant.

These women, Whitsett thought. These ironed women who rule the universe from their salons behind their teacups that grandaunt Jean brought back from Europe before the war.

"What is this all about, sir?" the mother asked.

"Just a few questions." Geyer showed her the picture of Holmes. "Have you ever seen this man?"

"Why, yes, that is the man who rented the St. Vincent Street house from me last October. He only occupied it for a few days." She took a register she kept out of a small desk. "October 20th Holmes rented No 16 St. Vincent Street. For six months at $10 for the first month and $12 per month for the remainder."

"How long did he stay?"

"I'm not sure. I heard nothing more until nearly the end of the month when I learned that the house was empty and that the key had been left with Mr. Ryves, the neighbor."

Whitsett hated how much everyone was fussing over the daughter. No one ever fussed over her. This pale, little, blue-eyed child had everything, everything in the goddamn world. A house, a doting mother and a shelf full of books. *I'll bet she can even read at night. I hate her*, Whitsett thought. *I won't be thrown away again.*

Cass was busily studying his ledger, cross-checking all the information. He was so engrossed in his ledger that he didn't realize he was still holding the teacup off to the side. He didn't even notice the sharp smell of the peppermint.

"Can I refill your cup, Mr. Cass?" The daughter couldn't get his attention. "Mr. Cass? Mr. Cass? Can I refill your cup?"

Whitsett became furious. *Don't talk to my friend*, she thought. She pulled her gloves off and put them away.

Everyone in the room was shocked at her violation of decorum.

"My goodness," Mrs. Nudel said.

Mr. Cass leaned over. "Are you alright?" he asked.

"Miss Whitsett, would you put your gloves back on?" Geyer said.

"No."

"It's very improper, Miss Whitsett," Geyer said through his teeth. "You're being rude."

"We're here because we believe that man murdered three small children and buried them in your home. We want to find their rotting bodies," Whitsett blurted out.

The women gasped and put their gloved hands over their mouths.

Geyer stood up and pointed at the door. "Get out," he said.

"It's true," Whitsett said. She was about to say something else when she saw that goddamn little girl grin at her, delighting at her humiliation. Whitsett felt her face go hot and she sprung at the daughter. She pulled at the girl's perfect bows and blonde hair.

"You vulgar witch!" the daughter said. "You trash."

Whitsett's hands were tingly and she became dizzy. Geyer lifted her off the daughter and threw her onto the sofa. Cass picked her up and carried her outside while Geyer struggled to apologize to the frantic mother and daughter.

Cass helped Whitsett walk away from the home. He was still holding his teacup. Whitsett took one smell of the peppermint and slapped his hand, knocking the cup onto the grass. As she was straightening her clothes and collecting herself, Geyer burst out the door behind them. Whitsett was frightened and grabbed Cass's arm. Cass was frightened as well, he held up his ledger, hoping to soften the impending blow.

Geyer stopped immediately. He saw Mr. Ryves looking at them with a large smile. He didn't want to cause a larger scene. His mind turned to the trunk.

"Everything alright?" Ryves asked.

"May I borrow that shovel?" Geyer asked. They walked over to No 16 and rang the bell. Mrs. J. Armbrust answered and Mr. Ryves introduced everyone.

"Would you please show us to the cellar?" Geyer asked.

The rented house stood back a few feet from the sidewalk, the narrow plot of lawn was enclosed with a wire-net fence five feet high and beautified with blossoming flowers. The front door opened into a hallway, which divided the house in half and continued to the kitchen. The cottage contained six medium-sized rooms on the first floor and four small rooms above. It was perfect for a small family and could always fetch a reasonable price, even in a down market.

Mrs. Armbrust led the group into the kitchen with oil lamps. She lifted a large piece of oilcloth from the floor and revealed a small trap door. The door was two feet square in the center of the room. Geyer and Cass descended into the cellar, each holding a lamp as though they were performing a ritual.

It's like they're descending into hell, thought Whitsett.

The cellar was ten feet square and four feet in depth.

Whitsett wouldn't follow Cass into the cellar. She tried to force her body, but she couldn't make her legs move. Her hands were trembling and she struggled to mask her discomfort. Cass handed her his hat.

"Just hang on to this," he told her.

She could hold on to the black felt of the brim and no one would see her hands shake. She was grateful that Cass understood.

Geyer had Cass hold his lamp as he searched the cellar, hunched over, stabbing the spade into the earth as he walked. Geyer found the outline of a soft spot in the south-west corner. Cass took off his coat, grabbed the shovel from the detective, and began to dig.

Mr. Ryves and Mrs. Armbrust waited in the kitchen with Whitsett. Mr. Ryves was laughing about Whitsett beating on the neighbor's daughter; he thought it was the greatest thing he'd ever heard. He offered to marry her on the spot. His smile, however, was eroded from a sharp smell that permeated the kitchen.

As Cass dug, he heard footsteps from above. Whitsett's footsteps. She was pacing again. *Poor girl*, he thought. *She must be nervous. I wish there was something I could do for her.* Cass thought he was known for being able to read people by their footsteps. The wood creaked from the thud of the shoe. It was like the house was an instrument.

After Cass dug only one foot into the cellar dirt, a horrible stench arose. A part of a waistcoat and, what appeared to be, a piece of ribbon was folded into the dirt. Geyer took the shovel so Cass could rest and continued to dig. The deeper Geyer dug, the more horrible the odor became. It was a thick, wet stench that made their heads spin. They could feel the decay on their skin.

At three feet, they discovered a forearm bone.

"We need to call the police station immediately," Geyer said. He moved some dirt back into the hole to keep the stench down. "Where's the nearest telephone?" Geyer asked.

"A couple miles over on Yonge Street, at the telephone office," Mr. Ryves said.

A small carriage took Geyer to the telephone office. He told the operator to connect him to Inspector Stark at the Toronto Police, it was an emergency.

"I've discovered a body," Geyer said.

Inspector Stark disconnected while he figured out what to do. Geyer spent the next 40 minutes drinking the entirety of his silver flask. Finally, the operator received a call.

"Detective?" Stark asked

"Yes, I'm here."

"Go to B.D. Humphrey, an undertaker on Yonge Street."

Geyer ran to the undertaker's office and quickly told him of the situation. As the undertaker was loading his gear, Geyer called out to him.

"I suggest you take several pairs of rubber gloves."

Geyer returned to the house with Mr. Humphrey. Cass helped to dig while the undertaker carefully unearthed the remains. The bodies were in an advanced state of putrefaction.

As they dug, they wrapped their handkerchiefs around their heads. They looked like bandits from the cover of one of Mr. Cass's dime novels or pirates digging for treasure. Whitsett watched from above, running Cass's hat through her sweating fingers.

One body was found lying on her side, with her little blue hands reaching out. Another was on her face, her plaited hair hanging neatly down her pale white back. The children were buried in the nude. *What an outrage! Why are they nude?* everyone thought. They couldn't believe that this man would violate them in such a way. *Were they nude before they died? Were they violated before they died? What did Holmes do to them?*

Everyone was rocked by a forceful wave of nausea. They were captivated with wonder and disgust. The skin was wet and discolored. Bugs crawled through the decomposing flesh. They studied the black and purple colors and the jagged texture of the rotting meat. It was as though they were staring at a painting in a gallery. They hadn't just been murdered; they had been tortured, disfigured, stripped of all humanity. *What the hell is this?* Geyer thought.

Whitsett looked at the remains. She realized it could have been her, dead in a cellar somewhere. She *was* almost dead in a cellar at one time. These girls weren't spoiled brats, they were just little girls, thrown away like used paper. She felt a stabbing pain in her stomach. *I wished for the children to be alright*, she thought, *but if wishes worked, I would have used them up a long time ago.* She almost tore Cass's hat in half.

The undertaker sent a messenger to arrange for two small coffins to be sent to the house immediately. The stench of death and decomposition hung in the air like the specter of the murdered children. Whitsett remembered the screaming image of the children from the séance.

The sounds of footsteps were amplified in the cellar. Dozens of heels making a hollow click, flexing the wood so that it made a gasping sound. The tempo of the music from the floors made them work faster.

No one could stay inside very long before they ran out coughing and gagging. The wagon arrived and the coffins were brought into the kitchen. The remains were lifted out of the cellar and carefully placed in the wooden boxes. As they lifted the head of the dead girl, the weight of the plaited hair pulled the scalp from her skull.

The remains were laid out on a sheet and then hoisted into the coffins.

Once the bodies were moved into the coffins, they were immediately driven back to Mr. Humphrey's establishment. The streets outside the house were flooded with people and newspapermen. As Geyer, Cass and Whitsett exited the house, they heard applause and cheers. Even the owner and her daughter were applauding and crying, forgetting all about Miss Whitsett and her attack.

St. Vincent Street became a sea of shouting newspapermen, sketch artists and pedestrians.

District Attorney Graham was so excited. In a newspaper interview, he proclaimed, "We win! We have proven that little children cannot be murdered in this day and generation, beyond the possibility of discovery."

"Hypothetically," Whitsett said. She knew there were still thousands of children that died in the streets every week.

"Can we go home?" Cass said.

"Our work isn't complete. We need to establish their identities. The bodies are badly decomposed, and identification looks impossible." Geyer found Mrs. Armbrust in the sitting room. She was being comforted by Mrs. Nudel. "I'm so sorry all this has happened here," Geyer told her. "To both of you."

"You are very kind," she said.

"Who occupied the house after Holmes left?" Geyer asked.

"A family named MacDonald who remained a very short time, but no one was able to tell us where they had moved."

"Thank you very much," Geyer said. He took Cass and Whitsett with him privately back into the kitchen. "We need to find the MacDonalds."

"Why?" Cass said.

"We have to find the trunk."

The following day the group began to search agents again. Cass suggested they search by name, house size and price. They spent the entire day going from agent to agent to agent. Cass and Whitsett searched on one side of the street while Geyer searched the other. All the agents were very cooperative and had been following the story in the newspapers diligently. They had done the same search for so many months that it was mechanical.

Whitsett couldn't get the smell of the corpses out of her nose. She could taste it in the back of her throat.

One late afternoon, they discovered the former tenant's new address through another newspaper tip and went there directly. Mrs. MacDonald answered the door.

"Mrs. MacDonald, did you ever see the man who occupied the St. Vincent Street house before you?"

"No."

"Did he leave anything behind?"

"All I found at the house was an old bedstead and mattress," Mrs. MacDonald said. She thought for a moment. "When I was cleaning the house after moving in, I noticed some rags and straw were hanging from the chimney in the north front room. I pulled down and found a part of a striped waistcoat of a grayish color, a piece of a woolen garment of brownish red, and a part of a dress of bluish color. The straw had been lit but had not burned, the clothing had been shoved into the chimney too tightly. I found a pair of girl's button boots in the wood box; also, one odd boot and other parts of a woman's clothing."

"Did you keep any of the fragments or the boot?" Geyer asked.

"I threw it all away."

"Do you have any children, Mrs. MacDonald?"

"Yes, a boy. He's 16 years old. But he's not at home."

"Will you please send him to police headquarters as soon as he arrives home, along with anything he found in the St. Vincent Street house?"

"Of course."

"Tell him he's not in any trouble. It's for these girls," Whitest added.

"Those materials match the description of what they were wearing. But I imagine that it is a very common color and material," Cass said.

"We need to find that trunk," Geyer said.

"Mr. Ryves said that a large trunk had been brought to the house," Cass said.

They spent the rest of the evening digging up every inch of the yard. They also examined the barn and outhouses. They found nothing.

The next morning the young MacDonald appeared at the police station. His mother had made him put on his Sunday church clothes. He was nervous and took small, timid steps. Geyer took him aside and the boy produced a small children's toy. It was a little wooden egg that contained a snake, which would spring out. He said he found it when they moved into the St. Vincent Street house in a small leather case in one of the closets on the second floor.

Geyer took the toy from him. As the boy was leaving, Whitsett gave him one of her dime books and a pencil. She felt bad the boy had to give something up and wanted to reimburse him somehow. *Do your best to make it to adulthood*, she thought.

Although the toy matched a list of the children's playthings, it wasn't unique. They would need more. They would need the mother to identify the bodies.

Poor Mrs. Pitezel

Jurors were reluctantly assembled, as they always are, while Geyer spent all day at police headquarters giving testimony in the inquest of the bodies that were found. He went through the same story he had been through thousands of times, yet again. He spent hours giving dates and addresses and interview summaries. He could tell it in his sleep at this point. As he sat on the stand, his mind wandered over the trunk. Trunks are much easier to think about.

When he was finished, Geyer and Whitsett drove a carriage to meet Mrs. Pitezel at the train station. District Attorney Graham had sent her to identify the bodies.

"When I was a boy, the town wouldn't wait for the trial. They just would've hanged him," Geyer said.

"I'm glad I didn't live in your town," Whitsett said.

"He killed those children in the heart of the city and no one suspected a damn thing. That would have never happened in my day. You kept your eyes on your neighbors in my day."

"Of course you did," Whitsett said. "Bad things only started happening a few years ago, right?"

By the time they arrived, the station was already crowded with reporters and newspapermen. They surrounded the track, shouting and whistling at each other. The tip of Mrs. Pitezel's train departure had traveled by wire hours ago.

Mrs. Pitezel stepped onto the platform. She was dressed for the first stage of mourning—black dress, bombazine fabric covered with crepe; widow's cap, lawn cuffs and long collars. The reporters rushed her and began shouting questions at her. She was confused and struggled to get her balance.

Geyer and Whitsett shoved their way to the front of the platform and escorted the grieving mother through the crowd.

They were devastated by the state of her. She was thin and frail. Her eyes sunk into her skull and her face was blank and white. A strong breeze would dissolve her like ash. She was skin and bone and despair held together with a bonnet.

Geyer handled the newsmen while Whitsett checked Mrs. Pitezel in at the hotel front desk.

"Very well. Here is her room, right across from yours, ma'am."

"Aren't you going to ask about her luggage?" Whitsett asked.

"I don't understand," the clerk said.

"Don't you need to look at her luggage first to know what to charge?"

"Oh, I see," the clerk said.

"It's okay, the city is paying for our stay so I don't care what you charge her. But, just out of curiosity, why don't you want to look at her luggage?"

"I'm afraid I've become a 'shut-eye,' ma'am. That was a little joke."

"What's that?"

"An occupational hazard for psychics and other con men. It's when they become so good at their con, they actually start to believe it. When all the scores of little things about a person add up in your head without thinking and you just do it by instinct."

"What does that have to do with her luggage?"

"Well, I don't need to see her luggage, ma'am. I already know what it looks like. And I know what to charge."

Geyer and Cass took Mrs. Pitezel up to her room. Whitsett slowly followed.

"How'd they know I was going to be there?" Mrs. Pitezel asked.

"The reporters from Philadelphia wired ahead," Geyer said.

Geyer and Cass both kneeled in front of her on one knee. They were so attentive and tender to the poor grieving mother. That's not fair, Whitsett thought. When I was suffering, all I got was a belt across the legs and a night in the cold cellar. Why does she get such special treatment? It was a woman like her that gave me up and put me in that cellar. Her crying is probably just a con, she thought. It's just a damn con. It's not fair. Everything is a con.

"Thank you," Mrs. Pitezel said with a broken voice. "Mr. Geyer, is it true you found Alice and Nellie buried in a cellar?"

"I found the children."

She began to cry uncontrollably.

She cried all night. Nobody could sleep in the hotel; they were kept awake by the muted wails and moans. She was like a restless haunting spirit.

Whitsett stared at the ceiling trying to ignore the horrible sounds. After a few hours, she became so enraged, she jumped up and ran into Mrs. Pitezel's room. She burst through the door in her sleeping gown and Mrs. Pitezel let out a shriek.

"Stop your blubbering, woman! No one's buying your con."

Mrs. Pitezel was sobbing too loud to hear anything.

"You aren't the only person who's suffered. If you don't stop your wailing, they'll put you in an asylum and then you'll find out what real suffering is."

Mrs. Pitezel looked up helplessly, as though they didn't share a common language. The candle Whitsett carried flickered as it struggled to stay lit with her wild movements.

"He murdered them! He murdered my babies! Why? Why'd he do it? He was like their uncle."

"You let them go!" Whitsett yelled. "Why'd you let them go? Why didn't you go after them? You left them chained in the cellar!"

Geyer came into the room. His eyes were blurry in the candlelight. Whitsett quickly blew out her candle so Geyer wouldn't see her cry.

"What's going on here?" The foot with the abscess had swelled to almost double the size of the other one and it reeked like garbage.

"Just trying to help her get some sleep," Whitsett said. Her eyes burned in the dark.

The next morning, newspapermen were waiting in the lobby. The investigators fought their way past them to a carriage on their way to the morgue. Mrs. Pitezel had to almost be carried up the steps of the red brick building. They brought her to a small room down the hall.

"Now, Mrs. Pitezel, I want you to prepare yourself. You'll only be able to see Alice's teeth and hair. And only Nellie's hair," Geyer said.

Mrs. Pitezel became overwhelmed with powerful, swelling nausea and had trouble breathing. Cass poured her a glass of brandy from a table the mortician had prepared for her. Her throat was sore from crying and the brandy burned on the way down. After the brandy, Cass used smelling salts to wake her back up so she could stand.

The thought of seeing her two daughters on the slab turned her own body against her. She couldn't breathe or see. She wanted to be sick but couldn't get awake enough.

With Cass on one side and Geyer on the other, they led her into the room as though they were dragging her to the gallows. Her shoes squeaked and made black marks on the floor as she kicked and thrashed her feet. Her arms became numb from where the men were holding her. The clicking of their footsteps echoed off the metal surfaces as they led her up to the slab.

The skin had been removed from Alice's skull and the teeth were cleaned. The bodies were covered with a tan canvas. A piece of paper was used to cover Alice's face and a hole was cut out so the teeth could be seen.

Alice's and Nellie's hair had been washed and displayed on the canvas on top of Alice. There was hardly anything to examine, just some teeth and hair.

"That's Alice," she said. "Where's Nellie?" Then she noticed the long black plait of hair lying on the canvas. She wailed and let out a scream that sounded like a wolf.

Cass tried to use the smelling salts but she thrashed and fought. They removed her as quickly as they could. They forced her to drink brandy, but the shrieking and crying made her spit most of it out.

Miss Whitsett was seated in the corner watching the men force brandy into Mrs. Pitezel. It reminded Whitsett of the belt and water treatments she received to make her behave. She remembered hoping someone would come to help her.

She dropped her papers and rushed to Mrs. Pitezel. She pushed the men away from the mother with violent thrusts and elbows. She hugged Mrs. Pitezel and pressed her head into her shoulder, where the tears soaked through to the skin. She didn't know if it was better than force-fed brandy, but it wasn't worse. She hated helping Mrs. Pitezel, but at least she wouldn't lie awake every night from not having done it.

The little girls were buried in the St. James' cemetery. Toronto picked up the bill. A woman from the Christian Endeavor Society took Mrs. Pitezel back to Chicago.

Case closed.

Cigar

Geyer was packing his bag to return home when he received a telegram, ordering him to return to Detroit and find the third missing child, Howard. There was even greater interest in finding the boy now that the two girls had been discovered.

Geyer appealed to the district attorney. They had found the girls and had the evidence to charge Holmes. There would be no need to spend further resources trying to find the boy. The decay of the bodies had been so great, that no real identification could be established; the same was probably true for the boy. The bodies may not even be those of the Pitezel children.

The district attorney wouldn't hear of it.

Whitsett sat up in her bed staring at one of her dime novel covers. She had been reading the same page for over an hour, but none of it would stick. She kept hearing the squeaking of heels against the morgue floor.

Whitsett reread the letters from the children. She reviewed the series of events.

Holmes didn't buy warm clothes for them because they would soon be dead. That's why they complained of being cold and miserable in their letters.

"Howard is not with us now," Alice wrote in a letter to her grandparents on October 14th.

The separation from Howard had taken place prior to the arrival of Alice and Nellie in Detroit. Howard was never in Detroit. Or he was in another hotel away from the girls. If the boy had been murdered there, his body had been disposed of. *Why does Holmes rent houses with large furnaces?*

Whitsett was getting a headache trying to keep track of Holmes. She imagined the frightened little children trapped under Holmes's boot. *They must have been so afraid*, she thought. *At least I made it out. They never got a chance.*

There was a gentle knock on her door. She was only wearing a sheer slip. She stood up and grabbed the pillow to cover herself. She opened the door a crack and saw Cass.

"What are you doing here?" she whispered.

Cass pulled out a cigar. She smiled and let him in.

"Close your eyes," she said. Then she ran into bed and pulled the sheets over her, being sure to keep her scarred wrists hidden under the covers. "Okay."

Cass opened his eyes.

"Don't look at me," she said with a smile. "Light the cigar."

Cass lit the cigar and handed it to her. She took a long puff and felt dizzy. She coughed and snorted as Cass laughed. The tobacco masked the taste of decay in her throat.

"How did you talk your way up here?" Whitsett asked.

"I didn't. I snuck in. With all the newsmen downstairs, the staff was too distracted to stop me."

"Where'd you get the cigar?"

"I stole it from Geyer."

She laughed. "Here's your hat back," She said, pointing to the end of the bed. The hat's brim was bent and distorted from her gripping and squeezing it. Cass put the hat on and looked like a clown. She tried to hide her giggling.

"Why do you hate Mrs. Pitezel?"

"I don't hate anybody," she said. "Don't look at me. When did you open your eyes?"

"I don't know." Cass had never seen a young woman in bed before. He couldn't stop staring. Her hair was unbraided and the thick frizzy locks looked like a wild shrub. Whitsett watched Cass stare at her with his funny hat.

"Are you just going to stand there?" she asked. Cass was so stiff he almost creaked like a wooden plank.

"I don't know."

"Say something."

"You have amazing penmanship."

"Sit down," she said, pointing to the wooden chair next to the bed. Whitsett hugged herself under the covers while Cass stood over her. "Take off that stupid hat," she said giggling. "I thought this insurance investigation was going to be fun. Instead it became not fun."

Cass leaned over and Whitsett let him kiss her. He was so ignorant and odd. But he meant well and had always been kind to her. 'We are investigators,' he would say. But we're not investigators and we are not detectives. We are resurrectionists. We travel around digging up the dead.

He sat on the blanket which made the covers wrap tightly around her chest. She tried not to think about Mrs. Jacobs and her cousin's son, who she was supposed to marry. She would deal with that mess later. It was more difficult for her to breathe, but she latched on to Cass's neck and hugged him.

They didn't smoke the cigar. They just watched it burn together.

Chicago

Late in the evening, Geyer received another telegram from District Attorney Graham, ordering him to go to Chicago. The police authorities had dug up the skeleton of a child at Holmes's block No. 701 West 63rd Street, Chicago. Howard may have been buried in Chicago all along.

The searchers took the first train to Chicago. They arrived midday in the heat of the day. After an exhausting trip, Whitsett wanted to get out of the crowd and stretch. Everyone was hot and hungry and fed up.

"Where are we going?" Whitsett asked.

"The platform," Geyer said.

"Why?"

"Will you stop asking 'why' all the time! Why do you constantly ask why?"

"I like knowing things."

"Well, stop it!"

"Why are you in such a bad mood?" Whitsett asked.

"All this travel and we don't have anything to show for it. We don't have a trunk and we certainly don't have the children."

"What are you talking about? We just found the girls!"

"No! He's alive. I won't hear any more talk of them being dead. Love, hate or money," Geyer said, taking a sip from his silver flask.

"I think Holmes killed Julia," Whitsett said.

"Who the hell is Julia?"

"The skeleton. The six-foot-tall woman."

"There are no women six feet tall." Geyer stood up and stepped onto the arrival platform. A train had just pulled up behind them.

As the cars opened, a flood of humanity poured onto the platform like a jar of spilled ink. They were fresh-faced young men and women. Most of them straight off the farm. Young boys with satchels and dirty faces, young girls with bright, clear eyes. They were all stepping off the train into what they thought would be a new life in the new, modern city. Children seeking adventure. It would be easy to approach one of them and offer them a job and a place to stay. You could have your pick of naive country girls and enthusiastic farm boys.

Young men and women with no local prospects surrounded the detective. Whitsett watched the young girls and boys try and talk to Geyer, begging for a job and a place to live. Whitsett had almost moved to Chicago for the world's fair. She could have been one of these girls begging to be taken, standing the line all over again. *Over 100 trains stop here every day.*

She could have left her small town hoping to find something new in the big city. The lure of the glamorous exposition and money and lights. The exposition was made from wooden marble and burned down. She shivered at the thought that she could have stepped off the train and into the clutches of monsters. This city wasn't a beacon of opportunity and prosperity; it was a killing ground.

"This would have never happened in my day. Everyone in the community knew each other."

"Everyone here knew Holmes," Whitsett said.

"But we wouldn't let a man come to the train station and pick up young women for his own perversion," Geyer said. "How many of these women will be forced to do God knows what? That didn't happen in my day. Nowadays, how do you stop it?"

"You're so full of shit," Whitsett said.

"Language!" Geyer said.

"While you get our papers, I'll go and follow up on a lead I had at the labor union," Cass said.

"Very good, just don't take too long. Meet me back here in an hour," Geyer said.

"Miss Whitsett," Cass said. "Are you coming with me?"

"No," Whitsett said. She had been distant towards Cass ever since they smoked the cigar together. She felt guilty about Cass because of Mrs. Jacobs's cousin's son. She shouldn't have let Cass into her room.

"But I'm going to the bookstore. Doesn't that sound neat?"

That does sound neat, she thought. Whitsett was very tempted with the prospect of a bookstore. She was confused about Cass and wasn't sure how to feel. The thought of possible happiness seemed distant and made her sad.

"Fine. You go with the detective; I won't bother you anymore," Cass said as he walked into the street to get a coach. His stomach swelled and his cheeks became hot.

Geyer went to the police headquarters to go through the usual preliminaries and introductions.

"I don't envy your position, Geyer. How long have you been searching for the children?"

"Months," Geyer said. He looked exhausted and his back was throbbing.

"Well, good luck. I'm praying for you."

"Thank you."

"Oh, and when you wired me the message you were coming, I had one of my men see if there was anything about this Holmes for you to go on. He was a very busy boy. Apparently, he was selling stock in a company that could make cheap gas from tap water. All he had to do was add a special chemical of his own design to tap water and he created gas.

"The gas company took one of my men over there to investigate and Holmes showed him the special machine in his cellar, installed into the wall. He poured water into the top, added his chemical and was able to burn a lamp. But when they did some looking, they found that the machine was just illegally tapped into the city's gas supply."

The two men snorted in mild amusement.

"Good con. What did the gas company do?" Geyer asked.

"They just took the machine away and fined him. It left a big hole in his cellar wall, exposing the water and gas pipes. I doubt he paid the fine. But what he did do, was use those exposed water lines to start selling a medicinal water elixir; Linden Grove Mineral Water. People were buying this water like it was whiskey, hoping to cure their bodies. It was just tap water. He has quite the reputation now as a hustler."

"He certainly is somethin'," Geyer said. He couldn't put his finger on it, but Holmes turned his stomach the wrong way. *There's no way he killed those kids*, he thought. "What about those bones they found?" Geyer asked.

"They only found one bone, in one of the rooms on the second floor of that castle."

"I want to see it," Geyer said.

The Castle

The investigators took the cable car to Englewood Station. They couldn't call a coach because an outbreak of strangles meant most horses in the city had to be quarantined. As a result, the cable cars were running full and slow.

Directly across the street from the station was a large imposing building. It was like a dark cresting wave over the curb. The people in the neighborhood had nicknamed the building 'the castle.' It appeared to have turrets and ramparts. It took up the entire block and was three stories tall. The dark brick stood out against the white paint of the surrounding buildings.

The crowds moved down the street like a swollen river. Lines upon lines of wires ran from poles staked from corner to corner.

"Well, that's obviously the castle," Cass said.

The ground floor was filled with shops. Stamped to the window was a notice left by the city explaining the building's owner's inability to pay contractors.

Geyer approached a collection of uniformed police officers. They were surrounding a set of building plans and drawings. A stocky man in a brown suit was pointing at parts of the plans as he was talking. He was Mr. Glenister, Secretary of the Bricklayers, from Union Street above 28th Street.

"If you knock that down, according to the plans here, the whole thing might come down. But, these plans are nonsense. Who knows how the actual construction is laid out? Probably more nonsense," Mr. Glenister said.

The police had asked Mr. Glenister to consult with them on getting into the building. A bone had been found in the upper floors and the police were anxious to search the entire building, especially since the story broke of the Pitezel children that were discovered buried in a cellar.

When the police entered to search the building, they discovered that the only door to the cellar was locked and heavily barricaded. The door was immovable. They contacted Mr. Glenister, a competent builder, to help them find a safe entrance. He spent an hour explaining that the construction was so poor that any demolition might cause the building to fall in on itself, destroying any evidence.

"I'm told a Mr. Hatch said there is nothing in the cellar," a police officer said.

"Is that right? Who told you about this Hatch person?"

"A man named H.H. Holmes."

"No wonder!" he said, laughing. "If Holmes told you, it's a lie."

"I take it you don't have a high opinion of Mr. Holmes?" Geyer asked.

"That man is a cheat, a liar and a fraud. Have you seen that monstrosity?" Mr. Glenister pointed to the castle across the street. "It looks like a terrible nightmare. He would hire my workers, then when the job was half-finished, he would fire them and refuse to pay for doing shoddy work. Then he would hire more of my guys to finish the work, then he would fire them and refuse to pay. He would never let any of the foremen see the plans or designs. Apparently, he designed it himself. Finally, I had to stop my people from working for him because he would pull that same nonsense."

"What do you think he was doing?"

"I don't know. These wasn't amateurs I was sending over. These was experienced craftsmen. This one guy told me he was supposed to finish a wall. He went in and saw a wall was half-built. He finished it up and was told to leave room for something four feet by four feet by four feet. He wasn't told what it was or where to stop the wall. Then one day, Holmes comes in, fires him and doesn't pay."

"Peculiar."

"It's ugly. And from what my guys tell me, its construction was a mess. You got walls that drop off, rooms that are bricked up, stairs that lead to bricked-up walls. If you start kicking doors down, the entire building might cave in. It's a nightmare, he's never gonna be able to sell it."

"Was he trying to sell it?"

"He was before he set fire to it."

"He tried to burn it down?"

"Yes, the boys at the fire union told me about it. He just set fire to the top floor. They said he tried to light the floor from both sides at once. Easy to spot. Especially once they learned about his reputation in this city. You go around and you mention the name Holmes and see what kind of response you get. He didn't get any money. Now he just has a half-burnt, shoddy building no one wants."

"He was trying to commit insurance fraud," Cass said.

"You got it, buddy. Everyone's after him. A group of creditors said they were owed $50,000. He somehow talked his way out of it though."

"That's a fortune! I could live the rest of my life on that. What was he doing with that money?"

"If I were you, I would find a locksmith," Mr. Glenister said.

"We did. The lock isn't the problem. It appears to be walled up from the inside. Like it has been hammered shut," an officer said.

"Well, none of my guys had anything to do with that." Mr. Glenister began to roll up the plans and put them away.

"What do we do?" Whitsett asked.

"I want to see this door," Geyer said as he took a drink from his silver flask. "Let me go ask the officer on the scene what they're doing." Geyer began asking police to point him in the direction of the ranking officer.

Crowds of newsmen and pedestrians were gathered around the giant building on 63rd Street. To Miss Whitsett, it looked like they were storming the castle, just like they did in dime novels. Whitsett wandered past the police officers to the front entrance.

She was stopped by a man in a suit guarding the front door.

"May I help you, ma'am?" he asked.

"I just wanted to look around?" she said.

"I'm afraid not. I'm not allowed to let anyone in. Run along."

"Oh, I'm an investigator for Fidelity Mutual."

"Sure you are," he said.

"No, really, I have papers." She began to dig through them when the man yelled at her.

"I don't care what you think you have, beat it!"

"Who the hell are you? You're not a cop."

"I'm a Pinkerton, lady. I'm better than a cop."

"Better at what? Being a snotty little twat?"

The Pinkerton grabbed Whitsett by the arm. Cass rushed the man and grabbed him by the shoulder. The Pinkerton took hold of Cass's collar and punched him in the face. Cass tumbled backward like a felled tree.

Whitsett began to kick and swing her bag at the Pinkerton. He grabbed the bag and threw it on the ground. Then Whitsett felt a gust of wind over her shoulder. She blinked and saw Geyer had run past her and proceeded to beat the hell out of the Pinkerton. The detective was using both fists and leaving the other man a bloody mess.

Whitsett tried to step in between Geyer and the Pinkerton and push the screaming detective back. She pushed forward, wrinkling and twisting her gloves into his large chest. Geyer shoved her aside, grabbed the Pinkerton by the collar and pushed him against the wall. The Pinkerton grabbed Geyer's coat and pushed back. They were choking each other. Geyer wound back to punch him on the side of the head, but the Pinkerton got his feet under him and forced Geyer to stumble back.

A handful of cops approached the fight and held back Geyer.

"I'll have you for this," Geyer said as the cops pushed him back across the street. The Pinkerton was forced to the other side of the street.

Another cop helped Miss Whitsett up from the ground.

"That Pinkerton is lucky I didn't get a swing in," Whitsett said as she straightened her gloves. The cop laughed and picked up her bag of writing supplies and handed it to her.

"Yes, ma'am."

"Will you please help my knight in shining armor to his feet?" Whitsett asked. The officer helped Cass stand.

"I'm fine, I just tripped. I just tripped," Cass said, grabbing his shoulder.

"No shame there, laddy. Just bend the knees and you won't trip next time."

The ranking officer was trying to calm Geyer down. He lit a cigarette and gave him a drink from his own flask.

"Thanks, Johnny," Geyer said.

"No problem, Frank. What was all that about?"

"Nothin'. Did you have a doctor look at the boy's bones yet?"

"Yes, too young to be the one you're lookin' for."

"I knew it. I knew that they couldn't be his. He's still alive."

"Not from what I read in the papers."

"He's alive!" Geyer screamed forcefully. "What's going on in the building: the castle?"

"We busted in and began searching the building when we discovered you found the little girls. We found some bones in the cellar, but the doctor doesn't know if it's a boy or girl bone. Or even if it's a human bone. We got 12 officers searching now."

"Probably just some animal bones," Geyer said. "What about the janitor. Mr. Quinlan?"

"At the station. They'll be done with him in a few hours. When they're ready, I'll take you there."

"Did he say anything?"

"Not really, just that Holmes is a mad man and tried to kill him. He says the hotel is a maze and he was never allowed in the cellar. He told us to stay out of the cellar."

"Thanks, Johnny."

"And listen, I was very sorry to hear about your wife and daughter."

Geyer flew into a rage. His face reddened and he began to spit.

"Yes! They're dead! They're fucking dead! Everywhere I go, people want to talk about the fire and my dead daughter and my dead wife and the dead Pitezel children. Just don't say anything. Can't you think of anything else to say? The next person that mentions the fire I'm going to put on the goddamn floor."

"Okay, Frank. Okay." Johnny walked backward so Geyer wouldn't jump him from behind.

Geyer sat on some steps, trying to stretch out his back. The pain was traveling down his back to his legs. *The trunk, think about the trunk*, he thought.

"Do you need a glass of preparation for your back?" Whitsett asked.

"No!"

"Easy!" Whitsett said. "What's wrong with you?"

"Nothing, dammit."

"Stop it!"

"Do we just wait?" Cass asked.

"No. The first floor of this building houses businesses. The largest business is called *The Holmes Drugstore*. We go ask them to open the cellar for us," Geyer said.

The Holmes Drugstore

The investigators entered the drugstore and took aside the man who was running the counter—Dr. Robinson. They asked if he knew how to get into the cellar. Dr. Robinson had never been allowed in the upstairs part of the castle and knew nothing of the cellar. He told them to talk to the owners of the drugstore across the street if they wanted any real information on Holmes.

"That Holmes is a no-good swindler son of a bitch. Pardon my language, ma'am," Mr. Jones said. His drugstore across the street was smaller and a bit more run down. "When we were looking to buy this place, that Holmes told us how much money he made from it and how busy it was. He paid people to be in the store when we came around so it would appear busy. Can you believe that?"

"He did the same thing in Fort Worth," Cass said.

"Then, I ask, why are you selling such a successful enterprise? He tells me it is too successful of a store. He can't manage it all on his own. He wants to branch out into other ventures. We'll have the entire neighborhood to ourselves, he says. Then after we buy it, he opened a larger, fancier drugstore across the street in his damned castle. Columns, frescoed stucco, marbled countertops, soda fountains, made this place look like a pigsty. We paid for him to build a better store and now I have to go through a bankruptcy."

"Where did he get this drugstore from? The one he sold to you?"

"I looked into that. Come with me." Jones took the investigators to the apartment building next door and introduced them to an elderly lady who knew everyone in the neighborhood.

"The first time I met Holmes was when he first got a job at the drugstore. Then it was called the *Holton Drugstore* and the castle didn't exist. Dapper young man. Very handsome. Mrs. Holton told me he was a great worker and could handle all the responsibilities. Which was good for her because her husband was dying of prostate cancer and he needed a lot of attention."

"Did you ever speak with him?"

"Nothing more than idle conversation. He was very polite and charming. Then the old man died, and Holmes asked to buy the store from her. Her only condition was that she would remain in the apartment above the drugstore. She had no family and this neighborhood was her only home. She had nowhere else to go. They struck the deal and the sign was changed from *Holton Drugstore* to *Holmes Drugstore*."

"Except he never paid, right?" Whitsett asked.

"That's right. Never paid her one dime. They would fight and fight. Then, she comes to me and asks for a recommendation for a good lawyer to file papers on him. I told her and she filed the papers. Then she was never seen or heard from again. Soon after that, that man moved into the apartment above the drugstore. Holmes said she moved away to be with family, but everyone knew she didn't have no family. Just the drugstore."

"And you think Holmes had something to do with it."

"What else could have happened? She would file papers and then leave? I don't think Holmes would have paid all that money in one day. Where would she go? She had no family. But Holmes was very popular around here, especially with the ladies. Then he got himself a wife and broke some hearts. His wife worked there in the drugstore as a clerk for a while, but there was some tension. Holmes was very polite with his lady customers and that caused some embarrassing scenes. When she got pregnant, she moved to Wilmette to be with her parents."

"That would be the second wife," Cass said. "Myrtle."

"Yes, Myrtle. If you want a real sad story, go see Ned Conner. He used to work for Holmes at the jewelry store in the castle. He would probably know how to get in. I'm sure he has a key."

They walked a block from the castle to find Ned Conner polishing display cases inside a small jewelry store. Geyer introduced himself and showed him his credentials.

"Have you ever been in the cellar of the castle?" Geyer asked.

"No. I don't think I would want to."

"Do you know how to get in? Do you know of a key or someone who has a key?"

"No. He keeps it locked. I've never even spoken to any one of his associates that has."

"How did you come to know Holmes?"

"We came to Chicago, my wife and I, because we couldn't find success anywhere else. Then I saw me the ad in the newspaper for a manager in a jewelry store. Twelve dollars plus room and board on the third floor.

"Holmes and Julia began to speak with each other and laugh. I should of seen it coming. That Holmes fiend tried the same thing with my sister, Gertie. He approached my sister and offered to divorce his wife for her and move east. She came back home after that. My sister was too smart for that bastard.

"Julia left me for him and got a job as the cashier in the drugstore. Julia wasn't a kept woman. She always wanted to be in the middle of it. Last time I talked to her she said she was going to learn accounting and manage Holmes's empire of businesses. She was always ambitious."

"What about Holmes?"

"I knew his business dealings were not all they appeared to be. I wasn't permitted to see the books, but it was obvious there was something going on."

"Why'd you stay on?"

"He paid me every week. And we needed the money, for Pearl, our daughter. Julia knew it too. She thought it was all so exciting. She liked the idea of money. Then she became pregnant and demanded marriage from Holmes and to be actively involved in the business affairs. She told me he agreed."

"What happened?"

"I never heard from my wife or daughter again. Every day I hope to get a letter from them saying they are okay. But…"

"People seem to keep disappearing around Holmes," Whitsett said.

"They're not dead!" Ned said, slamming his hand down. "They're alive!"

Whitsett leaned over to pick up her pencil.

"Why do you think he was interested in her?" Cass asked, hoping to change the subject.

"She was very attractive and lovely."

"Have you been following the story in the paper?"

"Oh yes. And that stuff ain't even the scary part. I know a machinist who can tell you some really scary shit about things Holmes does with dead bodies. He knows all about the cellar, he can get you in there. It's disgusting. But please don't mention my name. I don't want these people knowing I told you this."

Ned gave them the address to find Mr. Chappel, the machinist. Geyer and Cass filed out of the store.

"Miss?" he asked Whitsett as she was leaving. "If you happen to see them, my wife and child, will you send me word?"

"Of course. What do they look like?" Whitsett asked.

"Pearl was a brown-haired little girl with a button nose. And Julia will be hard to miss. She's six feet tall."

The Machinist

Cass followed Whitsett to the construction site where they were told she could find Mr. Chappel. She was haunted by Ned Conner's description of his wife. Could that six-foot-tall woman be the same skeleton they had seen in the med school office?

"What can I do for ya?" Mr. Chappel asked. He was a balding man with a pointed nose.

"Holmes. I was told you had some interesting stories about him. We want into the cellar."

"He's still in jail, right?"

"Yes."

"Thank God. He hires me when I responds to his ad in the paper for work on his crazy building. We gets to talkin' one day and I tells him I can articulate skeletons for medical purposes. He gives me some work that way a few weeks later."

"What is that?" Whitsett asked.

"It's where you strip everything off the bone of a dead body and put the skeleton back together for medical schools. You sees them in all the classrooms."

"That's a job?" Cass asked.

"We saw one of those, didn't we?" Whitsett said. "How do you do that?"

"There's a few different ways. You takes the bones and drill a small eye hook for the arms and legs. The hands and ribs and such, I use glue. Glue is cheaper."

"How do you get the bones clean?" she asked.

"Usually you lets the body decay for a while and then just strip the meat right off. After a few weeks, it slips off like a boiled potato skin, but the smell is unbearable. Fortunately, Holmes had a large vat that kept acid, so he could just dissolve the meat there. Alls I had to do was articulate the bones, he took care of the acid."

"He had a large vat of acid?" Cass asked. "Where?"

"Down in that cellar."

"You went into the cellar? What's down there?"

"There was a lot more rooms but I wasn't allowed in them. It was just a small room with that large vat. And the table with the bodies."

"Bodies? He had bodies?"

"In a manner. They were always cut open. The faces were always cut away."

"He cut away faces?" Whitsett was intrigued. "What was he doing down there?"

"You didn't find it odd that he had a corpse and a large vat of acid in his cellar?" Cass asked.

"At first I thought he was performing a postmortem on a patient. Doctors and surgeons have these kinds of things in basements all over the country. I didn't notice until later that they were all young women. One of them was a very fit woman. Six feet tall she was. Her bones were very healthy. I asked how she could have died so young, but Holmes never gave me a straight answer."

"A six-foot-tall woman," Whitsett said. "You made the six-foot-tall skeleton?" Her heart broke for poor Ned Conners. The man had been hoping and praying for his wife to return, and her skeleton was hanging in an office in the St. Louis Medical School.

"Correct. He paid me $36 for articulating the skeleton. And I think they sell for around $170."

"That's a fortune," Cass said. "How are you not living the high life?"

"I only did a few of them before I skipped town. I've only come back because Holmes is in jail. He's mad."

"Why was the cellar locked?"

"Trust me. You'd rather be locked out than in," the machinist said. "Once, while I was bleaching the bones he begins to tell me about these insurance swindles he pulled and he would get angry for no reason and he would throw things. He was half-cracked at best. He's a ghoul. I began to suspect he would do things with the bodies."

"Do things? What kind of things?" Whitsett asked.

"I don't know. It all seemed a bit unnatural to me."

"Do you have a key for the cellar?"

"No. I'd suspect Holmes is the only one with the key."

"Do you know how to get in?"

"Not in the slightest. But, I could help you save a lot of trouble. If you want to know where he sent the children, I can tell you. He would always have me run errands and send letters to the Chicago Children's Asylum. It's an orphanage down the road a piece. He was always picking things up and dropping things off there. I would bet my hat that is where they is."

Geyer leaned his head back and thought. He had considered Holmes sending the children to an orphanage as a simple solution. He was resolved to follow up on that lead. He tipped his hat and exited the construction site.

"Do the dead bodies scare you?" she asked. The machinist was charmed by her morbid curiosity.

"No. I'm used to it."

"Where do you think you go when you die?"

"Hopefully, you don't go to Holmes's cellar."

Standing on the Line

After packing themselves back into the crowded train, they followed directions to the Children's Asylum.

"That would be fortunate if they were in the orphanage," Cass said hopefully. "We could return the children to the mother and be done with this entire thing."

"I would rather be dead than at the orphanage," Whitsett said.

Cass was shocked at the venom in Whitsett's voice.

The carriage stopped in front of a two-story red-brick building. A sign hung on the door, 'Chicago Children's Asylum.'

Cass knocked on the door and a tiny nun answered.

"May I help you?"

"We're investigators in the Pitezel case, we were wondering if we could ask you some questions?" Geyer asked.

They were invited inside. Halfway down the hall, Cass noticed Miss Whitsett frozen at the door's threshold. He excused himself and returned to Whitsett.

"Are you alright?"

"I'm fine."

"Do you want to wait outside?"

"I'm fine! I don't need to wait outside. I'm not afraid of them."

Whitsett pushed Cass out of the way and entered the dark hall. She took a deep breath and smelled the familiar smell of bleach and coal. She knew it well.

They were brought to the mother superior's office, Sister Catherine. She was short and built like a bulldog. She had a big smile with rows and rows of crooked teeth.

"Yes, we read about those poor children in the papers," Sister Catherine said. "The poor children, we pray for them every day."

"Don't you have enough children to worry about?" Whitsett said.

"I beg your pardon?" Sister Catherine asked.

"With all these children you should be looking after, why are you praying for the Pitezel children?"

"I pray for all children. My mission is to help all children."

"How fortunate for them," Whitsett said.

"I must say, Sister Catherine, I'm impressed how clean your building is. The floor is spotless," Cass said, trying to change the subject. The room was sparse, with only a small wooden table and a secretary desk from 1797. Geyer was very relieved to be able to sit and take the weight off his back and foot. The pain was beginning to make him dizzy.

"Thank you, Mr. Cass. We try and keep a good home for the children."

"Tell him how the floors stay that clean, sister."

The sister's pleasant face melted as she glared at Miss Whitsett. Even though they had never met, they instantly knew everything about each other.

"Sister Catherine, as you have read, we're searching for these children," Geyer said. "We believe they may have been committed to an orphanage asylum or indentured to a farm or business."

"I see. I would be surprised if they could've been indentured. That isn't very common anymore. Not for children. That type of thing is only between families now, seldom with children."

"Have you received any children in the past year that look like these?" He showed her a photo of the children.

"We've had hundreds of children pass through these doors that look like that. They all begin to blur together; I see thousands of children through the course of a year."

"Would you be willin' to bring all the eight-year-old boys and ten- to fourteen-year-old girls into a room so we can take a look at them?"

"Of course," Sister Catherine said hesitantly. "But before we do, may I see your credentials?"

Geyer was shocked. It seemed odd that this nun would be so aggressive in her desire to keep the detective from inspecting the children. It was almost suspicious. "And if we didn't have any papers?" Geyer asked.

"Then I'm afraid I can't let you look at the children."

"Bullshit," Whitsett said.

"Mind your tongue!" Sister Catherine said.

"Or what?"

Geyer produced his credentials from the police chief and superintendent and unfolded them on her desk. She spent 20 minutes looking over it with her reading spectacles. The scrutiny she gave the paperwork made Whitsett want to slap her.

"Look how clean everything is," Cass whispered.

"That's because they make the children clean, every day, all day," Whitsett whispered back. "Quit stalling!" she yelled at the sister.

"I'm afraid not, we have a duty as guardians of these children, we can't just roll them out for anyone who comes in," she said. "Perhaps if you gave me the pictures, I could look for you."

"That wouldn't be very thorough on our part. As you just said, they all blur together for you," Geyer said.

"I can't let you see the children without proper credentials."

"What did I just show you?" Geyer demanded.

"I'm afraid this isn't enough. You don't have the proper authority."

"That's such a lie and you know it. Any idiot off the street says he wants a kid and you'll have them stand the line for him," Whitsett said.

"I'll not sit here and be called a liar." Sister Catherine stood up. "You will not see my children without the proper credentials."

Geyer stood up. "If you don't show me the children, I will go and see them myself."

"You would lay hands on a humble servant of Jesus?" Sister Catherine said forcefully, blocking his way. She had called Geyer's bluff. He couldn't lay hands on a woman.

"No. But I'll come back with the superintendent and we won't just be looking for children."

Sister Catherine lifted her head and removed her spectacles. The good sister knew she had to allow Geyer to inspect the children or he would invite more scrutiny of her institution. And she knew God wouldn't want that.

"Okay, then," she finally said.

"Thank you, sister," Geyer said. "Mr. Cass?"

"Did any children enter your care between September and November of 1893?" Cass asked.

"I can't be certain."

"Perhaps if you consulted your records."

"We don't keep records," Sister Catherine said. Cass almost fainted. "We don't have the resources to have bookkeeping of any kind. All of our effort goes to the children."

"Please bring all the eight-year-old boys and ten- to fourteen-year-old-girls into a room so we can look at them," Geyer said.

As they arranged the children, Sister Catherine gave her guests tea. Whitsett refused to drink. It took almost an hour for the children to be arranged. Whitsett knew the nuns were stalling.

After the children were ready, the sister escorted them to the cafeteria. It was a long narrow room with multiple benches and only one barred window.

"The boys are on the left side and the girls are on the right. Women are always right," Sister Catherine said.

Two rows of small silent children stood on either side of the door. They looked like a barn of staring owls, turning their heads and blinking their little eyes.

"Is anyone here named Howard, Nellie or Alice Pitezel?" Geyer bellowed.

There was no answer.

Whitsett could hardly stand still. She was staring at a line painted on the floor. A thick white line that had been almost worn away by the trampling of dirty little feet. It made her insides wring out.

"We aren't here to take one of you," she yelled out. "We aren't here to adopt. We're not here to make you stand on the line."

"You aren't in trouble. We just need to know if you are here?" Geyer added, unaware of Whitsett's distress.

Each child wore a similar set of grey and brown clothing that looked like potato sacks and they all had similar short haircuts. As the nun had said, indeed, they all looked the same. Geyer and Cass held up photos. But every other child looked like the missing Pitezel children.

"Boys with blonde and red hair may be excused. Girls with red hair may be excused," Geyer said.

Whitsett looked at each one of the clean children and was disgusted. She knew the nuns had spent the last hour preparing them for an inspection. They would have threatened the children to behave and violently scrubbed their frail bodies. Whitsett couldn't take their little eyes looking at her. She fled the cafeteria. *Those poor things with their little eyes.*

When Geyer was satisfied the Pitezel children weren't among those present, he joined Whitsett in the hall.

"As you can see, I don't think your children are here," Sister Catherine said.

"Perhaps Mr. Holmes committed them to a different institution," Cass said.

"No, this is the closest one to his hotels. Holmes likes things to be convenient. And this is the only one in this part of the city. You're sure those were all the children?" Geyer asked.

"Oh, yes, everyone within your criteria," Sister Catherine said, leading them to the front door.

"What about the naughties in the cellar?" Miss Whitsett asked.

The sister stood in hot silence, her eyes darting back and forth. "What do you mean?" Sister Catherine flinched.

"You know what that means. There are always a few children in the cellar. A punishment for the naughties. Or did you clear all them out this morning just for us?"

"I don't know what you're talking about. We don't punish our children. We are their guardians."

"Oh really?"

Whitsett stormed back into the cafeteria. The nuns were barking at the children, trying to round them back up. Whitsett grabbed one of the girls and pushed up her sleeve. There were bruises all over her arm.

"Let go of that child," Sister Catherine yelled.

Whitsett grabbed another little girl and lifted her sleeve. She also had dark bruises on her skin.

"No beatings, sister? No making children stand on the line? No making them drink their own urine? No rape?"

"You watch your tongue!" the sister yelled.

"No punishment, sister? You never touch them?"

"We have to maintain discipline."

She lifted another sleeve and another. Beneath, they all had black bruises over their skin.

"Looks like you have a lot of naughties here."

"Get out, you vulgar woman," the sister said.

"Not before we see the cellar," Whitsett said.

"Get out this instant before I have the police on you."

"I want to see the cellar," Geyer said. Sister Catherine didn't know what to say. "Now."

The Cellar

Sister Catherine led them to the cellar. Whitsett stepped in front of her and opened the small red door. She hated cellars. She hadn't been in one since she had been a 'naughty'. She wanted to run, her hands were shaking, and she was having trouble breathing. Then she turned and saw the angry, wrinkled face of the sister glaring at her. Whitsett snatched the candle from the nun, held her breath, and descended into the cellar.

The creaking old wood was rotting away on the stairs. She used the candle to light a small oil lamp in the corner. The stone walls were stained with moisture and spider webs. The mortar was crumbling away and the concrete floors had small pools of dirty water. Large pipes ran from the coal furnace to different parts of the building; they were a confusing maze of overlapping tubes.

The air was frigid and damp, like the dead room at the medical college. Even in the summer heat, the floors were unbearably cold. Miss Whitsett grabbed the lamp and took it to the furthest wall. Nailed into the stone were sets of chains. Attached to the end of the chains were small crooked binders. Whitsett grasped them, trying them on her own wrist, but they were too small for an adult.

As Whitsett inspected the binders, Cass and Geyer saw the small scars along her wrists. The scars they had seen so many times and ignored. Tears began to splash onto the iron bindings. Whitsett tried to pull and jerk them out of the wall. She heaved and pulled, but they wouldn't budge. Next to the chains were ropes to accommodate the overflow of naughties.

The footsteps from the children above were like hollow screams making their way down the pipes and into the cold, dark cellar. Whitsett kneeled to the floor and saw the faint graffiti etched into the wall. The mortar was old and easily rubbed away with a fingernail.

"What does it say, little one?" Geyer asked.

The words were illegible. She found the bucket used for the children to use as a toilet next to the gardening equipment. They used the waste as fertilizer for the vegetable garden.

Against the wall was a series of sticks and canes. Each with wear marks from excessive use. Her eyes became distant and harsh.

She found a button on the floor. It was dirty and smooth. She ripped off one of her own buttons from her new burgundy jacket and set it on the floor. She picked up the dirty button and put it in her pocket as she rose to her feet.

She tried to pull the chains out again, wrapping them around her arm. The dirt stained her white gloves and red dress. She pulled and pulled and thrashed and jerked. She felt the walls close in on her. She felt trapped. She hated cellars. She hated everyone. Everything was a con.

Whitsett ran.

She found herself upstairs. She ran into the cafeteria and called out to the children.

"Run!" She yelled. "Run!"

The children looked at her with nervous confusion.

"Don't just stand there! Run, you bastards!"

She tried to push the children out the door. They flinched and cowered when she tried to touch them. The nuns reached out to stop her but Whitsett began to push and swing. There was a sharp wave of nausea when she remembered there was nowhere to run to and nowhere to hide.

She looked down and saw the white line painted on the floor. She remembered being made to stand on the line quietly with the other children while prospective parents looked her over. The couples would walk up and down the length of that god damn white line and choose the child they wanted to take home, like picking out a horse.

For girls, young blondes went quickly. Tall or old ones were pushed to the side. Parents liked soft features, nothing that could be interpreted as ethnic. Whitsett was always made to take out her braids so the parents could see her hair. Her thick, frizzy hair.

"Oh, that just won't do at all. That doesn't look white at all," the prospective mothers and the fathers would say. "We can't have that."

She hated her hair. She hated the line. She wanted to be chosen to have a home so badly. She would pray and promise God that she would never act up or curse or say anything mean ever again if she were chosen to have a home. She would keep her hair in braids or cut it off. *I'll cut it off, I'll cut it all off. Why won't anyone choose me?* she would ask herself. For a child, nothing hurt more than standing the line and not being chosen. Whitsett would rather spend a week in the cellar than have to stand the line one more time.

Geyer put his large arms around her to restrain her. The constriction sent her into a rage. She began to kick and scream and twist and bite.

"It's just me, little one!" Geyer called. "It's just me!"

Whitsett became exhausted and stopped thrashing. Geyer released her and she struggled to catch her breath. She slowly picked up her stenographer equipment and approached Mother Superior, using every fiber of will to collect herself and straighten out her dress. The sister was as cold as iron and never blinked.

"I'm not afraid of you anymore," Whitsett whispered. "And I beat you."

She took one last look at the children before leaving the building forever. When she reached the street, the fresh air almost knocked her down. She walked around the corner and, when she was out of sight of the orphanage, fell on a dirt patch and began to tremble. She shook so hard her legs went numb.

"Can you explain this?" Geyer asked Sister Catherine. He was disgusted. "Can you explain this factory of misery?" Geyer could never hit a woman.

"We do the best we can," Sister Catherine said coldly.

Geyer punched the nun in the face. She collapsed immediately. Blood stained the white of her habit. She immediately began to pray to the good Lord to forgive Geyer.

Geyer and Cass found Whitsett around the block. Cass tried to hold her hand and arm, but she slapped him away.

"This wouldn't have happened in my day," Geyer said rubbing the pain from his knuckles. "There was less crime. Less degenerates. Less loneliness. You couldn't get away with this back then. The world is going to hell."

"Bullshit," Whitsett said. "Back then, I was alone! Back then, I was being beaten and chained and ravished. Back then, there was all this misery. You just didn't have to see it. Now it's in your face every day. This is the world your precious past has built."

Cass tried to grab Whitsett's hand but she ripped it away.

"Don't touch me."

"It's over, they can't hurt you anymore," Cass said.

"I'm not mad at them. They're just bastards. I'm mad at you and you," Whitsett said, pointing at Cass and Geyer. "You're the bastards who left me there. You're the bastards who let this happen. I hate you!"

Whitsett tried to run. She tripped on the street and rolled through old mud. She was dizzy.

"Why don't we just take three children from that place and say they're the Pitezel children?" Whitsett said.

"That wouldn't be true," Cass responded.

"Who cares if it's true. We're never going to find them. At least here, we can save three children."

"We can't do that."

"Why not?"

"Firstly, Mrs. Pitezel will know they aren't her children."

"She's half mad, she won't be able to tell the difference."

"You want three small children to pretend they're someone else?"

"They won't care. They'll be happy to do it if it gets them out of there." She was fighting the tears and screaming.

"Alright. Which three?" Geyer asked.

"What?"

"You pick the three children who we pass off as the Pitezel children," Geyer said.

Whitsett imagined the children in the cafeteria looking at her with their little eyes. She imagined the line. She remembered having to stand on that god damn line and wait to be chosen by family after family like a dog. She knew she could never make them stand on the line and she could never choose.

They would have to keep searching for the damn boy.

She slowly stood up, slapping away Cass's hand when he tried to help her. She straightened out her clothes and grabbed her stenographer's bag. She lifted her head as high as she could make herself and began to walk down the street. She turned back and saw the nun closing the shade on the window. Cass and Geyer followed her as they searched for a carriage.

Proper Burials

Whitsett stopped and remembered the machinist said he made deliveries to and from the orphanage. *What can you pick up from an orphanage?* she thought. *The only thing you can pick up is orphans.* Then she came to a hard realization; the only thing you can pick up is orphans.

Geyer and Cass remained on the street as she walked to the back of the orphanage through the alley. She found a small wooden door and knocked on the sharp panel. Someone stirred inside and grunted.

"What is it?" called a rough voice. The door swung open and a small, hairy man with black teeth and a blue scarf answered the door. "Oh. Excuse me, ma'am, what can I do for you?"

"Just looking around," she said quietly.

"Lookin' around? Well, look somewheres else. This is private property."

"Whose private property?"

"The Chicago Children's Asylum."

"Perfect." She walked past the man through the door. He rushed back and blocked her by putting his hands on her shoulders. The room only had space for a table and a gurney.

"Excuse me, miss."

"Get your damn hands off me," she said, with such force and determination that the man dropped his hands. When she tried to continue, he blocked her again.

"You're not allowed here. Shove off, you wench."

"I'm not a wench, I'm a resurrectionist."

When she was inside, the smell revealed to her that she was in a dead room. It was similar to the rooms where universities kept the cadavers that the students used in their studies. It was damp and smelled like garbage and salt.

There was a large block of ice on a gurney to keep the bodies from further decomposition. She remembered the man at the medical college in Philadelphia. He said he would have arrangements with institutions like this to procure bodies. Anatomical procurement, he called it. The children that died in the orphanage would be sent down here and sold on to a medical school or worse, people like Holmes. Her face grew hot with anger.

"Why do you have dead bodies down here?" she yelled, pointing her finger in accusation.

"Be quiet! Get out of here!" he screamed, pushing her with hard punches.

She dodged one of the punches and sprinted past the man into the room. He stumbled forward over his own weight.

The cold room was the size of a closet. The cramped quarters were easier to keep cool with ice. But there wasn't a lot of room for overflow. Next to the block of ice, two bodies were lying on the same gurney, head to foot. She positioned herself in-between the wall and the ice.

Propping her feet on the wall, she pushed the gurney with everything she had. Before the dirty man could get in front of the ice to stop it, the gurney had passed the threshold and was sent rattling through the alley and into the street. When the wheels stumbled from the curb, the gurney came crashing down and the ice block shattered into hundreds of little wet shards.

"Are you mad?" the man yelled, running after the gurney.

Geyer came limping towards the disturbance with Cass in tow.

"What the hell is this?" Geyer barked.

The man panicked facing the problem of having to explain dead bodies and ice. He immediately ran away in a full sprint, ducking through an alley.

Geyer looked back towards the room and saw Whitsett. She had found a shovel in the dead room and was digging a hole in a small patch of dirt next to the curb.

"What are you doing?" Cass asked.

"I'm going to bury these two children," she said.

She thrust the shovel into the hard earth and wrenched the dirt out with desperate heaves. Geyer looked inside the dead room and found the bodies of two children. His gut twisted into knots. They weren't the Pitezel children. They were too old. He finally understood why Holmes had an association with this place. He would send the machinist to collect the corpses of these poor children and make skeletons to sell to universities. *Disgusting*, he thought.

"You can't do that," Geyer said.

"Stop telling me what I can and can't do," Whitsett replied.

"You can't just bury them in the street."

"Why not? If we take them to the graveyard, some bastard will just dig them up and send them to be experimented on. If we call the city morgue, they'll just sell them on to the medical school to be turned into a skeleton."

"You can't just bury them in the street," Geyer said. He grabbed Whitsett's shovel and stopped her.

"This is the only place where they'll be safe," she said. None of us are safe, Whitsett thought. But that doesn't mean these kids don't deserve to feel safe.

Geyer kept holding onto the shovel as he looked into her face. She was right. There was nowhere to spare the children, living or dead, from the horrors of the world. He couldn't protect his own child and he couldn't protect the Pitezel children. This small patch of dirt by the curb was the safest place.

Geyer retrieved another shovel from the dead room, and together they dug deep into the earth. Once there was enough room, Whitsett, Cass and Geyer laid the dead bodies to rest. They gently covered them with dirt and wept for them. Whitsett was surprised to see Geyer weep with her. She grabbed his arm to try and console him.

Cass kept a lookout at the corner. Not one man, woman, or being paused to inquire or stop them. No one called the police or ran to find a beat cop. Cass thought about what Whitsett had told them when they left the orphanage. *She is right*, he thought, *we are all bastards. We are resurrectionists.*

Locked Doors

Whitsett was distant and detached like she was lost in a fog. They arrived at the castle, which seemed like it was covered in black tar. The police officers were white as ghosts.

"You there!" Geyer said.

"Not you again," the police officer said.

"Is the detective back yet?"

"Over there, sir," the officer said. Geyer and Cass walked to meet the gathering of detectives. Whitsett stayed at the door with the officer looking at the building.

"You alright, ma'am?" the officer asked. She was as pale as marble and her eyes were wide and vacant.

"Yes," she said. "Did they find a way into the cellar yet?"

"It's not right for a lady to hear, ma'am."

"Son, don't dick me around. There's nothing down there that can shock me."

"Yes, ma'am, there is. Your friend's waving to you."

"I don't have any friends," she said.

She walked over to Geyer and Cass. One of the detectives was going to take them to the station to interview the janitor. He grabbed the first cop he could find and had him draw out the trolley connections.

"What about going inside?" Whitsett asked.

"The detectives want us to wait until morning. It's getting dark. They haven't found a way into the cellar anyway," Geyer said. "But you can't go inside."

"I'm going to stay here," she said.

"Why?" Cass asked.

"Because I want to be alone."

"You can't stay here," Geyer said. Geyer stopped himself when he realized he was telling her what she couldn't do. "Alright, little one, just stay out of trouble."

Cass got out and stood next to her.

"I'll stay with you."

"No, go with Geyer. His handwriting is awful. You need to take notes."

Cass took out his tobacco pouch and rolled her a cigarette. "I'll be back shortly."

She asked for the tobacco pouch and Cass happily gave it to her. She felt guilty telling the cop she didn't have any friends. *Why do I say things like that?* she thought.

Whitsett returned to the police officer by the door and offered him the cigarette. He gratefully accepted it. She fumbled around with the tobacco pouch, trying to roll a cigarette for herself. She made a good show of spilling the tobacco leaves on the ground and tearing the rolling paper. The cop took the pouch and rolled it for her.

They smoked and watched the crowd thin away as it became cold and dark.

"How long are you going to stay here, ma'am? Don't you want to go home?"

"No, my home is dark. I have no lights."

"Do you work for the police station?"

"No, an insurance company. But we are working under that detective. Here's our letter from the district attorney of Philadelphia saying so."

"The DA, very impressive, that is. Who's the other fool?"

"He's an insurance agent."

"I knew it. I knew the other one was a pencil pusher."

"He's not so bad. Hypothetically."

"What does that mean, ma'am?"

"As an idea."

"Yes, ma'am. I loved what you said to the Pinkerton; we've all had a good laugh about that. Bunch of stuffed bastards, they are."

"Thanks. Was there anything on the third floor?"

"We can't get in; we can't find the key."

"No, that's the cellar. What about the third floor?"

"It was burned by the owner, that Mr. Holmes, to defraud the insurance company."

"Yes, Holmes is good at that. And the first floor is all businesses."

"Yes, ma'am. There's a jewelry store, restaurant, barbershop, glycerine soap shop. What's funny is that it's only a few years old and it looks like it has been rotting away for decades. This building was advertised as the 'World's Fair Hotel'. Just like the world's fair itself, everyone thought it was made of marble and stone. But it was made of paper and wood, and it went up like a match."

"Even the building is a con," she said.

The street corner was nearly deserted and the men that were trying to access the cellar had all gone home. The cop at the front door was one of a few sentries left to watch the building.

"What's on the second floor?"

"I can't tell you, ma'am."

"You can show me."

"Can't do that."

"I won't touch anything. I just want to see."

"I don't know about that."

"I'll be in and out real quick. You can come with me. Standing here is so boring, isn't it? Plus, you seen my letter from the DA, didn't you? You saw me punch that stuffed Pinkerton bastard." She knew she had him. "I'll even give you another cigarette."

"Okay. But you can't tell anyone."

"My lips are sealed."

The cop lit a small lantern and took her inside. They climbed a winding set of stairs.

"This is the third floor." It was burnt and charred. "From what the detectives can tell, it had a few small apartments. And this walk-in bank vault."

The large vault door was hanging open. It was three-feet thick and made of ash-stained metal. The cop led the way inside and the light from his lantern reflected off the metal like a mist. It was just large enough to stand in.

"Why's there a bank vault here?"

"Look here." The cop bent down on one knee and put the lantern to the floor. There was a small marking etched into the metal floor next to the door.

"Is that a footprint?"

"Yes. Detectives said that someone must have been trapped inside and the acid from the sweat etched this print into the surface." Whitsett ran her finger over the print and could feel the ridges.

The person who was trapped must have suffocated trying to push the door open. She tried to imagine being alone in the dark, screaming and running out of air. She began to panic and quickly stepped away from the vault.

"Unsettling, isn't it?" the detective said.

He took her down a flight to the second floor.

The hallway sloped to one side and veered to the left. The tiny lantern did little to illuminate the black halls. It was as though they were walking in a fog.

Through the doors on the right were simple sitting rooms and reading areas.

The cop came to a wall and knocked. The sound was hollow.

"There's a hidden room behind this wall. It's been walled up. The detectives broke through the other side. There was nothing in it. The door was bricked up and covered on the other side." The cop took her through the small hole created by the detectives. It was a long narrow room. "Look here," he said, holding up the lantern.

Whitsett saw deep marks on the walls and door. They were scratch marks; too high to be a dog. They were nail scratchings from a person.

"Someone was trying to escape," the cop said.

He took her out of the room and led her through a series of doors and switchbacks. Whitsett was reminded of the mermaid she had encountered at the sideshow she visited in Detroit. All she could hear in her head was the carnival barker in the top hat screaming, "Alive, alive, alive."

"Now we're on the side of the building facing 63rd Street. The only way to get through to the other side of the building is to cut through all the different rooms and closets. It's almost impossible. There are rooms with five doors, doors that lead into brick walls, false doors. One room had a series of walls that zigged and zagged like a maze to the center. These rooms here are shaped like a triangle. The doors on either side of the point can only be opened a little way before the opposite wall stops it. Each room is a different shape and size. No sense to the layout. The entire floor is a maze. It has secret rooms and rooms with no doors and trapdoors. Narrow passages close in on themselves. The floors have special doors that reveal a passage into the walls. Almost all the walls are false walls with a small passageway leading to different rooms."

As they walked, Whitsett felt disoriented. She was in a labyrinth. The walls blended into each other in the dim lantern light and blurred into infinity. The cop wasn't paying attention and became lost. The layout was hopelessly confusing. It was like walking through a nightmare.

He took her into a medium-sized room.

"Where are we now?"

"Holmes's office."

He took her to the wall and lifted out a piece of wood to reveal a secret panel. There were several turn valves with different color handles.

"What do these valves do?"

"They can fill the entire second and third floor with noxious gas. The entire building is set up with pipes that can fill each room with gas or steam. They are controlled here at this panel."

"Why would he need to have a gas panel."

"If he wanted to suffocate someone while they were sleeping, all he would need to do is turn on the gas and wait for them to die. Or he could turn on the steam and burn someone alive."

"Wouldn't people hear the screams?"

"No, they're all soundproofed."

"Jesus," she said.

"I know. But follow me."

He took her through a bathroom to cut through to the hallway. Whitsett stopped and giggled.

"You okay, miss?"

"Could you walk back this way please?" The cop, thinking she was going to faint, rushed back through the bathroom. "Did you hear that?" she asked.

"Hear what?"

"I have a friend who thinks they can tell the character of a person, just by their footsteps."

"Really?"

"Yes. He can't. But he says he can. Will you walk across there again? Please?"

The cop walked across the bathroom floor again. "I don't understand, ma'am."

Whitsett stomped her foot on the floor, then walking into the bathroom, she stomped again. The floor on the bathroom sounded hollow. "Did you hear the difference?" she asked.

"Yes, ma'am." He bent over and removed a piece of the floor.

"You're right, miss. There's a secret trap door that leads to a passage in between the floors. We got to tell the detectives about this."

"Let's keep going," Whitsett said. She got on her knees as if to squeeze through the trap door.

"We have to tell the detectives."

"What if there's someone down there that needs help?"

"Alright. But I should go first."

"I didn't want to go first," she said, snorting.

They entered the secret passage and slowly descended a set of stairs. There was a small table that looked like a butcher's table. The planks creaked and flexed under their weight and the light began to flicker. The cop tried to grab onto her arm. Whitsett pushed him away.

"I don't need help," she said. She followed the cop down the stairs into the darkness. She was exhausted. The cool air made her shiver and clench her stomach. It was stale and damp like the dead room in the medical college.

As she heard her heels click against the concrete floor, she realized she was walking around in a nightmare similar to one from her past. She was in Holmes's basement.

It was dark and wet. The brick and mortar on the walls were peeling away and weeping condensation. The smell was so foul that they coughed and gagged.

"There's a shoot that drops down here," the cop said.

The floor under the shoot was stained dark red. A few feet away were similar exam tables to those she had seen in the dead room at the medical college. They were stained with blood.

There was a large wooden table with two heavy hemp ropes at the foot and head. The ropes were wound into a pulley system which was controlled by a large wheel.

"What is this?" Whitsett asked.

"That looks like a rack. It's a torture device from the dark ages. The arms and legs are tied to that rope and the body is stretched until it breaks."

The rope and table were saturated with blood.

Whitsett backed up and bumped into a large metal container.

"Careful, ma'am." They examined the large zinc vat. It appeared to be full of acid. "What would he need this for?" the cop wondered.

"It's for removing flesh from a dead person's bones."

"How do you know that?"

"A machinist told me. I like knowing things," she said.

There were crates on the floor stacked to the ceiling. Whitsett tried to read the label.

"Chloroform," the cop said. "Bottles and bottles of chloroform."

Built into the wall was a kiln. The cast iron door opened to a sliding platform three feet by three feet by eight feet with rollers.

"Is this a furnace?" Whitsett asked. "Or maybe a stove? It looks like this thing gets as hot as the sun."

"A stove? What was he making?" the cop asked.

"The furnace has the measurements of a human body. He was incinerating bodies."

Every creak and twist of the building could be heard in the cellar. The walls and floors moaned. It was like being in the bowels of an old ship in a storm.

In the corner, next to a large shelf of tools, was a heap of clothing. Whitsett picked up one of the articles of clothing. It was bloody. Women's bloody underthings were collected in a pile; too large and formless to estimate the amount.

In the center of the cellar was a large hole. Whitsett's eyes blurred as she tried to focus, and she couldn't move. It was like a hole that led to hell. Dirt seemed to be scattered everywhere. The cop brought the lantern closer. It wasn't dirt, but a large pile of bones. Thousands of bones piled waist-high. They were different sizes and different shades of white.

Everything they had feared about Holmes was true. Everything spoken and unspoken. He was more than a con man, more than a thief, more than a killer. He was unambiguously a monster of the highest order.

Whitsett backed away from the bones and found herself against a cold stone wall. There was a rattling. There were chains with shackles bolted onto the wall. *More shackles*, she thought. She gave them a hard and furious pull. There were bloodstains and scratch marks on the wall.

She almost fell but used the chains to steady herself. She closed her eyes to stop the dizzy spell. She took the chains and threw them back against the wall. The sharp rattle left a ringing in her ears.

"What is all this?"

"He is a multi-murderer," the cop answered.

"What is that?"

"It's someone who kills lots of people."

"Why?" she asked.

"I don't know."

"He would kill them upstairs or put them to sleep with chloroform and then bring them down here to do God knows what to the bodies. This entire house is a killing apparatus. What the hell is this place?"

"I think you said it, ma'am. Hell."

"This is a factory of murder," Whitsett said. *Everything else is becoming industrialized, why not murder?* It was as though the entire Midwest had been abbreviated and stored in the cellar of this terrible hotel. *Welcome to the 20th century*, Whitsett thought.

Another Confession

In the morning Geyer and Cass were taken through Holmes's castle and shown all the horrors hidden inside. The following afternoon Geyer led the searchers back to Philadelphia to confront Holmes in his cell. Neither of them blinked during the long, rough trip back home.

Holmes had stacks of newspapers and transcripts from his trial in the corner of his cell. He had been charged with the murder of the little girls. He had grown a beard and looked exhausted. They had removed the second cot from his cell. His cons were wearing thin considering what they found in the castle. The confinement and the trial were washing away his polished veneer like hot melting wax.

"How's the trial going, Mr. Holmes?" Whitsett asked.

"As well as can be expected. I am representing myself now that I had to fire my attorneys. They were botching the entire thing."

"It's over. No reason to be dishonest now," Geyer barked.

"I am always honest, sir."

"What are the secret rooms for in your building?"

"There are no secret rooms."

"You have boarded up rooms and doors that lead into brick walls."

"Oh, I see. This was my first building design. I have no formal training as an architect, I'm a medical doctor. I had to make many field corrections and fix a few mistakes."

"Why is the entire building piped with noxious gas and steam?"

"That's a new heating and cooling system I designed. It wasn't very effective."

"Why are their secret shoots leading to the cellar?"

"Those are for garbage and clothing."

"Very big for garbage."

"People make a lot of garbage."

"Why do you have torture devices?" Geyer asked.

"Torture devices? What torture devices?"

"You have a rack," he said.

"A rack? No. No. That's not a torture device. That's an invention of mine. It's an 'elasticity determinator'. It can stretch a subject to twice his normal size."

"Why the hell would you want to do that?"

"To create a race of giants."

It was such a strange thing to say, Whitsett didn't know whether to laugh or cry.

"Why do you have a crematorium in your cellar?"

"You mean the kiln? That's for bending glass."

"Human-sized glass?"

"No. Large panes of glass."

"Make a lot of eight-foot glass panes, do you?" Geyer asked.

"I make all kinds of glass panes."

"How do you get an eight-foot pane out of the cellar? The only way in or out is through a small, red door that butts up against a wall."

"You just have to get the angles rights."

"What were the chains for, you bastard?" Whitsett asked.

Silence.

Geyer wasn't even upset that Whitsett spoke.

"There are no chains."

"Chains bolted to the cellar wall. I saw them."

"You were in my cellar?" Holmes asked with renewed excitement. His face lit up and he leaned forward; he was almost giddy. "You *were* in the cellar. You must have been mistaken." He could barely contain his excitement.

"I'm not. They had shackles to attach someone's hands to them. There were claw marks and bloodstains."

"I saw them too," Cass said.

"Those chains are for moving the glass pane. The scratches are when sharp edges hit the walls. The blood is probably from the many times I have cut myself moving them." He lifted his hands to reveal many scars along his fingers and palms.

"Bullshit," she said.

"You have an eclectic collection of things," Cass said.

"I'm an entrepreneur, sir. It is my job."

"Let me tell you what I think," Geyer said. "I think you have designed this entire house to be a killing apparatus. From what I can tell, you lure people into your hotel, gas them, murder them, dump them into the cellar and perform all manner of perversion and depravity on them.

Then you dispose of the bodies by burning them in your furnace or selling them to universities."

"That's quite an outrageous story, detective. Why would I do all that?"

"Yes, why?"

"There were thousands of bones dug into pits in the cellar," Whitsett said.

"Those must have been animal bones."

"No, sir. Most of them are human," Cass said.

"It must have been an old cemetery from before when the neighborhood was new. Why would I keep bones?"

"In this old cemetery, you think they would bury hundreds of people together in a pit and cover it with lime to mask the smell? And why would you keep women's bloody underthings?"

"I'm a doctor. I have very sick patients."

"I have a question for you. What color is this handkerchief?" Geyer asked, pulling a handkerchief from his pocket.

"It is blue," Holmes said.

"There, you have the capacity to tell the truth. Now we know you're just choosing to lie to us. Let me tell you why people kill, Mr. Holmes. For money, for love or for hate. This castle of yours, and you, make no sense. I understand selling bodies for money, but there are thousands of bones you didn't sell. I understand burning the bodies to remove evidence, but you left evidence everywhere. I understand stealing the insurance money, but why kill the children? Why keep their letters? What the hell is going on?"

"What letters?"

Cass and Geyer stood up.

"America isn't what you thought it was, is it?" Holmes asked.

Geyer stretched out his back; it was beginning to hurt and pulse with that familiar tingling pain.

"How long has your back hurt?" Holmes asked. "I have a health tonic for back pain. Linden Grove Mineral Water; two bits a bottle or five cents a glass. It uses special minerals that promote healing and flush out the body."

"Good con, Mr. Holmes," Geyer said.

They watched Holmes in silence.

"When I was a child, sent off to the schoolhouse," Holmes said, "I would have to pass the town doctor's building. Inside was an articulated skeleton. I was deathly terrified of it. I would run past the building screaming and crying. When the older children learned of this fear, they took it upon themselves to torture me. I was an exceptionally smart and bright child and they were always jealous of me. They grabbed me and took me into the office and locked me in a room with it. They used its white hands to grab me and touch my face. It was in that room that I was cured of my fear and became fascinated with skeletons."

"Where's Howard, you sick bastard?" Geyer asked.

"Like I said earlier, Hatch is the man we need to find before it's too late. He obviously murdered those poor innocent children in Indianapolis. We need to find him. I am willing to do everything in my power to help you find this villain and discover what he has done with poor little Howard-"

Geyer stood up while Holmes was still talking and left the room, followed by Cass. Holmes called to them as they disappeared down the hallway.

"I am not the killer. I keep telling you. It's Mr. Hatch. Why aren't you out there looking for Hatch?"

Whitsett remained and stood staring at Holmes. His face was expressionless, and his eyes had a vacant dullness to them. *He's a corpse*, she thought. *He has no more feeling than the bodies he steals. And we are here digging up his nonsense like resurrectionists.* She packed up her things and followed the detective.

Whitsett rode the train, staring out of the window and rolling a cigarette. They were traveling back to Detroit to search for Howard. The searchers had the demeanor of sailors bailing water out of a sunken ship.

Geyer and Cass were sleeping, their heads bobbing around from the rocking of the train. As Whitsett smoked, everyone stared at her. Ladies don't smoke, but she didn't care. Ladies didn't swear, but they could kiss her ass. She undid her braids and let her thick, frizzy hair go wherever it wanted. She was busy reading the girls' letters over and over, she didn't care if Geyer caught her doing it.

She didn't hate them. They were cold and hungry and alone. She wondered if she would have written similar letters. As she read the letters more closely, she noticed something peculiar.

"Holy shit!" she screamed. The passengers gasped at her outburst.

She grabbed Cass's head and shook it awake.

"What?!" he called out.

"When did the proprietor of The Circle House say the children left the hotel?" Whitsett asked.

Cass rubbed his face to remember as he woke up. "October 6th, I believe."

"That's wrong."

"What's wrong?"

"The date. The proprietor and the children got the dates mixed up. The first letter written by Nellie is dated October 6th. That's Saturday. In this letter, Nellie writes that Alice's eyes hurt, so she won't write at this time.

"In the letter written the next day, Alice says she had read so much in her book that she could not write yesterday when Nellie and Howard did. This letter is dated October 6th as well, but it should be October 7th, which is a Sunday. She even says it's Sunday later in the letter. She says 'this Sunday to pass away slower than I don't know what,' that 'Howard is too dirty to be seen out on the street today'.

"Then the third letter is dated as 'Monday Morning'. This is October 8th. And they were still at The Circle House. She got the date wrong."

Cass pulled down one of his suitcases. He took out the ledger from The Circle House. After looking through the cash-flow statement, he found that Whitsett was correct. The last payment was made on October 10th.

There are only 48 hours to account for, thought Whitsett. They arrived in Detroit on the 12th. Howard disappeared in those 48 hours before they arrived in Detroit. He must still be in Indianapolis.

They woke up Geyer and switched trains to Indianapolis at the next stop.

"Not a waste of time after all, was it?" she chirped.

Indianapolis

Geyer put out the word to the papers that they needed to find all the houses that had been rented in early October for a widowed sister. Holmes had given the same widowed sister story in Cincinnati, Detroit and Toronto. Many citizens contacted them at the Spencer House with clues.

"One morning Mr. H. told me to tell him to stay in the next morning, that he wanted him and would come and get him and take him out and I told him and he would not stay in at all, he was out when he came," wrote Alice in her letter to her mother.

This is exactly what Holmes did at the Albion Hotel in Toronto; he called for the girls and took them out on the morning of October 25th and they never returned.

Mr. Ackelow said Holmes spoke of Howard as a naughty boy and was trying to get rid of him. Holmes must have told that story so when the boy was separated from his sisters it wouldn't arouse suspicion or curiosity.

They spent several days searching hotels and boarding houses and interviewing real estate agents with no clues.

"The trunk must be here in Indianapolis," Geyer said.

With all the publicity and effort, why can't we find the house? Whitsett thought. She felt guilty for wishing they would never find the children. She thought uncovering the information in the letter would make her feel better, but she still hoped they wouldn't find the boy. Once they found the boy, she would have to return to her normal life and Mrs. Jacobs's cousin's son. She still felt guilty.

It seemed hundreds of shallow people had made up stories about Holmes and the boy, trying to get attention or fame. By Monday they had searched every outlying town, except Irvington. After Irvington, they would be out of towns to search.

Irvington was six miles from Indianapolis. There were no hotels and few real estate agents. It was a small hamlet with only a few streets. The sounds of construction in the city fluttered by on the wind like the march of an advancing army.

Geyer began to question the neighbors and local businesses. There was a grocer at the end of the street.

"I do remember that man. It was in early October," the grocer said. "He left a coat here with me one day, saying that a boy would call for it the next morning, but the boy never came."

"Do you still have the coat?" Whitsett asked.

The grocer leaned over his table and produced an old, dirty coat. Cass looked through his ledger and found it in the list of Howard's clothes.

"Did he say anything else?" Geyer asked.

"He wanted to know where the repair shop was. He had two cases of surgical instruments, which he wanted sharpened."

A short distance from the train stop was a very plain real estate agent's office. Geyer entered the office followed by Whitsett and Cass. They looked like a funeral procession. They were exhausted and worn down. They had been searching for the children during the hottest months of the year, which had left them frail and lethargic. They limped from worn boots and sore feet. Whitsett had barely spoken since the orphanage, and their train and coach rides had passed in uncomfortable silence.

Geyer asked a pleasant-faced old gentleman, Mr. Brown, if he knew of a house in his town which had been rented for a short time in October by a man who wanted it for a widowed sister. Cass handed him a photograph of Holmes. Mr. Brown put on his glasses and carefully studied it.

"Yes," he said, "I remember a man who rented a house under such circumstances in October of 1894, and this picture looks like him very much. I remember the man very well because I did not like his manner."

Dr. Thompson was the former owner of the house. The doctor immediately recognized the photo of Holmes and identified him as the renter. A boy who worked for the doctor, named Elvet Moorman, had seen Holmes and a little boy with him. Geyer showed him the photos.

"Why, that is the man who lived in our house and who had the boy with him," Elvet said. "I went over to the house one afternoon early in October and saw a transfer wagon unloading furniture, and a man and a boy were helping."

"Show us," Geyer said.

They were shown to a one and a half story cottage, standing on the fringes of the town. Across the street was a Methodist Church and 200 yards to the south were the Pennsylvania railroad tracks. The street was secluded with no other houses in the immediate neighborhood. To the west was a small grove of young catalpa trees.

A perfect location for privacy, Whitsett thought.

"Where is the entrance to the cellar?" Geyer asked.

A small hatch was lifted, and Geyer descended the wooden stairs into the dark cellar. He carried a lamp and left his coat with Elvet, the young boy. Cass handed Whitsett his hat again.

"We'll be right back," Cass said.

"I'm going down too," Whitsett said.

"Really?"

Whitsett clasped Cass's hand and they descended while she clenched his hat. Geyer saw them holding hands, but he didn't care to yell at them. Unmarried couples certainly didn't hold hands like that in public in his day. But he was resigned to the fact that his days had passed. This was the 20th century, and nothing could change that. Not a god damn thing.

The cellar was divided into two apartments. The rear had a cement floor and was evidently intended for a washroom and the front had a hard clay floor. There were no disturbances in the earth. There was nothing. Other than dust and webs, the cellar was clean and empty.

"Sounds like footsteps from above," Cass said. Whitsett listened with him. Cass thought the footsteps were of Whitsett. The clicks paced and sounded nervous. But they were not Whitsett's footsteps; she was right next to him. *Must be the type of wood used to frame the house*, he thought. *Footsteps all sound the same, like a distant thunderstorm.*

They left the cellar and continued their search outside. The right wing of the house was attached to a small piazza with open latticework under the floor. Geyer bent down through the pain of his back and, looking through the latticework, saw the broken remains of a trunk. He bent down further to grab it.

"What is it?" Cass asked.

"A trunk!" Geyer said. "Praise Jesus, goddammit." Dirt clung to the fragments of the broken luggage. A strip of blue calico had been pasted along the side seam, evidently intended to repair and cover it. The calico was two inches wide and had printed on it the figure of a white flower. This was the trunk that had kept Geyer up at night. He had thought more about this stupid trunk than the children. And here it was.

A numbness fell over his body for a moment. It was the hollowest of victories, just like finding an empty trunk. When he saw the mangled pieces of wood, he truly understood that the children were dead. All the children were dead, his child was dead, and he could no longer distract his mind with a missing trunk.

He wished he had never found the trunk.

"We need a shovel," Cass said.

Cass dug for the remains of the boy's body but found nothing. It was obvious by the hard flint clay that no one had been digging around the house.

"Did he ever say anything to you?" Geyer asked the boy.

"After I saw him with the furniture, I went over to milk a cow that was kept in the barn connected with the house. While I was milking, the man asked me to assist him in putting up a stove, which I did. I asked him why he didn't make a gas connection for natural gas and use a gas stove. He told me he didn't think gas was healthy for children."

They continued their search in the barn. The barn contained a large coal stove called the "Peninsular Oak". Barns usually didn't have stoves. The stove was three- and one-half feet high, and twenty-two inches in diameter. On the top, beside the pivot, Geyer found bloodstains.

The cow inside the barn bellowed.

Geyer found a long stick and began walking around the barn. He would plunge the tip of the stick into the ground. If the dirt was soft, he instructed Cass to dig for a body. They walked around the entire property stabbing and digging.

Whitsett sat by the stove and thought about the castle. She thought about Holmes and all the people he murdered. Why would he do it? she thought. Why would he murder the children? Why did I wish they were dead? I should have wished for them to survive. If I had wished for them to survive, we still would be looking for them, but they would be alive. Why didn't I think of that earlier? she thought. All of these dead people, over a simple insurance fraud.

In the barn, the three searchers waited for someone to bring lamps. They sat on a small bench, knee to knee. Whitsett was in the middle being pressed flat. Geyer took out his flask and took a drink. When he finished, he passed the flask to Whitsett. Her face lightened slightly, and she took a drink. It burned her throat and she held back a cough.

"In my day, women didn't drink," Geyer said.

"I know," she said. She passed the flask to Cass who took a drink. He let out a small cough.

"Jesus Christ," Geyer said.

Whitsett held on to the flask and Cass's hat, staring at them against her dirty white gloves.

Doctor Thompson arrived with a small bucket. "I'm glad you're here," he said.

"What's the matter?" Geyer asked.

"Two boys, Walter Genie and Oscar Kettenbach, were playing detective in the cellar with the cemented floor. There was a chimney which extended above the roof of the house. In the chimney was a pipe hole about three feet, six inches from the floor. Young Genie put his arm in the opening and pulled out, along with a handful of ashes, a piece of bone."

He showed them the bucket containing several pieces of charred bone, a femur and skull. The piece of the skull showed the sutures plainly which meant it was a small child between 8 and 12.

They used a hammer and chisel to take down the lower part of the chimney. Geyer found an old fly screen from the house and used it as a sieve for the ashes and soot, like a gold miner. The black ash billowed into the air as he shook dirt and soot through the screen. Remaining on top of the screen was an almost complete set of teeth and a piece of the jaw.

At the bottom of the chimney was a large, charred mass. Doctor Thomas used his penknife to cut it open and examine it. A portion of a stomach, liver and spleen had been baked together and had formed a large lump of coal. The pelvis of the body was also found. The chimney contained some of the iron fastenings which belonged to the trunk, some buttons, a small scarf pin, a tin man—which Mr. Pitezel had bought for Howard at the World's Fair—and a crochet needle that belonged to Alice.

Whitsett finally understood why Holmes installed furnaces in every house he rented. He was using them as crematoriums to incinerate the bodies. He was planning to kill them all along. He could have murdered scores of people and disposed of them inside the furnaces he installed in rented houses across the Midwest. Whitsett found a lot of corn rubbish on the floor that seemed to trail into the stove.

"Why did he use corn to fuel the fire?" Whitsett asked.

"Corn makes a hot fire," Geyer said.

Whitsett thought she would be disgusted or repulsed by the remains of the poor little boy. But she wasn't. She felt nothing. She wondered if there was anything left to get upset about.

The searchers returned to Indianapolis and spent the rest of the evening filling out paperwork and making statements.

"Did we win?" Cass asked miserably.

"It doesn't feel like we won," Whitsett said.

That night should have been the best sleep the searchers had in months. They should have been happy.

Case closed.

Skeletons in the Closet

The train chugged along as they rode back to Philadelphia. They were exhausted. They had been searchers for so long, it had become second nature. They were hot and dirty. They ached and the more they couldn't fall asleep, the more their minds wandered.

"I want you two to be ready. When we get off the train, there'll be scores of reporters wanting for us to sell them a headline."

"More reporters?" Cass said. "I'm not looking forward to that."

"You know what we should do?" Whitsett asked.

"No," Cass said.

"When the train stops."

"No."

"We could get off and switch trains."

"No. Not again," Cass said.

"We could go to Gilmanton, New Hampshire. It isn't too far out of the way."

"Why?" Geyer said.

"That's where Holmes was born."

"No," Cass said.

"Aren't you curious about where he came from? We could talk to his parents. See what they have to say."

"What do you think they're going to tell you?" Geyer said.

"I don't know. Maybe they know why he is the way he is."

Whitsett, Geyer and Cass stood at the train junction looking at each other for a few moments. Geyer would continue to Philadelphia while Whitsett and Cass switched trains for Gilmanton.

"Are you alright?" Geyer asked.

"I'll be fine," Whitsett said.

"Well, this is goodbye then, little one."

"Did you get what you were looking for?" Whitsett asked.

"What'd ya mean?"

"You didn't go for Holmes, he was already in prison. You didn't go for the crime, you said there was no crime. Crime, criminal, jail. Did you find what you were looking for?"

"No," he said. "Did you?"

"No," she said after a moment's thought. "What were you looking for?"

"My daughter," he said.

"You're a mean old goat. And you drink too much. And you have bad breath," Whitsett said as she gave him a big hug around his neck. "But you're a good papa."

Geyer shuffled his feet. "Good con, little one."

She smiled.

Geyer shook Cass's hand and told him to stay out of trouble.

Geyer boarded the train back to Philadelphia. Whitsett and Cass boarded the train bound for Gilmanton.

Geyer returned to his small apartment in Philadelphia. Everything was coated in a layer of dust. He hadn't been home in months. Everything seemed familiar, yet different; like a museum. He lit a lamp and sat down in his chair. On the table in front of him, he placed the three large jugs of whiskey he had bought. He didn't buy food or flour or sugar. He bought three jugs of whiskey.

He opened the first jug and began to drink. It slowly began to numb the pain in his back and his head. He peeled away his boot. The rotting leather dissolved from the sweat of his hands. The abscess had doubled in size and caused his two small toes to swell and curl. It was as though his foot was decomposing. He lifted his leg onto a chair and watched the liquid drain down his foot.

As the night went on, he just sat in his chair and drank from his jug. He had surrendered. He had given up. *Welcome to the 20th century.* He looked towards his front door and saw someone had slipped a letter under it.

Gilmanton was a very small community. It was different from the cities they had been searching through the last few months. It was an old country town with dirt roads and overgrown grass. There wasn't the looming bustle of construction agitating the town like water on an anthill.

Whitsett knocked on the door of a small farmhouse. Mr. Mudgett answered the door. Whitsett knew instantly it was Holmes's father. He had the same nose and forehead.

"My name is Miss Whitsett. And this is *Inspector* Cass. We helped catch Holmes and find the missing Pitezel children."

"Oh yes. What is it I can do for you?"

"I was wondering if you could tell me about Holmes. Or Herman Mudgett as he was called here. I'm trying to collect an explanation," Whitsett said.

"An explanation of what?" Mr. Mudgett asked.

"Of why he did what he did, why he was what he was," Whitsett said.

"Sounds like you need to go to church and hear the word. I don't know why he done what he done."

"But he was your son."

"I know what you're thinking. That this is somehow our fault. That we turned him into this monster. Well, let me remind you that my other children are God-fearing people. They've never done a wrong thing in their life. And his son Robert is the nicest young man in the state. He's gonna study accounting and work in an office."

"He has a son?"

"You leave that boy alone or you'll have me to answer to. You and those goddamn reporters come up here, bothering an old man. Trying to blame me. Telling me I'm the father of the devil. Well, I'll tell you what, I had nothing to do with it."

They were still standing at the door. Mudgett was not going to invite them in.

"Is that all?"

"What was he like as a young child?" Whitsett asked.

"Normal."

"What does that mean?"

"It means 'good day'." Mr. Mudgett slammed the door in their faces.

Cass's face went red. He was furious and pounded on the door. Mudgett swung the door open.

"What the hell do you people want?"

"Who do you think you are? I'm an inspector, sir. You can't slam the door like that."

"It appears that I just did. What are you gonna do about it?"

Whitsett stood in between the two men. "Let's just leave," Whitsett said to Cass. "No sense in making another headline."

They strolled down the main road. They weren't looking forward to a long ride to the nearest train station. They hoped they would have answers before they went back. It was a long way to travel just to have a door slammed in their face. Whitsett stopped at the end of the road.

"What's wrong?" Cass asked.

"This is the doctor's building." Whitsett remembered Holmes had told them he was locked up with a skeleton in the doctor's office. She marched up the steps and went inside.

Whitsett was greeted by an aged country doctor. It was a small office with an exam room filled with books and opaque jars. In the corner a dog was curled up with a blanket, snoring.

"Hello, young lady. Haven't seen you around here before."

"We're the investigators from Philadelphia. The Pitezel children case."

"Ah yes."

"We are here to learn about Holmes. Herman Mudgett. Do you remember him?"

"I don't know if I remember much, or anything, about Mudgett. I knew his father. They were a normal farmin' family as far as I knew."

"Normal? Even Holmes, I mean Herman?"

"Normal as any other child in these parts. I think he did ask me questions about being a doctor. Or maybe he even worked for me one summer as an apprentice. I can't remember, I'm getting so old now. He was pretty bright. I think he found a rich girl to marry and went to medical school in Michigan. There was some trouble when he worked at a pharmacy. I think a boy died or something. I don't really recall."

"That's all you remember?" Whitsett asked.

"Why do you sound so disappointed, young lady?"

"Just looking for some answers."

"Answers? I've read the paper. You found the children, Holmes is going to be hanged for it, what else is there?"

"I don't want punishment, I want satisfaction," she said. "I want to know why."

"I see. Well, I certainly have no secrets of the universe for you. I've been around for a while and things like this, there's no satisfaction to be had. Some things are just like that."

"Where's your skeleton, doctor?" Cass asked.

"What skeleton?"

"When Holmes was a child, he was locked in your office to confront the skeleton. He said this was a pivotal moment that shaped him into who he was," Cass said.

"We never had a skeleton. Do you know how expensive those things are?"

Goodbye

They arrived in Philadelphia in the middle of the day. There were no reporters but the station was as busy as a county fair.

Whitsett and Cass slowly walked away from the train station.

"Are you glad you came?" Whitsett asked.

"Yes," Cass said. "Are you?"

"Very." Whitsett was beginning to feel the dread in her stomach. The dread of returning home to Mrs. Jacobs and her cousin's son, who she was engaged to.

Whitsett stopped Cass only a block from the station.

"Well, Inspector the Kid, we should just say goodbye here." Whitsett stopped and pulled on Cass's arm.

"Don't you want me to walk you home?" Cass asked.

"Yes, but I don't think it's a good idea."

"I don't know what to say," Cass said.

"Me either," Whitsett said. "You can cry if you'd like. It doesn't help, but there's no shame in it. Oh, here." She handed him the notes and transcriptions from the case. She wouldn't need them anymore. Cass took the papers and examined the writing carefully.

"I hear you can tell a person's character by their handwriting. What do you see from my penmanship?" Whitsett asked.

"You have a great attention for detail. You are tough and persistent, and you are always ready for a fight. You are too smart for your own good and you swear a lot. But you are one of the most remarkable people in this entire Midwest."

Whitsett smiled. "You're learning," she said. "You knew your customer. You knew what I wanted to hear. Good con. Now you have to close the deal."

"I'm not trying to con you."

"Everything is a con. But you gave me a cigar. Thank you."

Cass's smile melted from his face and his eyes became distant. She wanted to hug him. She wanted to keep riding trains with him. But she couldn't explain Mrs. Jacobs's cousin's son and the hovel she lived in. She knew it would hurt even more.

Cass hailed her a carriage and made sure the driver was safe with a series of questions and instructions.

Whitsett ripped off the dirty button from the orphanage and put it in Cass's hand. She had sewn it onto her shirt in Chicago.

"What is the button for?" Cass asked. "Why was it there?"

"The cellar is always dark. So, you drop a button and then use your hands to find it. It's just a game you play to keep from going mad."

"I'm so sorry," Cass said. "How did you get through it? How *do* you get through it?"

"I just did. I just do. You don't think about it. But it's never one thing. A bunch of things had to happen. Scores of little things," she said.

"I can't take this," he said.

"It's okay. It's for you. Just don't drop it."

Cass held onto her hand and kissed it.

"I'll see you at work tomorrow, won't I?" Cass asked.

"I don't even know if I'll have a job. Mrs. Sappington will just fire me again." She laughed. "I should have taken that bitch's hat." She giggled thinking of Holmes's second wife and the nice hat in her luggage.

Cass gave Whitsett his hat.

"Your hat?" she asked.

"I can't really wear it anymore. It makes me look like a jackass."

"Inspector, it's not the hat."

She gave him a hug and kissed his cheek. As she got into the cab, Cass called out. "What's your first name?"

"Cindy."

Last Confession

The carriage shook through the streets. It was cramped and hot. Whitsett rang the bell for the driver to stop. She wasn't ready to go home. She didn't want to face Mrs. Jacobs and the life that was waiting for her.

The driver put his head into the back.

"What's the problem, ma'am?"

"I want you to take me to the prison house."

"The prison house? Why?"

"I have some questions."

"The gentleman who paid me said to takes you right backs to your home, ma'am."

"I won't tell him if you don't."

The driver changed direction and took her to the prison house.

Whitsett sat in front of Holmes's cell. He had somehow been able to acquire a nice cot, a desk and a chair to work at. Holmes saw her and his lips parted. She was wearing Mr. Cass's worn hat over her thick, wild hair.

"Mrs.—Miss Whitsett. What a pleasant surprise. How did you get in here by yourself?" Holmes asked.

"They know me here now. It's no big deal."

"I'll bet not. Good con," he said. "Nice hat."

"Go fuck yourself," she said. Holmes gave her a small smile. "We found the Pitezel children."

"Yes, I read that in the paper."

"What have you to say for yourself?" she asked.

"Oh well."

"Oh well?"

"What can they do, hang me twice?" His bright eyes had become vacant and pale. He was passive, disconnected from everything. "Aren't you going to write any of this down?"

"No. What's the point? Inspector Cass would say that if you don't write it down, it didn't exist. I don't want your nonsense to exist."

"That mark only knows what he's told, and all he's told can fit in his pocket."

"He knows a bit more than you think."

"He's a mule! And I hate to inform you that it doesn't matter if you don't want to write anything down. Reporters are lining up to write down things I say." He was more aggressive than usual, like a caged animal. There was no more pretense of being a gentleman.

"I know," she said.

"You found the poor babies and you don't want to write anything down, what are you doing here then?"

"J.A. Judson, Mr. Howard, G.D. Hale, Mr. Hall, Alex E. Cook. A.C. Hayes, Harry Gordon, G. Howell, H. Howell, Edward Hatch."

"Who are those people?" Holmes asked.

"They're you, Mr. Howard, Mr. Holmes, Mr. Mudgett. Why didn't you just put them in an asylum?"

"Who?"

"The children. You didn't need to kill them. You didn't need to kill anyone. Why not just put them in an asylum and move on? Why did you do it? Why?"

"I was committed to an asylum once, or I worked there, I can't really remember which."

"You can't remember?"

"I remember in that asylum they would line the walls with patients as the treatment. Being confined was supposed to help them with their ailments. It had terrible insulation. But the walls could actually hear you. The institute was a living place. The building was alive."

"Your building had some life to it."

"Exactly! Yes, it did. Thank you. Quite fun."

"What was fun? Your building is a murder factory. Was the killing fun? Is that why you did it?"

"Murder factory? Nonsense. I never killed anyone."

"What did you do to Minnie Williams?"

"Does it really matter?" he said, snorting.

"So, she's gone?"

"Gone like yesterday's sunshine," he said.

"And her sister? Not in the bottom of a lake, is she? Whose was that footprint found in the vault? Was that Nannie's?"

"Did you know that one of your buttons is missing?"

Whitsett looked down and remembered she had popped it off for Cass.

"Now," Holmes said, leaning forward. "Did it wear off, or did it tear off?" He laughed. "When I was incarcerated in St. Louis with the 'Handsome Bandit', we saw an execution. They tore off the buttons, the clothes, the hair and body parts for relics. Laughing and mocking the hanged; it was grizzly. I'm going to have them bury me in cement. I don't want them to tear me up to sell me for parts."

"You're a resurrectionist and you're worried about being desecrated; that your soul will be damned?"

"We're all just sacks of meat and fluid. Once the meat falls off and the fluid drains, you go nowhere."

"Like what you did to all those people in your cellar?" she asked, accusing him.

"You'd have had fun staying at my building," he said with a slow smile.

Whitsett had to fight back a shiver. She couldn't swallow. "What about Emily?"

"Emily?"

"The blonde. The most beautiful woman anyone has ever seen. The six-footer."

"Ah yes. She was beautiful. She's gone."

"Why?"

"Why do you ask so many questions?"

"I like knowing things. What about the children? Why did you remove their clothes? Why did you sharpen your surgical equipment? What was the trunk for?"

Holmes kicked his foot against the iron bars. "Stop it!" he yelled. The ground shook and the ringing lingered in the air. "Poor little dolls," he said in a sarcastic mocking tone, "with their naked bodies and little blue hands and dead black faces. Who cares? Do you really think you found those children? Of the hundreds of thousands of children dead in the hundreds of thousands of cellars across this great country? You really think you three idiots were able to trip over the exact three children you set out for? Wake up. When you walked down the street to get here, you had to step over 50 dead children. Did you bat an eye? If anything, I've shown you it's this city; these cities—these cities are the murderers. Churning out their misery. Life is a misery factory. And you lost. I beat you. You were terrible at this game."

"I wasn't playing a game," she said.

"That's how I won. Why are you still here?"

"I want to know why."

"You want to know why? Why? You're not a detective or a newspaperman. You called me a resurrectionist. What about you? Who are you?"

"I just like knowing things. I like knowing why."

"Why," he said, snorting derisively. "You want to know why? Do you know why the Chicago fire started? A cow kicked over a lantern. Why was Jesus crucified? Thirty pieces of silver. Why am I in here? Because I forgot to send the 'Handsome Bandit' $50. Not very comforting to know why, is it?

"Hearst offered me $7,500 for a story. That's right. I generate millions of dollars in newspaper sales every day. Millions read about me, like the modern-day Jesus. Reporters line up outside to get a statement from me. I'm the most talked about man in the country. I've killed thousands of people and no one knows anything. I'll live forever in their minds. I've found the secret to immortality. I'm the future of humanity. With superior intellect and strength. The next step in human evolution. Soon there will be an entire race of men like me. A complete metamorphosis. Kings among kings among kings."

"Hypothetically," she said. "Have you ever heard of the phrase 'becoming a shut eye'?"

Holmes didn't answer.

"When a hustler on the street pretending to be a psychic becomes so good at the con, he begins to actually believe he's psychic. You've become a shut eye. We all fall victim to our own delusions. Don't we, Mr. Holmes? How do you keep all the lies in your head? How do you keep up with the truth? How do you remember what's real and what is a lie?"

"Easy; there is no truth," he said. "Nothing is real. It's all a con."

"I'm real."

"You know, I've noticed you're a good stenographer. How would you like to come with me? When I'm done with this trial, we can travel and see the world. You aren't like these other people. I have business prospects all over the Midwest and east. You could work for me. And then, when you get tired of traveling, you could buy your own place and live off your pension. What do you say?"

Whitsett knew he was never leaving his cell alive. But the prospect still appealed to her. He must have known it was what she would want to hear. And she must have appeared desperate enough to think it would sell. *He really knows his customers*, she thought.

"Good con," she said.

Back Home

Cindy Whitsett walked down her street to the single woman's boarding house. She tried to avoid the sewage running through the street and the drunk men reaching for her chest. She saw the telegraph office and went inside.

Everyone was surprised to see this little woman blinking at them. She wore dirty white gloves and a mangled man's bowler hat that was too large for her over her wild hair. Her burgundy suit was too respectable for a working girl. She grabbed a form and began to fill out a message. She looked through her bag and found the telegraph address for Ned Conner. She noticed her stupid gloves were still on and she took them off with the aid of her teeth.

Ned had asked her to send word of his wife and daughter if she found them. They would never be found; Holmes had admitted as much. She struggled with what to say. She wanted to write something that would make him feel better. Something that would help him sleep.

She wondered about receiving a letter from the parents who abandoned her. She finally wrote a letter that she would have liked to receive.

Dear Ned Conner,

We found your wife and daughter. Holmes had left her for another woman. They are living happily in Canada. She was easy to find, not a lot of 6-foot-tall women. They want me to tell you, 'We are fine. Everything is going to be alright. We love you. Forces, beyond anyone's control, have forced us to abandon you. It is not your fault and it wasn't justified. We failed you. Our only wish is that you find ways to be happy. Please forgive us. You deserve it.'

Julia and Pearl

Care of

Cindy Whitsett.

It cost her a fortune to send that telegraph. That was an expensive lie, she thought. Not a lie, a con. A good con. No, not a con; a resurrection. He will want to believe it. And maybe it will help him get a little sleep at night.

I beat you, Mr. Holmes.

She entered Mrs. Jacobs's apartment and felt the world push down on her shoulders. She hung her boots out of the window from a bucket. The room was so small and dirty. It smelled and rattled as the wind blew through holes in the mortar of the brick walls. She shook the sheet and heard the bugs hit the walls and floor.

Mrs. Jacobs was yelling at her for being away so long, but Whitsett tuned most of it out. She was talking about weddings and cousins and names for her unborn babies.

The building had no gas and she couldn't afford candles. The bird upstairs was screeching in Hungarian and the Greeks and Italians next door were screaming at each other. She sat down on the bed.

It was all over. And here she was. She was in the dark again. She chastised herself for wanting to cry. *It doesn't help, but there is no shame in it.* In the dark, she composed herself and hardened her mind. She missed going to hotels and interviewing suspects and Mr. Cass.

She didn't know if she even had a job anymore. *The police station*, she thought. She would go and talk her way into a job at the police station. They knew her there now, maybe she could get a job there; if Mrs. Jacobs would let her.

She took her white gloves and threw them into the potbelly stove, setting them on fire. Mrs. Jacobs gave her her letters and messages. In the light from the stove, she flipped through the envelopes. She dropped everything onto the floor when she saw a small package from Detective Geyer.

Dear Little one-

Enclosed is a letter from an old detective friend of mine who needs some help working under him on a case. I think it's another multi-murderer. I'm too busy to help, but I have written to him telling him that you would be perfect for the job. You have experience and a good eye. I've also written to the DA telling him the same. I've enclosed some professional equipment for you. Don't forget your gloves.

Geyer.

Whitsett reached into the package and pulled out Geyer's old, dented silver flask. It was empty, that cheap bastard. She opened the letter from Geyer's old detective friend and began to read from the flame of her gloves.

www.ingramcontent.com/pod-product-compliance
Lightning Source LLC
Chambersburg PA
CBHW010729250626
47155CB00011B/3617
* 9 7 8 1 9 3 4 6 1 3 4 7 4 *